THE BOOK
OF PARADISE

ITZIK MANGER was born in 1901 to a Jewish family in Czernowitz (then Austria–Hungary; now Chernivtsi, Ukraine). He began publishing poems and ballads in literary journals after the First World War, moving to Bucharest, where he wrote for the local Yiddish press and gave lectures. Manger's literary reputation was made in Warsaw: he relocated there in 1928 and found considerable success publishing volumes of poetry and his own literary journal, doing public readings and composing lyrics for the Yiddish cabaret and the Yiddish film industry.

Manger began writing *The Book of Paradise* in the mid-1930s amid rising anti-Semitism. The novel was initially serialized in 1937 in the Warsaw-based newspaper *Naye Folkstsaytung*. Forced to leave Poland the next year, Manger negotiated the publication of *The Book of Paradise* as a stateless person in Paris. He later moved to England and then the United States, before settling in Israel, where he died in 1969.

ROBERT ADLER PECKERAR is a translator and cultural historian. He is the Executive Director of Yiddishkayt, the West Coast's premier Yiddish cultural organization, and the CEO of the Topa Institute, an intercultural arts and education center based in the Ojai Valley, California. After receiving his PhD in Comparative Literature from UC Berkeley, he was assistant professor of Jewish culture at the University of Colorado, Boulder. He lives in Southern California with his family.

THE BOOK
OF PARADISE

ITZIK
MANGER

TRANSLATED FROM THE YIDDISH
BY ROBERT ADLER PECKERAR

PUSHKIN PRESS CLASSICS

Pushkin Press
Somerset House, Strand
London WC2R 1LA

The Book of Paradise was first published as
די וווּנדערלעכע לעבנסבאַשרײַבונג פון שמואל אַבא אַבערוואָ
in *Naye Folkstsaytung* in Warsaw, 1937

First published by Pushkin Press in 2023

1 3 5 7 9 8 6 4 2

ISBN 13: 978-1-78227-925-9

Designed and typeset by Tetragon, London
Printed and bound by Clays Ltd, Elcograf S.p.A.

www.pushkinpress.com

Contents

Introduction

The Kaddish is more than a hymn of divine praise and mourning. In a mix of Aramaic and Hebrew, it is the most recited liturgical poem in the Jewish tradition, punctuating prayer services and forming the textual heart of the rituals of Jewish mourning. In Yiddish, *kaddish* is also a term of endearment for sons, who are destined, one day, to recite the Kaddish at the graves of parents over the course of days and months of prescribed mourning, and thereafter whenever called upon. When Yiddish was the everyday language of the majority of Ashkenazic Jews in the world, parents affectionately called their boys "my kaddish" or "darling little kaddish", a gentle, perhaps barely conscious, reminder of mortality and the sacred obligations of memory and memorializing.

The poet and writer Itzik Manger (pronounced with a hard "g" as "Monger") was born nearly with the dawn of the twentieth century, in the spring of 1901, in what is now Chernivtsi, Ukraine, and was then Czernowitz, capital of Bukovina, the easternmost province of Habsburg Austria–Hungary. He would be kaddish not only unto his mother and father, but, as it would turn out, unto his culture and his mother tongue. Manger's parents were born in the neighbouring province of Galicia. His mother, Chava Woliner Manger, was the daughter of a family of upholsterers from the city of Kolomea (now Kolomyia). His father, Hillel Helfer-Manger, was a tailor who came from a small town, Stopchet (now Stopchativ), just across the River Prut, about ten miles to Kolomea's south.

Manger was raised in the multilingual, multi-ethnic foothills of the Carpathian Mountains, moving between Czernowitz, Kolomea and Stopchet, where rivers and mountain passes marked out historical, ever-shifting boundaries between empires and nations and cradled a unique hodgepodge of local languages and peoples.

The streets of Manger's childhood Czernowitz resonated with a polyphony of tongues, including the official Austrian German (as well as the local Bukovinian dialect of it), Yiddish, Ukrainian, Romanian, Armenian, Polish, Hungarian and Romani. This diverse provincial capital proved a fertile breeding ground for poets and writers, Jewish ones in particular. In the city's schools, students recited Goethe and Schiller, and absorbed—through study or cultural practice—the Jewish sacred texts and liturgy from antiquity.

Even though he was one of the most popular and widely read Yiddish poets of his day, to date there are no monuments to Manger in his home town. There are some, though, to his contemporaries, including the Jewish German-language poets Rose Ausländer (1901–88) and Paul Celan (1920–70), who would both go on writing poetry in the former imperial language even after the shift of borders following the First World War. Ausländer and Manger were, in fact, childhood friends. The younger Celan grew up an admirer of Manger. The Czernowitz-born American Yiddish poet Beyle Schaechter-Gottesman (1920–2013) once recalled a strange encounter with Paul Celan in 1947. She remembered how, on Vienna's Seegasse, significantly the site of the city's ancient, enormous Jewish cemetery, Celan approached her and—out of the blue—declared, "Itzik Manger is the greatest Yiddish poet", and then disappeared, without a goodbye, "like an apparition".

Manger's poetic reputation was based on his unique blending of multiple cultural elements in his work, an admixture he called *Literatorah*—an apt portmanteau joining together the two dominant voices that informed his work. On the one hand was *Literature*, the high culture of European letters, and on the other Torah, which is far more than the biblical scripture and includes the oral and written Holy Law, as well as an entire Jewish way of looking at the world. Manger's *Literatorah* was not a simple amalgam of the literary traditions of Christian Europe and the Jewish people, but rather a deep engagement with the complex interfusion of lives and letters that once flourished in the places where Manger lived and wrote.

As Manger began to reach his poetic stride in Romania towards the end of the 1920s (Bukovina had, by then, become part of the Kingdom of Romania), he achieved distinction as a new type of "poet of the people" who bridged the Jewish folkloric traditions of wandering troubadours and itinerant balladeers with the legacy of restless, rambunctious and hard-drinking European poets from Anacreon to Villon. Arriving in Warsaw late in 1928, he fashioned himself as a kind of rabbinic Rimbaud; his work staked out a rebellious ground in Jewish poetry, centred around themes of *benkshaft*, profound melancholic longing, and *hefker*, which indicates a sense of both unbridled ownerlessness and abandonment. In the teeming Jewish metropolis, Manger deepened his engagement with particularly Jewish source material in a highly idiosyncratic and modernist manner.

After publishing two sparkling volumes of poetry, Manger more fully embraced the cultural world view of Warsaw's pre-eminent Jewish literary figure, I.L. Peretz (1852–1915), who had died thirteen years before Manger's arrival there. One of the central ideas that Peretz advocated in his influential salon was that all historical strata of Jewish literature accumulated to form a tell, an archaeological mound. Digging into this tell offered Jewish culture-makers a historical trove to plunder and draw on for innovative use. The work of excavation carried on an ancient practice, participating in creation *with* these texts in a way that kept them ever present, in every generation. The Midrash, the creative exegetical mode of reading holy scripture compiled by rabbinical sages well over a millennium ago, is a striking example of this type of continuous engagement and would serve as Manger's primary raw material.

On the surface, *aggadah*—the classical rabbinical storytelling mode—may resemble biblical storytelling of a non-Jewish variety. The entire genre of Christian children's religious literature is based on reworking the Bible's central characters and themes into easily digestible moralizing tales. But aside from some similar names and events, there is little that connects even the most whimsical classical rabbinical literature with, forgive the comparison, an animated VeggieTales video in which a tomato and an asparagus spear riff on "Josh and the Big Wall".

The sages' tales, as Dina Stein, scholar of rabbinical literature and folklore, has eloquently described, are overtly and intricately intertextual. Aggadic literature is uniquely given to characteristic self-reflexivity because the tales are first and foremost devoted to rhizomal networks of internal literary allusion. As Stein notes: "the seams of the rabbinic cloth are, at least partly, sewn on the outside, making visible the process by which it was made."* Manger mines in the same literary vein,

---

* Dina Stein, *Textual Mirrors: Reflexivity, Midrash, and the Rabbinic Self*. Philadelphia: University of Pennsylvania Press, 2012, p. 4. See also Daniel Boyarin, *Intertextuality and the Reading of Midrash*. Bloomington: Indiana University Press, 1991.

although sacrilegiously, extracting the raw ore of classical tales and their ancient scriptural sources for modern refinement. Like the rabbis of old, Manger proudly points at the textual seams, but rather than sewing them, the mischievous son of a tailor revels in their unravelling.

When Manger began to conceive his first long-form prose work in the mid-1930s, the radical, anti-Semitic right-wing movement led by Octavian Goga and A.C. Cuza was rising in Romania. Watching in distress from the Polish capital, where the virulently anti-Semitic *Endecja* movement was also gaining traction, Manger began writing *The Book of Paradise*. His first attempt at setting lyrical poetry in prose, while still including a good number of poems throughout, *The Book of Paradise* was the culmination of years of writing his own poetic volumes of "midrash". His novel was initially serialized throughout the spring and into the summer of 1937 in twenty-eight instalments as *The Marvellous Life Story of Samuel Abba Aberwo* in the popular leftist Warsaw-based newspaper *Naye Folkstsaytung*. Excerpts also appeared in Manger's home-town paper, *Czernowitzer Bletter*, whose editor lauded the new work as a "description of our times in grand style, a reflection of the tragic and the grotesque of our turbulent times". Turbulent times indeed. With the descent of central Europe into fascism and the accompanying ascent of the violent anti-Jewish political Right in Poland and Romania, the world appeared to be on an inexorable, postlapsarian decline. Manger's novel probed the roots of a peculiar, universal type of nostalgia that has us yearn for people and places who aren't all that lovable when recalled in full detail—yet our love for them remains real, immense, and overwhelming nonetheless.

Late in the summer of 1937, as Samuel Abba's adventures were still hitting the news-stands, Manger, together with his partner, Rachela Auerbach, returned to Romania for what would be the last time. They stayed until autumn, visiting his home town, the Carpathians, as well as his former haunts in Iași, before heading on to Bucharest. Just two months after Manger and Auerbach returned to Warsaw, the Goga–Cuza government came to power and began the process of stripping Jews who were born outside the pre-war borders of the Romanian Kingdom of their basic rights. To extend his Warsaw residency permit, which was set to expire at the end of April 1938, Manger needed to acquire proof of employment and to renew his passport. After getting the requisite credentials from Yiddish newspapers in Romania and the United States, Manger set off to the Romanian consulate. There he learnt that he was no longer a citizen. With a passport valid for only ten more days, Manger boarded the overnight train to leave the city he had inhabited for a decade—a time he would describe as the loveliest in his life—to become a stateless person in Paris.

From his Parisian exile, Manger negotiated the contract for the publication of *The Book of Paradise*, which Auerbach signed on his behalf in Warsaw, and he revised the work for release as a single volume in February 1939. His precarious state—legal, financial, physical and psychological—left its stamp on the final draft of the book. The deceptively outlandish and childlike tone, characteristic of all of Manger's work, with its vacillation between elusive joy and melancholy, now intensified the novel's peaks of delight and troughs of despair. The outbreak of the war also amplified his insecurity and anxiety, leaving him dependent on friends and supporters for the rest of his life, first in France, then in England, the United States and, finally, Israel, where he died in 1969.

Manger returned once, if only briefly, to an entirely different Poland in the spring of 1948, almost exactly ten years after he had left. The real invitation to visit Poland, he said, was not from the official organizations responsible for the dedication of the memorial at the site of the Warsaw Ghetto, for which he had ostensibly come, but rather "from my dead readers in Poland. I was drawn here to visit them. Amongst the nations of the world, people journey to the graves of their poets, but now the Jewish poet must make the pilgrimage to the graves of his people."*

As I was finishing work on *The Book of Paradise*, I spent some time in Bukovina and Galicia, tracing Manger's youthful footsteps—in Chernivtsi, Stopchativ and Kolomyia, all found today in Ukraine. This was a few months before the Russian invasion in February 2022 and, although there was a lot of public sabre-rattling, all felt cool and crisp and peaceful. The trees of the Carpathian autumn were vibrant with golds and reds, and pools of mist filled the twilight in the towns and country meadows. My thoughts turned to Manger, who never returned here. Perhaps he wanted to preserve the landscape as it was that last day he saw it, so that it and the throngs of people who had crowded the railway station to bid him farewell in October 1937 could live on endlessly in memory and in poetry.

For his last two decades, Manger published sporadically, acutely aware of the absence of an audience. A poem published in his final collection, *Stars in the Dust* (1967), is divided into two parts. In one we encounter the bereft Prophet Elijah beside the ash and bone at the crematorium of Majdanek, where the ancient messianic messenger strokes the ash heap with his sad fingers:

---

* Marian Gid (I. Moskowski), "Poet Itzik Manger Visits Warsaw", *Forverts*, 29 May 1948, p. 6.

And he will stand here all alone,
With dishevelled beard and *payess*,
An eternal memorial stone.

And against this image is an "Evensong", in which we find the poet, who sits with a glass of wine, struggling to write, his days endlessly slipping into shadow and shine:

Silent evening. Murky gold.
A grey Jew past his prime
Piously prays away the dust
From fairs of days gone by—
May just a mumble off his tongue
Come to me in rhyme.

Manger's late poetry remains devoted to a credo he adopted early in his career: that through the transformation of the everyday into poetry, people, objects and landscapes transcend their earthly trappings to become divine. And the divine, as the Kaddish insists, will be forever magnified, lauded and exalted.

ROBERT ADLER PECKERAR

A Preface

I T STRIKES EVEN ME as a bit odd to have such a gloomy prelude to my happiest book.

But maybe it must be so? At the edge of the abyss, laughter becomes even more audacious.

Stripped of citizenship from my Romanian homeland, far away from my beloved Jewish-Polish enclave, left hanging with no passport, no visa between borders, I bow deep in this grotesque pose before my esteemed audience and present my dear Samuel Abba Strewth and the extraordinary story of his life.

The Book of Paradise is actually the first part of what I imagine to be a trilogy. *The Book of the Earth* and *The Book of the World of Chaos* will perhaps be written someday.

Still, quite a few of my most intimate experiences are found in this book of joyous abandon, much of my own life, suffering and love.

I dedicate this volume here to myself, in memory of my lonely days and nights, wandering the streets and boulevards of Paris.

The happiest moments in this eternal abandon were those spent in nocturnal watering holes with the shadows of French troubadours, those derelict singers that, perhaps, even in their own homeland, were no less lonely than I.

And that is but small consolation. But now, let's not dispirit this happy tale of Samuel Abba Strewth.

Samuel Abba, the floor is yours!

ITZIK MANGER
Paris, January 1939

THE BOOK
OF PARADISE

THE MARVELLOUS LIFE
OF SAMUEL ABBA STREWTH

I

My Last Day in Paradise

T HE TIME I SPENT in Paradise was the loveliest in my entire life. Even now I feel a pang in my heart and tears fill my eyes when I think back on that joyful time.

Often, I'll shut my eyes and relive those happy years. Those years, gone forever, will never return. Unless, of course, the Messiah comes.

In such minutes of reverie I forget that my wings have been clipped and that I was dispatched to the other world. I spread out my arms and try to fly. Only when I fall to the ground and feel the pain in my bruised nether parts do I remember that it's all gone and wings belong only to the creatures of Paradise.

So I've decided to record everything that has happened to me, both before and since my birth. I do not wish to write all this down simply to beguile the disbelievers, but rather to console myself. I know that many people have recounted their own lives in the various languages of the world. I have read a hundred or so such life stories myself and I must admit that they can really put you off. At every step I sense human pride doing the talking and that it is all, at bottom, lies. Lies that paint oneself in rosier and others in darker colours. Such a life story is nothing more than drivel, which sets out to pull the wool over the eyes of the fool who believes it and, at bottom, the selfsame writer.

Rather, I will tell everything just so, as it was. I won't alter a single hair. I don't want to delude anyone into thinking I'm some kind of holier-than-thou saint. God forbid! I've made my share of mistakes and done some good, too, and I'll admit where I have strayed and also, wherever I have done the right thing, I'll accurately tell how and what and when.

I know that many people will ask me: how can it be that a person can remember all that happened before he was born with such accuracy? They, my questioners, will even offer evidence that such a thing is not possible. Everyone knows, after all, that before a person is born an angel comes and gives a flick to the nose and, with this very flick, all that happened before is immediately forgotten, even the Holy Torah that the angels had taught this newly birthed being before being brought into this wicked world.

Those who assert this would be correct. That's really how it is. So it happens with every human being who comes into this world. An angel really does flick everyone's nose and everyone indeed forgets everything. But a miracle happened to me, an extraordinary miracle. And I want to tell of this miracle straight off so that I can spare folks the trouble of whispering their doubts in each other's ears that this Samuel Abba Strewth is just talking nonsense, stretching out lies like a housewife rolling dough for noodles.

On the day that some angel signed off on sending me to the Earth, I was just sitting there, under a Paradise tree, taking pleasure in the canaries singing amongst its branches, as it is written in the Psalms. By the way, I should tell you that compared to Paradise canaries, Earth birds are just chickenshit. In the first place, Paradise canaries are twenty times bigger and they sing like, well, you simply can't describe it in any human language. Such a thing must be heard by your own ears in order to understand the distinction.

It was twilight. Our Talmud teacher, Mr Meyer Scabies, an angel with hefty, dark-grey wings, left class for the late-day prayer in the angels' synagogue and, in the meantime, the students all took off. Some played Red Rover with other little angels and some were telling tales of pirates. I went to my favourite Paradise tree to listen to the canaries sing.

I admit: the song of the Paradise canaries was my greatest weakness. When they were singing, I forgot everything else in the world.

So there I was, lying under the Paradise tree. The canaries sang, enormous butterflies flitted amidst the Paradise grass, playing tag. When I speak of the Paradise butterflies, you shouldn't think that these are just some run-of-the-mill butterflies that you see on the Earth in summertime. If you think that, you're grossly mistaken. A Paradise butterfly is nineteen times as big as an earthly one. Each butterfly has its own different colour. One may be blue, another green, another red, another white, another black. In brief, how could I even take stock of all the colours when human language possesses not nearly enough words for all the colours in Paradise?

I had just laid myself down under the tree when I suddenly heard a voice, a familiar voice, that sounded like a silver bell: "Samuel Abba! Samuel Abba!"

I looked around and saw my friend Little Pisser, a clever angel with wise, dark eyes. As usual, his mouth was smeared with jam. He flitted over to me with his delicate bright wings and descended at my feet.

"What's up, Little Pisser? What's happened? Tell me quick or else I'll burst!"

Little Pisser wiped the sweat from under his little wings and whispered in my ear: "Samuel Abba, it's awful. I learnt that today you'll be sent to Earth. Your fate is to become a human being, you get what I'm saying?—A human being!"

My heart started pounding: *thump-thump-thump.*

"What are you talking about, Little Pisser? Who told you that? Where did you hear it?"

So Little Pisser told me how he just happened to be flying by the Paradise tavern, Righteous Noah's Inn. In the pub sat the angel Simon Bear, the biggest souse of all the angels. "He had already downed ninety-six shots and was swearing a blue streak—at whom, I don't know," Little Pisser explained. "But I saw that he was mad. He was being sent on assignment. He was to guide *you* to Earth and flick your nose and make you forget everything: Paradise, the Holy Word you've learnt, and even me, your friend Little Pisser, too."

At that, Little Pisser started to cry. His tears rolled down on to my right hand. They were gigantic tears, and hot.

My friend Little Pisser's tears moved me to tears. I patted his head and tried to console him. "Don't cry, Little Pisser, who cares what a drunken lout of an angel blathers about in a barroom? Come on, let's see if he tries to take me. I'll rip out his red beard. I'll scratch his face. I'll take a bite out of his red nose, as sure as you see me here!"

Little Pisser, however, could not calm down. "Don't you know what a bandit he is, this Simon Bear? He's a butcher," blubbered Little Pisser.

I knew that what Little Pisser was saying was the truth. Everyone trembled before the angel Simon Bear. He was almost never sober. Falling into his hands was worse than into the flames of hell. Yet they had picked him to be the one to accompany the children who were to be born and to give the famed flick to the nose.

I was quivering like a fish in water. I imagined how this drunk would take me by the hand. If I didn't go nicely, then he'd hoist me over his shoulders. And there we'd be, on the frontier of Paradise, and I could hear his drunken voice: "Gimme that honker there, ya punk. Lemme flick it and then scram!"

Everyone was afraid of this flick. It was even scarier than being born on Earth. Not just one child has had the misfortune of being flicked by this drunken angel. If you ever see some snub-nosed kid on Earth, you ought to know that he got that from an extra-forceful flick on the nose delivered by the angel Simon Bear.

"But what can we do about it, Little Pisser?" I demanded.

"Nothing," Little Pisser answered sadly. "Your fate is sealed and what's decided is decided. There's no evading the hands of Simon Bear, even with eighteen heads you couldn't. What I mean is, it would be for the best if you'd…"

"What? What?" I asked, looking him straight in the eyes.

"… If you'd go nicely, without resisting and without tears. Simon Bear detests insubordination, he detests crying. If you cry you could end up receiving a flick to the nose so hard that you might, God forbid, wind up without any nose at all. And then what a face you'd have, goddamn that Simon Bear."

Little Pisser made it clear: there was no escaping Simon Bear. The whole time Little Pisser was speaking I held my hand to my nose, which deplored with all its heart the sad fate that it might, God forbid, meet, and, deep in my heart, I beseeched the Almighty to preserve and protect it.

The entire time that I was silently praying that the Almighty would preserve and protect my nose from all prospective peril, Little Pisser was sitting beside me in the grass and scratching his forehead with his finger to indicate that he was thinking something. His wise, dark eyes suddenly gave a flash. Anytime Little Pisser thought of something, his eyes would gleam. "You know what I think, Samuel Abba?"

"What, Little Pisser?"

He looked all around to see if anyone could overhear and then he whispered in my ear: "Over in our cellar we have some holy wine that my dad was given once as medicine. I'll give you that bottle to bring with you on your way."

"What do you mean you'll give it to me to bring on my way?" I wondered. "It's yours, isn't it? What use would it be to me?"

"I see you really need it all spelt out for you," Little Pisser smiled. "What's so hard to understand, I ask you? You give the bottle to the angel Simon Bear, which he'll gladly take, then he won't give you—well, you'll have to work it out with him—a powerful punch on your nose."

"What do you mean, Little Pisser?" I cried out loud. "Do you mean you'll pinch the bottle? What about 'Thou shalt not steal'?"

"Oh, my dim-witted birdbrain," Little Pisser laughed. "Don't you know that 'Thou shalt not steal' applies to people, not angels? Go on then, show me where it's written in the Bible that the Lord of Hosts has commanded the angels not to steal!? Maybe in the Book of Numbskulls?"

I realized my friend was far smarter than me and that he was right. Yet I still didn't fully understand. Let's suppose that I gave the bottle of holy wine to the angel Simon Bear and, in return, Simon Bear would only give me a mild flick on the nose—forgetting everything that happened to me in Paradise and who I am would still be a terrible shame.

Little Pisser made it clear that he understood what I was thinking and took out of his pocket a wad of clay that he moulded in his hands until it formed a nose. Then he handed it to me and said: "While Simon Bear is drinking the holy wine, stick this clay nose on your face. When he flicks you, he'll touch the clay and you'll be left intact. Remember everything and be sure not to forget to tell the people on Earth that there's a Little Pisser here in Paradise."

He stood up, adjusted his wings, and in a loud voice said, "Come! Soon Simon Bear will be looking for you. It would be better if you go find him. Now let's fly over to my place."

And so we flew. It would be my last flight over Paradise with my dear friend.

It wasn't long before we landed at the house where Little Pisser's father Solomon-Zalman the tailor lived, an angel with a bulging Adam's apple and eyes like a calf's.

On the wall hung a sign and on it was painted an angel with patched wings, showing that Little Pisser's dad was a botcher, that is, a patchmaker who repaired worn-out angel wings.

Little Pisser went into the house and I waited outside. Not long passed before he was back, and tucked under his wing was the holy wine. He handed me the bottle and said: "Here, take it, Samuel Abba, and fly straight away to the Righteous Noah! It would be far better for you to come to Simon Bear than for him to come to you."

We hugged and kissed and then hugged and kissed some more, and who knows how long we would have stayed there if Little Pisser's mom, the angel Hannah Deborah, hadn't bellowed out the window, "Little Pisser, the tripe stew is getting cold. Come and eat!"

Again we embraced and wrapped our wings around each other. Little Pisser went into the house to eat dinner and I set off flying towards the Righteous Noah.

Paradise was pretty dark by now. The lamps were all burning in the houses where the angels lived with their families, bearded angels were poring over yellowed holy books. Fat angels with three-storeyed chins were mending shirts, young angel mothers were rocking cradles, sending their newly born angels off to sleep with a song:

> Sleep little angel, my angel sweet;
> Lovely little angel, go to sleep.
> Lay to rest your fledgling wings,
> And listen as your mama sings,
> Ay-lu-lu…

As I flew I peeked into this window and that. I was terribly envious of all the young and old angels. They would get to sleep through the night, and when they woke up in the morning they would still be in Paradise. But me? Where would I be? Fortunately, the wind cooled the tears rolling down my cheek, and if it hadn't been for that wind my tears would have seared a crater right into my face.

I touched down just in front of Righteous Noah's tavern. I peered in through the window and saw a couple of everyday angels, the ones who toiled for the tzaddikim, the holy sainted ones, ploughing their fields, reaping the harvest, getting only insult and injury in return. They sat at the tables, drinking their whisky, smoking their peasant's tobacco, and regularly letting jets of saliva spray from between their teeth on to the floor.

The angel Simon Bear sat to the side at a table, his red beard dishevelled, his eyes rolling back in his head. Clearly, he had already downed a good amount. As I caught sight of him my heart pounded with fear. *This* here is supposed to lead me out of Paradise, I thought. I simply could not get my head around it; I had to go inside.

For a good while I stood there indecisively, until I said to myself: "At some point the situation must be faced." Then I marshalled all my courage and went in.

As soon as he saw me, he wanted to stand up and greet me with a "Welcome!" But he was far too drunk and his wings were all crumpled, so he just slumped back into his seat.

I went over and helped him straighten out his wings. If he can't stand on his own two feet, he may as well fly. And it wasn't long before we took off flying to the border that separates this world from the other.

We flew out on Thursday at ten in the evening and we got to the border on Friday just before the Sabbath candles were to be lit.

You should know that it wasn't so easy to get there by flying. The angel Simon Bear, as I mentioned, was well stewed. He continually lost his sense of direction. We had been flying for three hours when the chimney of Righteous Noah's came into view once more. Simon Bear was simply drawn back to the pub where he always spent his days and nights.

Very narrowly we avoided a bit of a catastrophe. The night in Paradise was pitch darkness, without even the trace of a star. Simon Bear had forgotten his lantern at the pub, so we were flying blind through the night, not knowing where in the world we were.

In the blackness, Simon Bear crashed into another angel. It was the dream angel, who was just flying off to Earth. This crash mangled one of the dream angel's wings. Simon Bear let loose a torrent of curses at him and the dream angel started to cry. Now he wouldn't be able to fly any further and the people on Earth would sleep the whole night dreamless. With his one good wing, he lamely headed over to Solomon-Zalman the patchmaker so that he could repair his damaged wing and we—that is, Simon Bear and I—continued on our way towards the border.

The crash sobered Simon Bear up a little. He took out his pipe, stuffed it full with peasant's tobacco, struck a match and puffed as we flew on.

With every draw he took from his pipe a little glow blazed and, from time to time, we could just make out where we were in the world.

We flew past the Paradise mill, which stood on a hilltop open to all the winds that could turn its wings.

This mill inspired many tales told in Paradise. During the daytime it was a mill like all other mills. It ground wheat and rye, like any mill. But by night it was the haunt of devils and demons.

I know that you're looking at me astounded: how could there be demons in Paradise? I wondered this myself when I heard about them. It was my friend Little Pisser who told me about it. I never saw these demons for myself, but every angel will tell you how the angel Raphael, Paradise's local medic, one night went out to a patient. As he was passing by the mill he heard strange voices. Suddenly, he saw a long tongue sticking out through the window opening of the mill. The angel Raphael let out a yelp, prayed "*Hear O Israel!*" and fainted on the spot.

He was found at dawn, lying beside the mill, and they could barely get him to stir. From then on he was left with a severe defect. He stammered when he spoke; really it was such a pity.

We, that is, the angel Simon Bear and I, were still flying. We didn't exchange a word between us. Whatever Simon Bear was thinking, I could not say. How could I know? But all that I thought and felt—all that, you see, I still can recall, and other memories still.

I thought about my friend Little Pisser, asleep now in his bed, all tucked in. His feet have kicked his blanket on to the ground. Even in sleep his impudence had no equal. He slept with his finger in his mouth. Who knows, perhaps he dreamt of me, his friend, whom he said goodbye to forever?

I wanted to cry. The sobs were already in my throat. But I remembered that Simon Bear detested tears, so I choked them back and let out a barely, barely audible sigh. By daybreak the angel Simon Bear had fully sobered up. The morning wind was sharp and cold. We both caught a chill and our teeth chattered.

"What goddamned cold!" the angel Simon Bear kept grumbling, and shivered his downy wings to warm up. With every shiver of those wings he looked back in the direction of Righteous Noah's tavern.

I quickly understood that this was the right time to offer him the bottle of holy wine that my friend Little Pisser had given me.

"Simon Bear, sir," I called, surprising myself with my boldness. "Simon Bear, a nice snifter of hooch would warm you up, no? What do you say, Simon Bear, sir?"

Upon hearing the word "hooch" the angel gave a clap with his coarse, downy wing and, in doing so, scared a few Paradise swallows that had just gathered to sing a paean to the Creator.

"Hooch, oh for a snifter of hooch," he cried in a voice so loud that ten Paradise bunnies fainted out of fear and two lionesses went into labour.

I took out the bottle of holy wine from under my right wing and showed it to him. He somersaulted in the air with joy. At first I thought he had gone off his rocker.

I was terribly scared right then; having to deal with a mad angel is no picnic. Even today I shudder when I think of a young angel named Pearl, who went mad because of a disastrous love affair. Awful, it was just awful what she went through. All of Paradise was nearly upended by it.

But, to cut to the chase, as soon as Simon Bear saw the bottle in my hand he flew over, snatched it from my hand, pulled out the cork with his teeth and started guzzling. This holy wine, you should know, is pretty heavy stuff; each drop weighs about two and a half pounds.

"You know what, Samuel Abba," he said to me, "let's head down! We still have some time before we have to be at the border." He took out his brass pocket watch and looked at its red face and then we descended on to a ploughed field of Paradise.

After the angel Simon Bear had fully gulped down the entire bottle, he became so cheerful that he pinched my cheek and roared: "You're a fine lad, Samuel Abba."

Then we flew on. We prayed the morning prayer in flight. At exactly five o'clock in the evening we arrived at the border.

At the border checkpoint, Simon Bear told me that I needed to stand on one foot and recite the entire Five Books of the Torah that I had learnt. I did what he asked. After I had finished he took out an enormous pair of scissors and cut off my wings.

"All right, now, pal, let's have that honker and let me give it a flick…"

While Simon Bear had been clipping my wings, I had already stuck on the clay nose. He was so soused from the holy wine that he didn't even notice.

"Simon Bear, sir," I pleaded, "just a little flick, please Simon Bear!" I could see that he really liked me. He gave me such a light flick to the nose that I just barely felt it.

"Now vamoose, scram!"

I took a look behind me for the last time. I saw the entire Paradise panorama spread out before me, sparkling in glittering gold. I caught a last glimpse of my wings, lying on the ground.

"Farewell, Simon Bear, sir!" I said to the angel with the downy wings, and I headed down to Earth.

2

My Birth

M Y MAMA had a difficult labour. She wept and screamed and cursed my pop something awful: "Murderer!" "Bandit!" "Killer!" My pop wanly paced the room, tugging at his short black beard, not understanding why my mama was bestowing such lovely epithets on him.

He kept looking beseechingly at the midwife, Sosia-Deborah, a woman with bloated hands and a mannish voice. This midwife evidently grasped the meaning of his glances and kept grumbling under her breath: "How can I help it? See for yourself how this little fatso digs in his heels and refuses to be born."

The midwife Sosia-Deborah wasn't lying. She had tried a variety of methods already, attempting to coax me into the world by any means necessary, but to no avail. I heard her loud and clear but turned a deaf ear.

I scorned all her propositions. I scoffed at her dumb promises of the "golden watch" or "football" that she would present me with the moment I saw the light of day.

I could tell she was a great liar. In Paradise we had heard plenty of stories about her. My friend Little Pisser even warned me about her, saying that I shouldn't trust her "as far as I could throw her", and indicated that was not very far indeed.

I remembered my friend's warning and held firm, not giving in a jot. Like a yapping dog, I thought, enjoying her anger, her flapping hands, her unkempt hair.

In the end I prevailed and she left furious. She wrapped herself in her shawl and slammed the door behind her as I doubled over in laughter.

My pop stood in a corner, terribly anxious. "What is going to happen?" he muttered to himself, wringing his hands.

I felt terribly sorry for my pop, even though there was nothing I could do to help. I knew that if ever I gave in to this sense of pity, I'd be done for.

This was, as I mentioned, Friday evening. People were already heading off to pray and yet Pop was standing lost in his corner of the room.

All of a sudden he gave a wave of his hand, indicating that he wasn't going to wait for me any longer. He cast another glance at my mama and went off to pray.

Mama was left alone in the house. She had no more strength left to scream and no one remained for her to curse. She lay in bed with eyes full of tears.

I felt terribly sorry. She is, after all, a mother, I thought to myself. Yet against all this remained my dread of seeing the light of this world. The fear of being born was stronger than my pity for my mother.

By now, women were blessing Shabbos candles in all the Jewish homes. But on our table the brass candlesticks stood forsaken.

Mama looked at those brass candlesticks. It was already growing dark outside and she was still lying there as if nothing was happening, as if the holy Sabbath weren't starting.

Suddenly she hoisted herself up. No, she would not bring shame to the Shabbos candles. She dragged herself out of bed and slowly made her way to the table where the candlesticks stood.

I observed everything she did, every movement of hers, and I've got to admit her piety made a deep impression on me.

She lit the candles, her hands slowly circled the burning little flames, and then she brought her hands to cover her face. Her lips quietly whispered something, but what it was I could not hear.

It was the very first time that I saw my mama bless the candles. I was touched and troubled and made a decision: no matter what, I had to be born. I gave some thought as to how I'd manoeuvre this and decided: I would tiptoe into this new world so quietly that my mama wouldn't hear. Because of the great pains I had already caused her to suffer, I wanted to surprise her.

My mama was still standing covering her face with her hands and whispering, piously whispering, through her lips. I stealthily snuck out and she didn't notice at all.

I stood behind her and waited for her to finish her whispering, for her to take her hands down from her face. Only then would I let her see me.

I waited and waited. Every moment felt like a year. But my mama didn't know that such a distinguished guest was standing right behind her.

Finally, my wait came to an end. My mama lowered her hands from her beautiful face, swollen from crying. My heart began to flutter like a bird. I couldn't hold myself back any longer and I shouted out loud: "Good Shabbos to you, Mama!"

My mama could not believe her eyes. For several moments she stood there, as if petrified. I could see she was short of breath and I immediately regretted my little joke.

All at once her eyes lit up, her face beamed. She stretched out her arms to me, wanting to hold me, embrace me, kiss me, as is the way of all mothers.

I wouldn't allow it. I ran straight into the nook where there was a bowl filled with water. I cleaned up and dried myself off with a towel before heading back to my mama and said, "Now you can hug and kiss me as much as your heart desires."

Then she took me into her arms. She stroked me and kissed me. My forehead, my hair, every bone of mine, she kissed. And she started to call me all sorts of names: "my treasure", "my precious", "my prize", "my sweet angel".

I liked it best when she called me "my sweet angel". Little Pisser's mama used to call him that too, and all the Paradise mothers as well.

My mama wanted to lay me down in the cradle that was next to her bed. She probably thought that I'd be tired from the long journey. I thanked her for her devotion, which I genuinely adored.

"Thanks, Mama," I told her, "but I don't want to sleep just yet. I'd like to stay up until Pop comes back from shul. I'd like to hear him make the Sabbath blessing over the wine."

My words delighted my mama. Again she took me up into her arms and started kissing me: "My brilliant little kaddish, may you live a hundred and twenty years!"

This word "kaddish" that she said made me sad. This word reminded me that earthly mothers are mortal and it seemed a terrible shame that, one day, my mama would have to die. From that very first moment on I was overwhelmed by my deep love for her and, as a result, felt an intense envy of all the Little Pissers out there whose mothers would never die.

My mama didn't understand why I suddenly became so sad. She looked into my eyes and made kissy sounds with her lips and tried to cheer me up.

I looked at my mom's lovely bright face, looked into her blue eyes, but I couldn't get rid of that nagging feeling.

All at once, my mama turned pale. She clapped her hands together: "Oh! What kind of mother am I? I completely forgot!"

She ran over to a dresser, opened a drawer, rummaged about and then fished out two red ribbons that she had prepared.

She wrapped one little red band around my right arm and the other around my left. It would be a charm against the evil eye.

I took great delight in these red ribbons. I began to play with them, trying to slip them off my hands, which I could not do at all.

My mama watched as I played. She loved seeing all the faces I was making and laughed at them wholeheartedly.

Eventually I got bored playing with the ribbons. I turned my head towards the Sabbath candles still burning on the table. I saw how two little flies were circling the flames. Any closer and they would be incinerated.

I was filled with pity for these two little flies and I begged my mom: "Mama, tell them they shouldn't get so close to the flames. Something awful, God forbid, could happen to them."

As soon as my mama heard these words come from my lips she scooped me up into her arms and started kissing me again: "Oh, what a splendid child you are! May you only be healthy and strong, my darling soul."

I was greatly annoyed at my mama. Instead of warning the flies, she went on kissing me. Meanwhile, the flies succumbed to the flames of the Sabbath candles.

My mama noticed the gloom that swept over my brow, she understood that I was angry with her, and she began to respond: "Don't be angry at me, my treasure, don't be angry at your mommy…"

I told her curtly that indeed I was angry at her, terribly angry that two once-living beings were now dead on account of her carelessness. "You should have warned them, Mama, it was your duty. Why didn't you warn them?"

My mama looked at me with her big eyes, shocked by my reproof. "What are you talking about, my child? Even if I had said something, would they have understood? I don't understand the flies' language and they don't understand mine."

All this that my mother said was news to me. On Earth, one doesn't understand another's language. I was suddenly overwhelmed by the distress that could result from such bewilderment. I recognized the limitations of these earthly creatures and felt very sorry.

My mama looked into my eyes. I knew she was not to blame. She couldn't make herself understood to the flies. The real guilty one was me. I could have spoken to them in their language, yet I hadn't. I wanted to give my mother the merit of saving them. In my attempt to observe a principle of "honouring thy mother", in the end I committed a grave sin.

I comforted my mama, soothed her, and asked her to forgive my anger. "You know, Ma," I said, "I am a bit on edge and nervous after my long journey."

She immediately forgave me. Like all mothers on Earth, she didn't need to be asked repeatedly. She stroked my head with her tender hand and then she asked again, "Maybe you'd like to rest, then, my little man? Come, lie down in your cradle and Mama will sing you a lullaby."

I could see that the lullaby was already hovering at her lips. Even though I was very curious to hear it, I still insisted: "Please, Mama, let me stay up. I want to wait until Pop comes back from shul. I want to hear him sing the blessing on the wine. I'll have my first Friday-night supper at the table with my mama and pop. And after we eat, I'll join in with Pop to sing some Shabbos songs."

My mama said nothing. She stood up and took out a bottle of brandy from the cupboard along with two glasses: one for Pop and one for me. She set them on the table by the covered challah and then sat down beside the window to wait for Pop.

In the window, a star shimmered: a pious, Sabbath star. It seemed somewhat familiar to me and I asked it, quietly so that my mama wouldn't hear, to send greetings to my friend Little Pisser.

My mama looked out through the window. I was sitting on a chair and observed her, ceaselessly astonished by her beauty.

All of a sudden she turned to me, laid her finger on my mouth and said: "Shh... Your poppa's coming."

I ran over and asked her not to tell him that I was here. I would hide in the cabinet to make an unexpected appearance.

Mama agreed to it. I won her over to everything I wanted that first Friday night.

As soon as I heard my pop's footsteps, I quickly ducked into the cabinet. Pop opened the door with a cordial "Good Shabbos".

I took stock of my pop from the cabinet: a guy of average height with a black beard, dark eyes, a furrowed brow—a face full of worries. The only thing that I didn't like about him was his adenoidal voice.

Pop went about the house, saying "*Sholem aleichem*, peace upon you," sending greetings to all the angels that were, apparently, somewhere in the room. I looked in every corner, yet I saw not a single angel. My mama stood with a pious expression, listening to my pop's nasal pronouncements of "*Sholem aleichem*." I, however, grew annoyed. He's either a liar or some kind of idiot, I thought. Otherwise, how could you explain his walking around the house greeting angels when no angel whatsoever could be seen.

My pop poured out a tumblerful of the brandy and began to say the blessing. I quietly crept out from behind the sideboard. I tiptoed over to the table and, just as he was about to raise the glass to his lips, I took my little glass in my hand and belted out the blessing.

The glass dropped from his hand. He stood aghast, looked over at Mama and then back at me, apparently not comprehending a thing.

"Heaven bless you and your guest!" Mama said to Pop, pointing her finger at me. "What are you gaping at, Feivel? It's our only son, our kaddish."

Pop kept standing there, as if in a daze. Little by little he recovered. He reached out a hairy hand to me and offered a "*Sholem aleichem*".

"*Aleichem sholem*," I responded, "and peace also upon you, Pop!" And we all sat down at the table.

Mama served the meal. Looking at Pop with his son, she delighted, taking proud pleasure in them both, and in her heart she wished that such joy would never be disturbed.

We kept silent the whole time we ate. Pop and I didn't say a word. From time to time we examined each other and then went on eating.

I could tell that my father wondered how I could handle a fork and spoon like a grown-up. Pop didn't know that I still remembered the entirety of the holy books from back in Paradise. And really, how could he have known, since we hadn't even exchanged two words between us.

I noticed that my mama had eaten almost nothing. She barely picked at her food: at most a morsel of meat or a scrap of challah or a spoonful of chicken soup. For her, it was sufficient that I ate—no evil eye—with a hearty appetite. I didn't budge an inch from my pop's side. She gazed at me and couldn't take her eyes away.

Pop started singing the Shabbos songs. I didn't care for this at all. I remembered Friday nights back in Paradise, where the singing of those hymns would tug at all the strings of my heart.

My pop was unaware of my opinion and continued to drone on nasally, thinking God knows what kind of wonders he was showing me. It really started to get my goat. Soon enough I'd just keel over.

When I couldn't hold back any longer, I said to my pop, "You know what, Pop, why don't you take a break and let me sing some on my own."

My pop went red. A vein bulged in his forehead. He raised his hand to pay me some respect as only a father can.

My mama was in the kitchen just then. Who knows whether or not my pop would have given me a pop in the teeth and I'd be down for the count, as they say. But fortunately I just opened my mouth and started singing. Pop's hand was left suspended in mid-air. And it remained hanging there until I finished.

As I sang, all the birds of the city flocked together and perched on our window and our rooftop and wherever there was an open space.

Mama was standing in the entry to the kitchen, holding a pot with one hand and wiping the tears from her eyes with the other.

The flames of the Shabbos candles danced, bowing at my side, greeting me like I was aristocracy, a noble of the highest rank.

The cat, who was in the midst of cleaning her kittens, stopped mid-lick with her tongue sticking out.

Our neighbour, Samuel Zanvil, who was just sitting down to a bowl of chicken noodle soup, remained transfixed with a noodle on his bearded chin and a spoon in his hand as he listened to my hymns.

At our door and window, men, women and children gathered. They stood with their ears pricked, anxious not to miss a note.

The men kept their hands on their beards and the women held theirs to their hearts. And the children held their fingers in their mouths.

Deaf Shachna yelled over to Deaf Berel that everyone ought to hear this, himself included: "It has the flavour of Paradise."

Deaf Berel nodded his head to indicate that he agreed. He had never heard such a thing as long as he had lived. And Deaf Berel is not just anybody, he's heard some things in his life.

The priest at the Orthodox church later swore that when he was in his orchard that Friday night his apples burst into bloom, instantaneously ripened and dropped right to the ground.

I do not recall how long I sang. I only remember that, by the time I had finished, my father had lowered his hand. Apparently, he had forgotten that he had raised it to give me a slap.

An entire river of tears had amassed around my mother. Had I sung for another half-hour, her tears would have flooded the house.

As soon as I finished my hymns all the birds flew off, each to its own nest. The cat went on washing her kittens and our neighbour slurped the last of his chicken noodle soup.

The door opened and a whole host of people barged in. It was the first time in my life I had seen so many caftans and beards.

"Who's singing so beautifully here, Feivel?" they asked Pop.

He, pointing his finger in my direction, answered: "Him! That's my boy, my son, who was born just this evening."

"Congratulations are in order then, Feivel," the folks said, wishing Mama and Pop "*Mazel tov!*"

Each of them greeted me with a "Peace upon you" along with wishes for my future piety. After so many peace-upon-yous I was left with a sore hand. But the door was not shut just yet. Barely had one bunch left before more piled in, splitting my ears with their *mazel-tov*s and their peace-upon-yous nearly dislocating my wrist.

Fortunately, my mama intervened. She couldn't bear to see my distress and shouted to the guests: "Maybe you could let the child rest and please come some other time. To his bris, God willing."

It took some time before all the folks had cleared out. When I was left alone with my parents I said: "Tomorrow, after the close of Sabbath, would you be so kind as to invite over the rabbi, along with his juridical assistant, and the town magnate, too? I'd like to tell you and them about what I have seen and heard and experienced in Paradise."

Again, Pop was left speechless. He barely spluttered out: "What do you mean you'll tell us about Paradise? You still remember what happened to you there? Didn't the angel flick your nose so that you'd forget?"

I assured my pop that I remembered everything accurately, that I hadn't forgotten a thing, and to prove that I was telling the truth I told him the whole story about Simon Bear, who brought me from Paradise to the border of this world.

Pop was flabbergasted. He would not let up for a second. Over and over he asked and re-asked about every detail. And over and over I recounted it for him, and surely we would have been sitting there all night if my mama hadn't interrupted: "What are you hounding the child for, Feivel? You can see that he's tired. Tomorrow is another day and you'll have plenty of time to discuss this with him as much as you want. Now come, my little pussycat, come to bed."

Mama took me by the hand. She laid me in the cradle and tucked me in. As she rocked the cradle, she sang me her lullaby for the very first time.

I lay in the cradle with my eyes open for a little while, unable to fall asleep. But with the cradle's rocking and my mama's song, finally I drifted off.

3

My First Saturday on Earth

POP GOT UP EARLY on Saturday morning. I lay in my cradle and observed everything that he did, having woken up much earlier than he had. Wonderstruck, I watched as two golden sun spiders crept out from two sides of the room. One from the southern wall and the other from the eastern wall. They crawled out slowly, approaching each other. Just above Pop's bed, they shook hands and—*boom!* Down they fell into my pop's beard.

My pop woke up, his beard gave a quiver, and both sun spiders fell to the ground. I really enjoyed this show.

Pop clambered out of bed and started to dress. Before you knew it, he was all ready. He poured out the water to wash his hands and began pacing the room, if I'm not mistaken maybe two hundred times.

This pacing grew tiresome after a while. I saw him approach my cradle and I quickly shut my eyes.

My pop stood above me, looking me over. He was probably wondering who I took after, him or my mama. Then I felt him poke me. "Wake up," he said, "enough snoozing. It's time to go to shul."

I shut my eyes even tighter, pretending to be sleeping still.

I have to admit, it felt pretty nice in my mama's cradle and I had no desire to go to shul with my pop.

But Pop insisted. He poked me harder and harder and was nearly shouting: "What will it take to wake you up, you little stinker?!"

His yelling awakened my mama. Her lovely eyes sparkled at him and she offered him this earful: "What do you want from the child, Feivel? Where on earth did you ever get such an idea to drag a newborn baby, not even a day old, to shul? What has got into you? Let the child rest now, you blockhead."

Upon hearing "blockhead" Pop shrank a bit. He was no match for my mother's tongue-lashing. He smiled dumbly and answered: "Never mind then, Zelda. If you say not to, then we won't."

I learnt just then that my mama was called Zelda. I loved that name.

My pop thought he was done with her, but he was sorely mistaken. "*Never mind?!*" my mama scowled. "Just look at the blockhead! 'Never mind!' He hasn't even got enough sense to know that you can't go dragging a newborn to shul. What a blockhead! Such a villain! You'd have to search the world to find his equal."

Pop stood there as if flogged. He hadn't expected such a raking over the coals, especially so early on a Saturday morning. He snatched his tallis and ran off to shul like he was escaping a fire.

My mama got out of bed and dressed. She leant into the cradle and stroked my head. "Sleep, little man, sleep, my pussy-cat, I wish I could take on all your distress."

I grasped my mama's hand and began kissing it. I thanked her for my rescue. "Many thanks, Mama," I said, "may you live a hundred and twenty years for how you told off Pop. He didn't seem to care that I needed my sleep and went and woke me up."

I had told my mama an outright lie. The devil (may his name be blotted out) made me do it. I straight away regretted it and wanted to confess immediately, but my shame stopped me in my tracks.

This was, by the way, the only untoward incident on that particular Saturday morning. The rest of the day continued like any other Saturday, solemnly and a bit dull. Pop came back from shul and we ate. Then Pop took a nap. Mama sat down to read her Ladies' Home Bible.

I must note that of all that Saturday's dishes, I liked the cholent the best—the only dish that had a real taste of Paradise.

Pop snored. Mama murmured barely audibly above her Bible. Butterflies hovered at the windowsill. My eyes started to feel heavy. I dozed off and woke up again around dusk. The house had already grown dark and Mama was quietly and piously bringing the Shabbos to a close with a blessing.

My mama's prayer roused a sharp longing in me, drawing me back, back to Paradise. In my mind I could see Paradise one dusky Saturday evening. Here was Sovereign King Avenue: young angel ladies strolled, making eyes at the young angel gentlemen passing by. Since it was the Sabbath, you should understand, there was no flying in Paradise, you could only go by foot.

"God of Abraham, of Isaac, and of Jacob," Mama chanted from her seat in the corner, and I could picture our holy Patriarchs as they strolled in Paradise. Our forefather Abraham walked with his hands clasped behind his back. Our forefather Isaac wore a pair of thick-rimmed dark spectacles (his vision was always pretty lousy), and Jacob our forefather always brought along his little tobacco box, taking pinches of snuff and then sneezing so loud it echoed throughout Paradise.

Everyone in Paradise was terribly envious of our Patriarchs. Each of them had his own lovely villa, each with an orchard, and vast swaths of land as well, that the poor angels tilled.

I recalled that Paradise Saturday twilight, when the Patriarchs were strolling down Sovereign King Avenue as usual. They talked amongst themselves and were getting a little hot under the collar to boot. I was very curious to hear what they were talking about. Probably, I assumed, they're discussing the Holy Law. It would be worth finding out.

My friend Little Pisser was walking beside me. "You know what, Little Pisser?" I turned to him. "Let's have a listen to what the holy Patriarchs are talking about."

I quickly convinced Little Pisser. His wise, dark eyes shone. "All right, Samuel Abba, let's go listen."

We took each other's hand and quietly trailed the holy Patriarchs. They were so engrossed in their conversation that they didn't even notice us.

"Listen to me," Isaac our forefather was saying to our forefather Jacob, "you've got to break it off with those two handmaids of yours. Only then will you have peace in your home. You can see that Rachel and Leah can't live together with your concubines. And your wives' squabbles at home are an embarrassment for all of Paradise."

Abraham, who was walking on their right, nodded his head, indicating that Isaac was correct. "It's just not right, Jacob. You hear what we're telling you? Go and get rid of both of those concubines."

"Grandpa," countered Jacob our forefather, "I won't do that. I lived a full life with them on Earth and it was hard enough to get them into Paradise. And now I ought to go and drive them from my home? You think that's fair, Grandpa?"

"Fair-*shmair*," Abraham gestured dismissively with a flourish of his hand, "you do what your pop tells you and what your grandpa tells you, too. It's for your own sake."

"What? To repeat what went down with Hagar, but times two?" Jacob said angrily. "I don't wanna and I'm not gonna. The women can go ahead and claw each other's eyes out."

Jacob's insinuation about the whole Hagar affair clearly ticked Abraham off. He turned beet red and screamed, "Scoundrel! Is that how you talk to your grandfather?" and he gave Jacob a resounding smack.

I was stunned. I grabbed Little Pisser by the arm and begged, "Come on, Little Pisser, let's get out of here. I'm scared that punches will be flying soon. I just wanted to hear a little discussion of the Law and in the end it came to blows."

Little Pisser smiled. "Whatever you want, I'll do, Samuel Abba. Anything you like."

"How about we go back to the Paradise tree and listen to the canaries sing."

"Okay, Samuel Abba, let's go!"

On the way to the canaries I asked my friend: "You think Jacob will really kick them out?"

"Who knows?" Little Pisser's eyes gleamed. "Patriarchs are a pretty pig-headed bunch. The more you live, the more you learn."

My mama lit a candle and announced: "Here's to a good week!"

I was so deep in my recollection that I didn't even hear Mama's good week blessing. She walked over and gazed at me: "What are you thinking about, pussycat?"

"Nothing, Mama, just daydreaming."

I felt that I shouldn't tell her about this indelicate scene from Paradise. She's quite pious, my mama, and this would have made a shocking impression.

But she wouldn't let me off, my mama simply had to know what I was thinking about. I was in a terrible fix. Luckily I recalled another episode that happened to me in Paradise. "I was just remembering, Mama," I told her, "how Jacob our forefather once gave me a pinch on the cheek back in Paradise."

"Tell me about it, pussycat!"

"There's not much to tell, Mama. Jacob was heading to pray in the Forefathers' Synagogue. His kerchief was poorly tied to his caftan and it fell on the ground. I picked it up off the ground and handed it to him saying, 'Jacob, sir, you lost your kerchief, here it is.' He took the kerchief from me and asked, 'What portion of the Torah is read this week?' 'Genesis 47 through 50,' I answered, and he gave me a pinch on my cheek. 'You're a fine lad!' he said, and went on his way."

"Where?" Mama asked, her eyes gleaming. "Which cheek did he pinch?"

"Right here, my left cheek, on this spot." I pointed to the place with my finger.

Mama kissed the spot maybe a thousand times. It was not her usual kind of kiss, but rather each was devout and tremulous. Was it not a big deal that her son's cheek had been held between two fingers of our forefather Jacob himself!?

My mama was very religious. With all my heart I couldn't begrudge her this joy.

Pop came home from shul and recited the blessings that separated the holy Shabbos from the start of the new work week. I observed the ceremony with great interest. When he finished the blessings, I asked him: "Pop, did you invite over the people I mentioned to you earlier?"

"They're due any minute," Pop answered. "But behave politely towards them. You think it's no big deal that these are the finest Jews in town coming: the rabbi Isaiah, his juridical assistant Zadok, and a genuine town magnate, Mr Michael Hurwitz?"

I promised my pop I'd be on my best behaviour for these local bigwigs and that I would be especially polite.

"And for God's sake, tell them nothing but the truth. You hear what I'm telling you: nothing but the truth!" Pop added.

"What do you take me for, Pop?" I asked, feeling rather insulted. "You think I'm just some jerk who goes around shooting his mouth off?"

My mama, bless her, dove into the fray. She was always ready to tell off my pop, especially when she could tell that I was being insulted.

"What do you want from the child, Feivel?" she roared at my pop. "He just came into this world and here you go suspecting him of lying. Have you ever once heard him lie, Feivel? Now have you?! What are you gawking at?"

Pop wanted to respond or, rather, to defend himself, since he meant, God forbid, no harm, he just wanted… "You see, Zelda?"

But my mama wouldn't let him talk himself out of it. No one was more of an expert in talking than she was, and once a storm was under way there was no turning back for her. She would continue until complete victory.

"Just look at him: the father of this delight! And there he goes accusing a baby of lying. Are you a poppa? You're a brick, a pest, a blatherskite, but you're no poppa."

Mama calling Pop a "blatherskite" nearly knocked me off my feet. Pop stood there bewildered. This was his second coal-raking of the day and there was a full week still in store.

"Now, I didn't say… I didn't say anything," he stammered. "Let's change the subject, Zelda!"

Looking at my pop as he stood pitiful and perplexed, I was seized by an urge to yell "Blatherskite!" right in his face. Fortunately, I remembered the commandment about honouring thy father and I held back.

Pop pulled a holy book off a bookshelf and sat down at the table thumbing through its yellowed pages. I got the impression that he was hiding his face in shame.

Mama went into the kitchen to heat up the samovar so she could serve our guests, who were due any moment.

I sat on the floor and watched as my pop's shadow swayed back and forth on the wall. His shadow appeared three times as large as Pop himself. I was curious as to whether Pop's shadow was as big a coward as Pop. And what would happen if my mama's shadow met his on the wall? What a fine wedding that would be. I'd be very interested to see.

I crept over to where my pop was sitting and, out of curiosity, started tickling his foot. At first, just softly, but then in earnest. Pop got mad. He wanted to give me a thrashing. At that very moment my mama entered with the boiling samovar. Pop sat back down on his chair, as if nothing had happened.

Not long passed before the invited guests arrived at our house. First in was the rabbi, followed by his juridical assistant, and then the town magnate, Mr Michael Hurwitz. They offered their *mazel-tov*s to my mama and pop and greeted me with a "*Sholem aleichem*."

I took a good look at them. I liked the rabbi the best: a small, skinny man with a long white beard, trembling hands and a kind smile in his squinty, rheumy eyes. His assistant was somewhat taller and much younger, maybe in his forties. He had a mole on his right cheek and spoke in a calm, unhurried manner, relishing every word that came out of his own mouth.

I reserved a particular distaste for the magnate, Mr Michael Hurwitz, a stout man with a trimmed little beard. He flaunted his gold excessively: gold rings on his fingers, a gold chain attached to a gold watch, and a mouth full of gold teeth. But the most irritating thing was the respect that the rabbi and his assistant paid him, as if he were some kind of genius.

Our guests took their seats at our table. The rabbi sat directly across from me, observing me with his bleary eyes, wondering at how I sat and conducted myself like a grown-up.

Everyone sat in silence for a while. My mama sat to the side, taking pleasure in watching me. Anyone who didn't see my mama that Saturday night never saw true beauty in his life.

The rabbi was the first to open his mouth. He passed his hand over his long white beard and remarked, "So, it seems you wish to tell us about Paradise, eh? By all means, let's hear what's doing there."

I sat up in my chair and said that I was prepared to tell them everything that I had experienced in Paradise before my birth on one condition: that they—the rabbi, his assistant, the magnate and my pop—all swear that they would tell no one else. I exempted my mama from taking this oath because I knew Mama's word was good enough.

Even though they didn't take this seriously, they had no choice in the matter. All had to stand up, raise their hands and repeat after me: "By the moon and the stars, we give our word—we shall keep this secret, so help us O Lord."

After swearing, they all sat back in their seats and I turned to my mama: "Mama, please draw all the windows and seal up any cracks, so that no one, God forbid, would be able to sneak over and listen in. The wind, by its very nature, likes to blow the whistle, to be a snitch. The wind can spread any news to anyone and it makes no difference if it's to the cherry tree in the garden or the vanes of a windmill."

Mama obeyed immediately, bless her! She plugged all the cracks in the walls and shuttered the windows. The room's atmosphere grew quite sombre. If I'm not mistaken, I even saw the rabbi's beard trembling.

I gave my brow a scratch with my finger, trying to figure out just how to begin. After reflecting a moment I decided, first and foremost, to tell how the angel Simon Bear accompanied me from Paradise and the story of the clay nose. I painted a picture of Simon Bear with the sharpest detail, as if he were right there before us. The rabbi was nearly grasping at his hair: "Oh, my! Oh, my! Could an angel be such a drunk? Oh, my! So that's why everyone is so mum about what goes on in Paradise, huh?"

I explained to him that no moralizing ever helped with Simon Bear. In Paradise, you simply got used to such tribulations. You were content when things went more or less smoothly, and when Simon Bear occasionally forgot to beat his wife.

"He beats his wife, too, the scoundrel?" the rabbi exclaimed in astonishment. "Goodness gracious, folks, goodness gracious!"

"And how, Rabbi! His wife, Candy, an angel who's continually in the family way, is always going around with black eyes and bruises all over."

"If such things happen in Paradise, what's the point of it all," the rabbi sighed woefully, and was joined in sighs by his assistant, the magnate and my pop.

The entire time I was telling them about the angel Simon Bear, the magnate Mr Michael Hurwitz kept running his fingers over his nose. As he listened to me it dawned on him, for the first time in his life, that he had a bit of a pug nose himself and he had only come to learn this from me.

"Hmm, hmm," he grumbled, "it's a good thing he doesn't live on Earth or else I'd have him brought up on charges."

You ought to know that the magnate Michael Hurwitz had a thing for legal affairs. "Well, well, if he were hauled off and indicted in court: in the matter of the angel Simon Bear, the case would be one hundred per cent open and shut."

I already regretted bringing them my story. What good can come of this, I thought, stirring these religious folks up. They simply can't handle the truth. But since I had already begun, I decided to continue to the very end.

The juridical assistant, Zadok, gave a little cough, then turned to me to ask if I would tell him approximately how big Paradise is. That is, he added, he was interested in ascertaining the overall area occupied by Paradise.

I told him that Paradise is, no evil eye, big enough. It stretches approximately four hundred thousand square miles. On the east it borders Turkish Paradise and on the west Gentile Paradise. To the south Paradise is separated from Earth by two thousand curtains of mist, and in the north a sea of fire separates it from hell.

"Oh my! Oh my!" said the rabbi's assistant, grasping his face with his hands.

"Will wonders never cease!" said the rabbi, grabbing at his beard.

"*Sonderbar!* Most peculiar!" said the magnate, fondling his gold watch.

I continued:

*

Our Paradise is populated mostly by angels and pious Jews. You only seldom meet Jews from Lithuania and White Russia. And then there are a great many Polish and even more Galician holy tzaddikim. There aren't a lot of warm feelings between the angels and the tzaddikim. The angels maintain that there are too many tzaddikim in Paradise: a thousand per square kilometre. There's hardly enough room to breathe, the angels complain, and they curse the tzaddikim terribly.

There's not a lot of affection amongst the tzaddikim themselves. To a Galician tzaddik, your Polish tzaddik is no more than a scrap of treif. And vice versa to the Polish tzaddik. But when it comes to the Lithuanian ones, both groups of tzaddikim are in full agreement. Such a tzaddik should never have been admitted into Paradise.

The main issue that bothers the angels is that the tzaddikim go around idle all day. They loaf about as if they're in their own private heaven, not lifting a finger, and they boss around the angels as if the angels were created to serve them alone during the six days of Genesis.

At one general assembly of the angels, things went so far that the angel Jonah Taub put forth a proposal that demanded that the Master of the Universe curtail the rights of the tzaddikim and introduce a quota system for Paradise.

Nearly all the angels applauded this proposal, and it would have certainly got a majority of votes if the tzaddikim hadn't got lucky. At the very last moment, a tow-headed angel named Raziel, who was a bit of a mystic, spoke on their behalf.

He took the floor and gave a speech. Nobody understood a word he said. In general, this angel's turn of phrase was difficult to follow. But soon they got the gist of what he was saying: he was defending the tzaddikim and was opposed to the proposal made by the angel Jonah Taub. At a certain moment, he even referred to this same Jonah Taub as a "Haman" and a "Heathen".

This caused quite a stir. Raziel was a prestigious angel in Paradise. So, even if they couldn't understand what he said, many thought: "Who knows what kind of wisdom lies hidden in his words?" One side was all for the angel Jonah Taub's proposal. The other supported the angel Raziel. It nearly came to blows. One side argued passionately: the tzaddikim keep calling the shots in Paradise. They go on behaving as if they live some Edenic ignorant bliss, ruling the roost, and if you say so much as a word they answer with the famous opening word of the Song of Songs: "*Yishokeini*", which means, in plain Yiddish, you can go kiss my…

Ever since that assembly meeting the angels were divided into two factions, I explained further. One faction was known as B.A.ST.A. (that is, the Bloc of Anti-Sainted Angels) and the other as F.O.TZ. (Friends of the Tzaddikim).

*

I outlined the various fighting strategies of both sides, told them about a whole series of pamphlets that one faction launched against the other, and one camp's organized attacks against the other.

"Oh my! Oh my!" said the rabbi's assistant, grasping his face with his hands.

"Will wonders never cease!" said the rabbi, pulling at his beard.

"*Sonderbar!* Most peculiar!" said the magnate, and fondled his gold watch.

I should explain that the magnate Mr Michael Hurwitz often travelled to Leipzig on business and was fond of peppering his speech with High German words.

"At least the tzaddikim weren't harmed, God forbid." My pop breathed a bit easier, and then looked over at the rabbi. I understood my pop's look. His eyes clearly said: "You ought not to be afraid of entering Paradise, Rabbi. If I were a tzaddik like you, you'd see what I would accomplish there."

With all his heart, my pop longed for Paradise, and I knew why. Here on Earth, he was my mama's footstool. In Paradise, she would be his footstool. Then he could put his feet up on her and avenge all the indignities that she heaped on him in this world.

The rabbi asked me if I had seen the Font of Wisdom and, when I said I had, he gave a deep sigh. The magnate asked if there were gold coins in Paradise. And the rabbi's juridical assistant asked me if the angel women were punctual with their ritual ablutions.

Every question they asked disgusted me. I had barely answered one query when they posed yet another. Really, I had invited these people so that I could tell them about my experiences in Paradise, but now I was in the midst of a full-on interrogation. It really got my goat.

I lost the will to go on talking. A few times, I gave a deliberate yawn to drop a hint that I was tired and they should get out of my hair already.

They appeared to take my hints, but made a comfortable footbath for themselves out of them and continued asking their questions. The rabbi, for instance, wanted to know if I had seen the Behemoth set aside for the great Feast of the Righteous, and whether it really was such a substantial beast that its flesh would be enough for all the Jews in the world when the Messiah came.

I could take no more and told them that I was tired and would tell nothing further. But if they'd be so kind as to come again the following night to sit quietly and listen, I would tell them tomorrow about how I met my friend, the angel Little Pisser.

"Oh my, oh my! An angel called 'Little Pisser', oh my!" blurted out the rabbi's assistant, and grasped his face in his hands.

"Will wonders never cease, an angel with the name 'Little Pisser'!" said the rabbi, grabbing at his beard.

"*Sonderbar!* Most peculiar!" said the magnate Mr Michael Hurwitz, clasping the gold chain of his gold watch.

I, for one, wanted nothing more of them. I called my mama to tell her that it was high time that I be nursed. I hadn't had a thing to eat since five o'clock.

After my mama nursed me, she carried me to the cradle that stood next to her bed. She laid me down in it and started rocking it.

I lay there thinking that these creatures on Earth are rather odd, indeed. And, thinking this, I drifted off to sleep.

The rabbi, his assistant and the town magnate sat awhile longer at our house, drinking tea and chatting with Pop. After some time, they all left. In the doorway the rabbi said to my pop: "So, tomorrow then, God willing, Feivel."

4

My Friend Little Pisser

O N THE SECOND NIGHT, when we were all assembled around the table again, I rolled up my sleeves and began:

*

I first met my friend Little Pisser at Hebrew school when we both were put in Meyer Scabies's Talmud class. I loved Little Pisser from the moment we met.

I should note that everybody who met this little angel, with his wise, dark eyes, loved him too. Except, of course, our Talmud instructor, the angel Meyer Scabies, who caused him nothing but grief.

To be fair, the Talmud instructor had reason to be irritated by my friend Little Pisser. My pal very nearly caused him some misery with one of his pranks.

It was a Tuesday afternoon. The Talmud angel was holding forth and brandishing his whipping rod over us for so long that he tired himself out. His eyelids started getting heavy and it didn't take long before he was snoring. As was his custom, he nodded right off. The little whip fell from his hand.

Little Pisser's eyes gave a sparkle. He turned to us, the other students, and asked: "Can you fellas keep a secret?"

"Yes!" we all answered, waiting with great interest for what was in store. We knew that Little Pisser was up to something.

Little Pisser extracted a wad of tar from his pocket and approached the Talmud instructor on tiptoe. The Talmud angel's wings hung wearily down. Little Pisser delicately lifted the instructor's right wing, smeared it with tar, and then stuck it fast to the bench. After he finished with the right wing, he repeated the same with the left.

We were all choking with laughter, picturing the moment when the Talmud angel would wake up.

We waited and waited, but our instructor kept on sleeping with no intention of waking up soon.

Seeing that we could hardly wait, my friend Little Pisser went up to the sleeping Talmud angel and shouted in his ear: "Teacher, it's time for the evening prayer!"

The Talmud angel perked up and wanted to fly over to the shul. He gave a jerk with his wings, which were glued with tar to his bench, and both ends of his wings tore right off. The teacher fell on the ground, screaming in agony.

His wife Golda, an angel whose right eye was clouded by a cataract, flew in from the kitchen, hooting and hollering. The local medic, the angel Raphael, was called in immediately. He ordered a special bandage from the Paradise pharmacy and stuck it on to the Talmud angel's wings.

From then on, our Talmud teacher harboured a grudge against my friend Little Pisser. Whether he was guilty or not, the very first one to get a lashing was always Little Pisser.

But my friend Little Pisser was the sort of prankster whose mischief no whip in the world could tame. That's why I loved him so much. The two of us were permanently joined at the hip. Any issue I had, I'd discuss with him first and he would counsel me on everything. "Little Pisser, can you give me a little advice?"

And Little Pisser would give his forehead a scratch with his finger and think awhile until he came up with some guidance. "What do you say about that, Samuel Abba?"

I told him everything that crossed my mind, never holding anything back from my best friend, who was as dear to me as one's own brother, maybe even dearer than one's own brother.

I know you'll tell me that the gag that Little Pisser played on the Talmud angel wasn't all that original. All schoolboys on Earth boast about the tricks they play on their earthly teachers. To that I'll just say that, first of all, this prank was not the only one that Little Pisser pulled in Paradise, and second, Earth schoolboys are known liars and braggers, to boot, while Little Pisser really did pull off these pranks.

Once Little Pisser came over to me. He was very sad. He looked at me for a moment with his sorrowful little eyes and then exclaimed: "You know what I say, Samuel Abba? Life in Paradise is simply unfair."

I looked at him astounded. I had no idea why he said this to me. Little Pisser heaved a sigh and continued: "You know, Samuel Abba, I have this uncle. We call him Baron Haim. He lives in his own brick house on Prophet Elijah Boulevard, a split-level building with a new tin roof."

"I know, Little Pisser," I responded, "your uncle is the lease manager for all the distilleries in Paradise. They say he's as rich as Croesus."

"He's also an enormous pig," added Little Pisser. "If he lived in Gentile Paradise, they'd roast a great holiday feast from a swine of his size."

"But what did you want to say, Little Pisser? Tell me, you've got me curious."

"Listen closely," Little Pisser said, "this uncle of mine, the pig, has a goat that gives twenty quarts of milk every twelve minutes. We've got to get this goat out of her pen and take her away."

"But where will we take her, Little Pisser? The suspense is killing me!"

"To my Uncle Joel the bookbinder, who lives over on Johanan the Sandalmaker Street. He's sick with consumption and needs that goat's milk far more than the angel Baron Haim."

"You're right, Little Pisser," I had to admit, "life really is unfair in Paradise. Your rich uncle, healthy as a horse, has a goat that gives milk that he needs as much as a fish needs a bicycle. Meanwhile, your poor uncle, suffering from consumption, all he's got is misery—but no milk, which he needs for dear life."

Little Pisser gave his brow a scratch, as he usually did when he thought. "You know what, Samuel Abba?"

"What, Little Pisser?"

"We ought to sneak that goat out from Uncle Baron Haim and get it over to Uncle Joel."

"Sure, Little Pisser," I agreed, "but when? Seems like we'd have to do it at just the right moment."

"It'll be fine, Samuel Abba," Little Pisser laughed. "Uncle Baron Haim always takes a little nap around midday. That's when my aunt, the angel Yenta, goes to her seamstress to get fitted for new wings."

"And then, and then?" I prodded my friend.

"And that's when I'll take the goat from its pen and bring her to my poor uncle. You'll stand lookout on the street and let me know if my aunt is coming."

"All right, Little Pisser, I'm ready. When do you reckon we should do it?"

"Let's think, when?" Little Pisser shrugged his wings. "Let's not commit to anything, but, say, tomorrow, just after noon."

We fixed a place to meet. Little Pisser described the place precisely. The rest of the day I spent in a daze. The goat that gave twenty quarts of milk per minute trampled over my dreams the whole night long.

The next day at exactly the appointed time I met my friend at our predetermined spot. We headed straight off towards Prophet Elijah Boulevard, where Little Pisser's rich uncle lived.

Prophet Elijah Boulevard was a very beautiful street. All of Paradise's upper crust lived there. The finest building on the block belonged to the sainted Rebbe of Sadagura. He was accustomed to spreading out over as wide an expanse in Paradise as on Earth. It's worth pointing out that on the same boulevard, Rahab, the former Jericho harlot, opened a nail salon where rich lady angels got their manicures. You should know, by the way, that in Paradise she became exceedingly pious. She's read all sorts of religious books and pamphlets and had them all nearly memorized. She didn't much care for her work, but a living's a living. In Paradise you almost forgot she was once a whore.

My friend Little Pisser and I stationed ourselves outside the angel Baron Haim's house and began our wait for his aunt to leave. This would be our sign that his uncle was having his nap.

We waited for about half an hour until the angel Baroness Yenta emerged from the house. We watched after her until she disappeared.

"May she have nothing but trouble," my friend Little Pisser cursed after his aunt. "There she goes off to blow a fortune on the latest fashions while my Uncle Joel the bookbinder's wife Riva can't even afford to patch up her wings, which are so worn you'd think she was a beggar and offer her a handout."

My friend Little Pisser wanted to go straight into the yard where the pen was. But, at that very moment, an old man with a thick walking stick in his hand came by. He stopped my friend and asked: "Little angel, where are you off to?"

Little Pisser recognized the old fellow right away. It was the Prophet Elijah. In the past, he used to head down to Earth from time to time to help a pauper, perform a miracle or make sure that some pitiful creature had something to eat for a Shabbos supper. Lately, he had got depressed. The wretched of the Earth had given up having faith in awaiting his assistance. They had decided to help themselves. "Let them," the Prophet Elijah said scornfully, "let them help themselves, those… what do you call them… those Barksists."

Ever since the Prophet Elijah stopped descending to Earth, he did nothing but loaf about in Paradise, strolling all day long on the boulevard that bore his name. He wouldn't stroll down any other street for love or money.

"Little angel, where are you off to?"

I was frightened, certain that our whole endeavour was doomed. Out of thin air, now, you've got old Prophet Elijah, who just loves sticking his nose in everywhere.

But my pal Little Pisser did not miss a beat. He knew the old man's weakness: he loved when you recounted the miracles he performed back in the days when he enjoyed doing such things. Now, even though he still could perform miracles, he didn't feel like it.

"They can go help themselves, those, what do you call them there? Those, those Barksists," he said, spitting with contempt as soon as he uttered the word.

Little Pisser told him he was right. Then he told some stories about the prophet and the old man smiled, believing that everything Little Pisser told him was true. Agonizingly, we waited for the old man to leave. Little Pisser wiped the sweat from his brow, having put in quite an effort.

"Now, Samuel Abba," he said to me, "go and watch out to see if anyone is coming. If, God forbid, someone is, then put your two fingers in your mouth and give a whistle."

"All right," I answered, "but make it quick, Little Pisser."

My friend took his time. Every minute seemed like an eternity. My head was twisting from right to left to see if anyone, God protect us, was coming. My heart was pounding like crazy.

My friend Little Pisser appeared. He was leading his uncle's goat by a cord.

"Quick, Little Pisser, quick! Let's fly to your Uncle Joel's!" My heart was telling me that something was going to happen.

"Dummy," said Little Pisser, "we have to go by foot. A goat doesn't have wings."

We had barely taken a few steps when we saw Little Pisser's aunt, the angel Baroness Yenta, flying hurriedly homewards. Evidently, she had forgotten something. His aunt saw us and started to create a scene. My friend Little Pisser and I flew off to make an escape, dangling the goat in the air. Every "*meh*" of hers resounded alarmingly over the entire boulevard.

Little Pisser held on to the cord. Breathlessly we continued flying. Shmaya the cop, an angel with a green uniform who was standing on the corner directing traffic with a little baton so that the angels wouldn't, God forbid, crash into each other, started blowing his whistle.

A genuine pursuit was now under way. Shmaya the cop kept blowing on his whistle and chasing after us. Aunt Yenta, a rather portly angel, flew through the air, wheezing like a goose and screaming: "Thieves! Give me that goat! Oh, for crying out loud, give me back my goat!"

"Little Pisser, hold that cord tight!" I called. The goat floundered in the air. Her "*meh*" was deafening.

"Old Prophet Elijah held us up for too long," gasped my friend, clasping the cord tighter.

"When you least expect him, that's when he turns up the most," I responded, and my friend and I flew on.

We were flapping our wings so fast I could barely catch my breath. We were young and our wings were pretty sound. We zigged and zagged. Just when we thought we had shaken our pursuers, we'd hear the beating of their wings at our backs.

Out of her terrible fright, the goat opened her udders and milk started to pour down. Wee little angels, who could not yet fly, stood below with their mouths open, delighting in the drops of milk that sprinkled from above.

We reached Johanan the Sandalmaker Street a good twenty minutes before our pursuers. We made our descent and landed. Little Pisser knocked on his Uncle Joel's window. His uncle, the angel Joel the bookbinder, came out. He coughed a bit and then asked what was the matter with us.

"We brought you a goat, Uncle Baron Haim's goat. It will be more useful for you."

"Who asked you for such a favour?" hollered the book-binder, and gave Little Pisser two resounding slaps across the face.

Just then, our pursuers arrived. Aunt Yenta was as red as a beet. She screamed and yelled: "My goat, you thieves, give me back my goat!"

Shmaya the cop, the angel in the green uniform, took a full report. He wrote down my name and Little Pisser's name. Aunt Yenta took the goat on the cord and promised us that she would report this all to Meyer Scabies the Talmud angel.

Aunt Yenta gave a little tug on the cord and began walking the goat back home. My friend Little Pisser and I looked at one another, sad and embarrassed.

Then we went home. What Little Pisser was thinking, I can't say. But I was feeling heavy-hearted.

Little Pisser kept quiet for a long time. I didn't want to ask him anything: no "what if this?" or "what if that?" But suddenly my friend lifted up his head. He looked at me with those wise, dark eyes: "You know what I think, Samuel Abba?" he said.

"How should I know?" I answered. "Am I some sort of prophet?"

"It strikes me," Little Pisser said, "that as long as rich uncles don't allow it and poor uncles don't desire it, life in Paradise will never be fair."

Little Pisser was absent from school the next day. I thought he didn't come because he was afraid of the beating he might have received from the Talmud angel, Meyer Scabies. But later I learnt that it wasn't on account of fear that he missed school that day. Little Pisser told me that he was no coward; rather he didn't come because he had to help his father, the patchmaker Solomon-Zalman, remove the tacking threads from hundreds of pairs of worn-out wings.

"Little Pisser," I turned to my friend, "why do you never let me go inside your house? Are you ashamed of me?"

"By no means!" Little Pisser said with dismay. "What kind of nonsense is that, Samuel Abba. If you'd like, you can come with me. Right now, even."

The two of us took off flying for Little Pisser's home. Little Pisser's pop, Solomon-Zalman the tailor, an angel with a bulging Adam's apple and big calf-like eyes, lived not far from the pasture fields of Paradise, where they tended the great wild ox, the Behemoth.

The Behemoth was an enormous, fat steer. How much he weighed, no one knew. There wasn't a scale in Paradise that could bear such a load. On his right side the Behemoth had a huge brown blotch that looked like a map of Paradise.

When we arrived at the angel Solomon-Zalman the patchmaker's house, we came across the angel Gabriel standing in front of a large mirror. Solomon-Zalman was taking measurements on a pair of wings that the angel Gabriel had brought in for mending.

The angel Gabriel was a tall, stout angel. He was very rich, but also very stingy. In his whole life he had never ordered a new pair of wings to be made for himself, but rather kept darning his old ones.

"Over here on the right side, it's a little too tight," the angel Gabriel said. "Right there, Solomon-Zalman."

Solomon-Zalman the patchmaker made a mark with his chalk and measured with the tape measure. All the while he kept popping up and assuring the angel, "It'll be just right, Gabriel, sir. It'll be just right, you can rely on Solomon-Zalman."

But the angel Gabriel hated relying on anyone. He just lifted up his shoulders and found a flaw here and another there. Solomon-Zalman found this extremely irritating. Gabriel bothered the poor patchmaker for a solid hour. Then he left.

When he got to the door he stopped once more, and once more warned the patchmaker: "Remember, Solomon-Zalman, I need these wings by Passover. Don't forget!"

As soon as the angel Gabriel was gone, Little Pisser's father was like a new man. He did a little jig and burst out singing:

> When Messiah comes at last,
> What shall we eat at the Great Repast?
> Leviathan and wild Behemoth,
> The wild ox and the great sea beast,
> Shall we all eat at the Final Feast.

At the sewing machine sat the angel Seymour, a journeyman tailor. He was stitching the hem of a wing and grumbling quietly. At the pressing table stood the angel Barney, another journeyman, tall and gaunt with small, blazing eyes. He continually checked to see if the iron was hot enough with his finger.

The angels Seymour and Barney, the two journeymen tailors, were once the best of friends, like two peas in a pod. But after they both fell in love with the angel Rosie, the daughter of the Paradise shopkeeper Israel Moses, they were always at daggers drawn, always provoking each other. They were forever driving each other up the wall.

The angel Rosie, young and beautiful, made the greatest sport with the two of them. She would lead one on and then the other. At one particular time the two former friends came to blows. They threw pressing irons at each other's heads and for weeks they returned to work with their heads bandaged.

Seymour the angel once even tried to kill himself. He hanged himself with his own braces. He had apparently forgotten for the moment that there was no dying in Paradise. After he had spent an entire day and night dangling in the air, he took the braces off from around his neck and cursed Paradise, the journeyman tailor angel Barney and—he wanted to curse the Paradise shopkeeper's daughter, the cause of all his suffering… but his heart wouldn't allow it.

I really liked Little Pisser's home. A room with a little sleeping alcove, and a kitchen. This was all that made up the entire house. In one room they worked. In the little alcove they all slept, and in the kitchen Little Pisser's mama, Hannah Deborah, fussed away all day, preparing lunch and dinner for everyone in the house.

The window was open. Through it you could see the pasture fields of Paradise and the Behemoth grazing there. Three barefoot angels tended the Behemoth to make sure he didn't wander into anyone else's garden. One of them played a pastoral tune on his flute as the other two sang along.

In the evening, the two journeymen angels slipped their needles into their lapels and went off dreaming of their mutual love. Little Pisser's pop went to pray in the Tailors' Synagogue. Little Pisser and I stood at the open window, watching as the pastures of Paradise grew dark. We could hear the silvery chirp of the Paradise crickets. The Behemoth munched at the grass. His appetite was astonishing.

Then the three herdsmen began to sing. That is, one played his pipe and the other two sang. If you never heard the song of the herdsmen of Paradise, you've never experienced true beauty in the world.

> On the pastures of Paradise
> On greenest fields of green earth

We humble herders head out at sunrise,
To tend the great Behemoth.

A bird sings out in Paradise,
Its song, full of delight.
A calf springs upon the meadow,
Its leap, full of delight.

Crickets chirp amidst the grass,
Trill-trill, trill-trill, trill-trill,
And the old rascal of the wind,
Spins the vanes of the old mill.

The flute faded away, sweet and haunting. We could still see the silhouettes of the three herdsmen and hear the ruminating Behemoth.

The moon rose through the trees. I gave a little nudge to my pal Little Pisser, who was standing quiet and lost in thought. "Little Pisser, you know what?"

"What, Samuel Abba?"

"Let's go for a little walk."

"Where to, Samuel Abba?"

"I think we should go for a little stroll on the Avenue of the Patriarchs."

"All right!"

We spread our wings and took off. Little Pisser inhaled the air of Paradise deep into his lungs.

"Your pop's a very fine angel, Little Pisser. He works hard and still he looks so down and out."

Little Pisser didn't say anything. He hated it when anyone mentioned his father's poverty.

The Avenue of the Patriarchs was filled with young couples. Many were flying and some were sitting on benches, whispering quietly to each other. Whatever it was they were whispering, we didn't understand, but we liked it just the same. We promised each other that when we grew up we'd each find an angel girl to whisper with on the Avenue of the Patriarchs.

We heard a deep, heavy sigh. We looked around to see who this sigh came from and immediately recognized the journeyman tailor Seymour the angel, walking lonesome down the avenue.

On the other side of the avenue we could hear another sigh. It was the sigh of the angel Barney, who did not know what to do with himself.

"When we grow up, we'll also sigh like that," said Little Pisser.

"Maybe even worse than these two journeymen tailors," I added.

"Yes, indeed," Little Pisser affirmed as we descended into the very centre of the avenue.

We strolled up and down, overhearing the murmurs carried between the branches of the trees. With every possible pledge, one angel was swearing his love to an angel who didn't believe him. He threatened that if she didn't believe him he would throw himself down to the Earth.

"What are you doing here, Little Pisser? Come home!" We turned and saw Little Pisser's sister Ethel. She was strolling with one of her girlfriends down the avenue.

"I don't want to go home," Little Pisser answered, "I want to walk a bit with my friend Samuel Abba."

His sister left and the two of us watched after her.

"Your sister is a beauty," I said, "her wings are like roses."

"She is engaged now," Little Pisser responded proudly. "She'll be married on the Saturday after the Shavuos summer holiday."

"Will you invite me to the wedding, Little Pisser?"

"Of course," my friend assured me, and we parted until the next morning.

The whole night I dreamt of the wedding. Little Pisser was my in-law and the groom was me. Wedding musicians were playing. The bride wept. I woke up and realized that it was a dream. And I felt very sorry that such a fine dream should come to an end.

5

Phantoms of Paradise

ALL THIS TALKING had worn me out a bit. I took a little breather and looked at my listeners to see if they were dozing off as I shared my experiences in Paradise. But when I saw the rabbi, who was clutching his beard tight with his fingers, the magnate with his hands on his paunch, and the rabbi's assistant sitting upright with his mouth agape—may the evil eye stay out of it—I knew that I had to go on…

*

I woke up from that strange dream in the middle of the night. In my dream, as you remember, I was the groom, my pal Little Pisser was my in-law, and Little Pisser's sister, the rosy-winged Ethel, was the bride.

I wanted to go back to sleep and to keep weaving that beautiful dream, but I simply couldn't. I lay in bed for some time with my eyes closed, but sleep would not come and the lovely dream was already far away, beyond the mills of Paradise.

I got out of bed. Barefoot and pyjamaed, I walked over to the window to have a look outside.

The street was soaked in silvery moonlight. Such a radiant moonlit night was a rare thing in Paradise. I opened the window to inhale the gentle midnight air and exhaled my greetings to my friend Little Pisser and his beautiful sister with the rosy wings.

On the pavement across from me I saw two shadows converge. They each spat out a grunt and stepped back in surprise.

"Is that you, Seymour?"

"Is that you, Barney?"

"What are you doing out in the street so late at night, Seymour?"

"And you, what are you doing, Barney?"

I recognized the two lovelorn journeymen tailors who worked with Little Pisser's father, Solomon-Zalman the patchmaker. I strained my ears to catch their conversation; it would have been a shame to miss even a single word.

"I just can't sleep, Seymour. Whenever I shut my eyes, all I see is her, the Paradise shopkeeper's girl."

"It's the same with me, Barney," Seymour sighed back. "I… I can't stand it any more."

The two remained silent for a while. I could see the needles sparkling in their lapels in the moonlight.

"I'm envious of even the lowliest tailor on Earth. When things don't turn out for him in love, at least he can take poison or drown himself in a river."

"We have no choice," responded the angel Barney. "We must bear our misery for all eternity. What a nasty idea that is: 'eternity'. Who thought that up? And why?"

I saw the two question marks following the "who?" and the "why?" hovering in the empty space of Paradise, illuminated with the sweet moonlight.

They walked on together, Seymour on the right and Barney on the left. The two luckless angels wandered on through the nights of Paradise and I felt real pity for them. A profound pity.

I thought about the Paradise shopkeeper's daughter, the source of their grief. She was probably asleep now, her hair spread out on her pillow. The wings that usually covered her body now dropped down languidly beside her. Perhaps she smiled as she dreamt, unaware of the grief that she provoked, an unrelenting grief that sought death but could never die.

Even a moonlit night in Paradise, I thought, can be haunted.

At that very moment, I couldn't have guessed that I would be destined this night to hear so much more than the sighs of these two hapless tailor angels.

I heard a wailing, sharp and desperate. I lifted my head and, for the very first time, saw the angel Simon Bear. He was, as usual, dead drunk. He towed along two little as-yet-unborn children by their hands and they were trying to wrest themselves free, screaming and crying.

"You shut your bloody craws, ya bastards," the angel Simon Bear roared at them. "Are you going to put a cork in it or what?"

His red beard was unkempt and his eyes were rolling back into his head. He was that far gone.

"We don't want to be born," the two unborn children were crying, "we don't want to go down to Earth. Have mercy, Simon Bear, sir!"

One of the kids was a girl and the other a boy. Simon Bear had got orders to haul out that very night for Earth. They were due to be born as a pair of twins.

"We don't want to be born…" Simon Bear parroted mockingly. "Who asked ya little bastards anyway?"

The boy, whom Simon Bear was dragging with his right hand, hatched a plan of his own. "Simon Bear, sir," he said to the drunken angel, "let my hand loose for a second, I've got to wipe my nose."

Simon Bear didn't realize what was happening. He let go of the lad's hand and the little fellow made a run for it.

Then, on this lovely moonlit Paradise night, a real race started. Simon Bear flapped his fat, downy wings as he chased after the fugitive, clasping the girl tight by her little hand as he dragged her behind him.

I saw it all with my own eyes. My heart was pounding. I prayed to the Creator to work a miracle so that Simon Bear wouldn't catch the runaway child.

But apparently my prayers did not help. In the end Simon Bear caught up with the little fellow. He snatched him by the ear and dragged him along.

"You just wait till we get to the border, you'll both get a blow to your noses then, ya misbegotten cretins."

The little girl was absolutely blameless, but guilt or innocence didn't much matter to an irate Simon Bear. He had to vent his anger. I watched Simon Bear drag the girl by her hand and the boy by his ear as they flew towards the border.

I watched after them until I could no longer see them. I thought of the fate of these unborn children. I wanted to understand their fear of the Earth but I simply couldn't. I was still too young and too little to comprehend it all.

The next day I would tell my friend Little Pisser about everything I saw and encountered that night. I'd be curious to know what he might say about it.

"I know very well that Simon Bear is a scoundrel and a drunk," I'd tell him. "I've already heard lots about him and last night I saw it with my own eyes. It's all true what they say about the villain. But, please, Little Pisser, tell me: why are unborn kids so terrified of being born and why are they so scared of the Earth?"

I tried to imagine how Little Pisser might answer. Just like my friend, I gave my forehead a scratch with my finger, thinking that this might help somehow. But how could I know? Everything remained a puzzle, just as before. I could reach no conclusions.

I heard a flapping of wings. As I looked up I saw distant flashes of flames—many, many flames. Now the flames were getting closer and closer and the flapping became more forceful and swift. I was dumbfounded. I had never heard such a flapping before. Who could it be, I thought, squinting to see.

I saw an angel with huge black wings. This angel had a thousand eyes that glowed red and menacingly through the pale moonlit night. In his hand the dark-winged angel clutched a sword.

"It's the Angel of Death," I recognized. "He must be flying down to Earth." Here in Paradise no one was afraid of him. But down on Earth they were terrified. Everyone there was seized with dread just hearing the flutter of his approaching wings. Men would rush into their shuls to recite verses of Psalms and women would wail at the graves in the cemetery. But all for naught, as they say. Whomever the Angel of Death must take, he takes. No weeping or praying is of any use at all. The dark-winged angel was coming closer and closer. He flapped his way through the air with his enormous sword to make it clear that he was flying on a serious, very serious, mission.

A star tore itself from the Paradise sky, flew over to the dark-winged angel and stood in his way.

"Where are you off to, Angel of Death?" the star asked with a quiver. I couldn't tell if the quiver was out of fear or pity.

"I'm flying," the dark-winged Angel of Death responded, "down to Earth. I must collect the soul of a young bride-to-be and bring her before the Heavenly Entourage."

I felt a flutter in my heart. The soul of a young bride, I thought. Little Pisser's sister was also a bride-to-be. But then I remembered that the brides of Paradise had no reason to fear the dark-winged angel and I calmed down.

The star trembled and flickered, pleading with the Angel of Death: "Turn back, dark-winged angel! What do you want with this poor young bride-to-be on Earth? Have mercy on her. Let her be happy with flowers and love and her dreams."

"Would you look at that, a new heavenly intercessor," the Angel of Death snarled. "Who asked you for your pity? You were ordered to shine, so go ahead, shine on and mind your own business."

But the star wouldn't relent. He started arguing with the Angel of Death and trying to convince him. "This earthly young bride is not my sister or any relation of mine. But I've caught sight of her eyes as she looked up at me. And once, I heard her murmur and sigh as she asked me to send greetings to her sweetheart."

"What are you telling me all this for?" responded the dark-winged angel curtly. "Perhaps you could move out of my way, if you would be so kind. What an impression that would make, if I were as sentimental as you!"

The star started sobbing in earnest now, trembling and pleading through his tears. "Isn't it a pity, angel? Such a young life! She's only nineteen years old. Think about that: just nineteen years old."

"You're quite the poet," said the angel scornfully. "Maybe you should fly over to the Heavenly Throne and sing some songs of praise? It would sure be a lot easier and you'd save yourself the bother of interfering with my work."

"You're nothing but a scoundrel and a thug," the star said sadly. "Your heart is stone and you won't listen to anyone's pleas. But just remember this…"

"Remember what? What do you want me to remember?"

"Remember," the star piously continued, "what's written in the Passover song, '*Had Gadyo*'…"

"Oh yeah? What about it?" the Angel of Death scoffed.

"In that song about that lone little goat, at the end, the Master of the Universe comes and slays the Angel of Death…"

I saw the Angel of Death give a shudder as the star reminded him of his own end. It was a most unusual shudder: Death's fear of himself.

I was eager to see what might happen. Would the dark-winged angel at last be deterred? Would the earthly bride-to-be open her eyes the next morning, just as on any other day, to delight in the sun and flowers and her sweetheart?

Apparently not. The Angel of Death gave a flourish of his sword and sparks started to fly. He spread his enormous, dark wings and took off in flight.

"You're still going?" the star called after him, his voice catching.

"I must!" answered the Angel of Death sharply, and in an instant he was gone.

From far off, I could still make out the sparkle of his eyes and hear the flutter of his wings. The star fell somewhere into a field of Paradise, seeking solace amongst the Paradise crickets.

Strange thoughts came into my head. On this same moonlit night, I had heard the cries of two children who did not want to be born and the harsh and stern "*I must!*" of the angel with a thousand eyes, as he flew off to extinguish a life on Earth.

Across from my window a cherry tree was in bloom, and even though its canopy was flooded with moonlight its shadow spread on the ground below. I observed the shadow there and saw how it trembled. Could it be, I wondered, that even a shadow might tremble? But for whom? Maybe it trembled for itself?

For the first time ever in Paradise, I felt afraid of shadows and phantoms. I tried to calm down and suppress my fear. I started talking out loud, so I could hear myself better. "You fool," I admonished myself, "what are you scared of? Simon Bear didn't have his sights on you, he wasn't leading you off to be born. And the angel with the thousand eyes wasn't flying down to pluck you off the face of the Earth."

A breeze was murmuring quietly in its sleep in the canopy of the cherry tree across the way. The tree's shadow on the ground was chasing its tail without success.

Maybe you should move away from the window, I thought to myself. But still I remained there, fixed in place. My heart told me that this Paradise night had more phantoms in store and they would be revealed in their turn.

Then I heard a voice singing. Quiet and sad, the melody resounded through the moonlit Paradise streets.

I listened closely, trying in vain to figure out where the tune was coming from. The melody approached the street where I lived. Only now could I make out the figure singing the song, weaving this melody through the moony streets of Paradise.

It was the madwoman Pearl, an angel who lost her mind over a love affair gone wrong. My friend Little Pisser had told me that this Pearl had carried on a romance with Getzel, the Paradise bookkeeper. Getzel's job was to record the deeds of the folks on Earth. At the close of every year he would add these deeds up and register them in the angel Michael's ledger.

For three years, Pearl went out with the Paradise bookkeeper. He had pledged his "immortal love" to her and Pearl believed everything he said as if it were the Five Books of Moses. She, with her pure and good heart, was unaware that there were swindlers in Paradise that liked to play with young girls' hearts, only to toss them away.

Pearl worked as a modiste in Paradise. She set aside every cent that she earned, forgoing her own sustenance, saving up for the happy day when she would marry the Paradise bookkeeper. And on that day, the nest egg that she scrimped and saved for years while toiling away in the shop would come in handy. In the end, though, it all went up in smoke. Her sweetheart cast her aside and he went and married Evie, the angel Michael's youngest daughter.

Pearl wept for nights on end. She didn't eat or sleep. She was inconsolable.

One fine day, she came outside with unkempt hair and dishevelled wings. She caused quite an uproar, throwing herself on to everyone until they had to restrain her. Two angels carried her over to a tap and let the cold water run over her until Pearl calmed down.

From that moment on she went mute, she wouldn't say a word to anyone. Anytime she saw an angel coming she ducked away. She sat for days alone in her room. When anyone spoke to her she didn't respond. She looked at them straight in the eyes, seeming to comprehend nothing.

On moonlit nights, my friend Little Pisser told me, when all the angels—big and small—are fast asleep, Pearl would leave her room and wander the streets singing her songs of love.

On this night, suffused with moonlight, I saw Pearl, tall with blazing eyes, as she walked. Her hair was tossed over her shoulders. Her wings were rumpled. As she went with her bedraggled head towards the stars, she sang:

> As I went a-wandering
> Through fields of wheat and corn
> I lost my dearest sweetheart,
> And I was left forlorn.
>
> Between a yes and a no—
> My love he slipped away,
> Tell me, birds in the skies above,
> If you see him on the way?
>
> If you do, please tell him, birds,
> That I shall wait and grieve,
> And if you do, please ask him, birds,
> Why did he deceive?

I could swear I saw tears in her eyes. The wind played with her dishevelled hair, dishevelling it even more. The wind seemed to be ridiculing this mad angel and I resented it.

Pearl passed by close to my window. She paused for a moment and heaved a deep sigh. She doubtlessly sensed that there was a heart close to hers that could feel her sorrow. I wanted to say something to her, I wanted to tell her that this Getzel could just go to bloody hell, that this swindler wasn't even worth a single tear from her beautiful eyes.

But I said nothing. Until this day, I don't know why I kept my mouth shut. Maybe, if I had said some kind words to her at that very moment, she would have been comforted.

Or maybe I didn't say anything because in Paradise words don't exist that can heal the wounds of a love gone wrong.

Pearl went on walking. Two jokers of Paradise, Teddy the South Wind and Sammy the East Wind, kept playing with her hair.

I could not stand by my window any longer. I was drawn to the madwoman angel. And so, dressed only in my pyjamas, I went out after her.

I stepped barefoot into the moon's cool, silver glow, which ran riot over the streets of Paradise.

Pearl walked ahead as I followed. She did not even notice me. With each deliberate footstep forwards she sang:

> The angels now are sleeping soundly,
> In the midnight moonlight fair,
> But for me, oh Mama dearest,
> There is nothing but despair.
>
> At love, at love I gambled,
> With a soul so radiant and light.
> In the jewelled crown of Paradise,
> He was my diamond bright.
>
> He held me in his arms
> And kissed me and caressed,
> He called me his precious darling,
> As he clasped me to his breast.
>
> Oh, angel maidens hear my song,
> and how my heart does break,
> Trust the angel man who pledges love
> Like, in the grass, a snake.

This song that Pearl sang moved me deeply. I watched as Pearl approached the King David Forest and followed her.

The jokers, Teddy the South Wind and Sammy the East Wind, now started playing with my nightshirt and kept blowing it up over my head. I begged them to leave me alone. This was no time for games. Some other time, maybe. The two jokers started whispering—one into my right ear and the other into my left:

"This game with your shirt is better than the game of love, Samuel Abba. Playing with a shirt certainly doesn't cause as much grief as playing with a heart. Take our word for it and let's keep playing the shirt game."

I shooed them away and harshly berated them with some sharp words, telling them that I wasn't always in the mood for mischief-making.

Pearl stood at the edge of the King David Forest. She spread out her arms and sang as she went into the forest:

> Once in these very woods,
> By the moonlight and stars of fire,
> I offered my love as a sacrifice
> And burned it on a pyre.

I remained there, my hand clutching my heart as I listened to her song, which sounded at once like a prayer and a dirge:

> Ask the wind out in the field,
> Ask the tree that stands in bloom,
> Why did you take my world once bright,
> And leave nothing left but gloom?

By all means, I thought, go on and ask away until daybreak for all the wind will answer.

> Ask the birds on every treetop,
> Ask the fish in all the streams,
> If they know what it is to lose
> All their splendid dreams.

Pearl went into the King David Forest and I followed her no further. To tell the truth, I was scared. This madness, combined with the forest, was pretty daunting.

I stood as if frozen at the entrance to the King David Forest, unsure if I had been dreaming or if this was all real.

I spread my wings. The morning dew glistened on them. I flew back home, intent on forgetting all these nightmares, all these phantoms that appeared to me on this moonlit night.

But I could not forget. These phantoms of Paradise stand before my eyes until this very day. The two lovelorn tailor angels who longed to die, the two unborn children who did not want to be born, the star's appeal to the Angel of Death not to snuff out the vibrant life of a young bride. But most of all, the singing insanity of unrequited Paradise love…

*

"How could you ever forget such a night?" I asked my listeners, who sat in the room with my pop listening to my stories of Paradise.

"What's that?" The rabbi gave a start, as if waking up from the world beyond. "What's that you ask, little whippersnapper?"

The magnate drummed his fingers against his belly, presumably wanting to exclaim his German "*sonderbar*", but he couldn't manage to get it out.

The rabbi's juridical assistant, who had been sitting the entire time with his mouth wide open, finally shut it, gulping down a dozen flies that had taken up residence amongst his teeth while I was talking.

My mama wiped away a tear that was hanging suspended in her right eye that wouldn't come down.

My pop's fingertips tapped on the table. What he was trying to convey with this, I couldn't be sure.

I felt that I could tell no more that night. I excused myself and laid myself down in my cradle without supper.

I could still hear as the rabbi, his assistant and the town magnate said their goodbyes to my pop. I heard them kiss the mezuza. "So then, Feivel," the rabbi said, out of the blue, "he'll continue his story tomorrow, God willing?"

I fell asleep.

6

At King David's Estate

THE FOLLOWING NIGHT, when the rabbi, his juridical assistant and the town magnate, Mr Michael Hurwitz, were sitting around the table waiting for me to go on with my tale, I paused for a moment to reflect. They all looked pale, as if they hadn't got much sleep. The rabbi's beard appeared to have turned whiter. The stories of the phantoms of Paradise, it seemed, had rattled him.

"Go on!" my pop grumbled, "go ahead and start! You can see that we're all waiting for you to talk and you just sit there like a dope."

Upon hearing the word "dope" my mama, who had been standing in the doorway, wanted to jump in on my behalf and tell my pop what's what, but I didn't allow it this time. I gave my mama a look and she stayed put. Pop, who was nearly trembling before the expected storm, calmed down. I began to tell:

*

After all the visions that I had seen on that pale, moonlit night, I could not sleep. I could hardly wait until it was light enough in Paradise for me to fly straight over to my friend Little Pisser.

I knocked on his window. Little Pisser was still asleep and didn't hear me knocking. I rapped at the window until my fingers were sore. With difficulty, I managed to rouse him.

"Little Pisser, come quick! Hurry!"

"What's up, Samuel Abba?" my friend asked as he rubbed his eyes.

"Come outside and I'll fill you in on everything." Every limb of mine was shaking. My friend came out. I took him by the hand and looked directly into his sleepy eyes and said: "Let's fly to the King David Forest!"

And off we flew. On the way, I told him all the nightmarish things that I had seen. Little Pisser gave a heavy sigh. My story made a deep impression on him. He gave a shudder with his little wing and said: "Until now I have never witnessed any of the things you told me about, Samuel Abba. It seems that such things can only be seen on sleepless nights. You've had the privilege of one such sleepless night and I envy you that, Samuel Abba."

I didn't understand what he meant. All that he said seemed odd to me. What was there to be envious of? I told him so and he stared back at me. He had a strange and distant look about him…

"All that the daytime keeps muted in silence and dazzled with golden sunlight, the night can reveal. It lifts the veil off everything so you can see into the abyss. What a pity that I slept the whole night through."

We continued flying. The dawning sun warmed our wings. The Paradise wind was young and fresh and played with our hair and surprised itself with its audacity.

We came to the King David Forest and the wind went its own way. It bounded nimbly into the forest to tell the Paradise rabbits that guests were coming and not to be afraid: these two "flyers" had come unarmed.

My friend and I dropped down close to the entrance to the wood. "Right here"—I pointed with my finger—"is where Pearl the madwoman angel went into the forest. I was too scared to follow. Come on, Littler Pisser, maybe we can find her."

We entered the forest and searched for the madwoman's footprints, but found none.

Birds were twittering on the trees. On the grass enormous silver drops of morning dew glistened.

"Maybe these dewdrops are the tears that miserable love has let fall on to the grass?" I said to my friend.

"Yeah, maybe," Little Pisser replied quietly. We came upon a huge Paradise rose bush, which was full of these drops, and with piety and dread in our hearts we recited some verses of the Psalms.

"Pearl's tears remain," I said, "but where have her footprints gone?"

"The Paradise janitor probably swept all traces of her away. That's how it's done in Paradise. The daytime mustn't find out that nights of Paradise are filled with grief and madness."

"Then our search is in vain, Little Pisser. Let's go back."

Little Pisser thought for a moment, scratching his forehead with his finger. I stood, waiting for him to finish thinking.

A bird flew over Little Pisser's head, chirping "Pee Pee". All the birds knew my pal Little Pisser and they loved to greet him. "Pee Pee" was how you said "Pisser" in the Avian language.

"We're not going to school today," Little Pisser decided.

"What about our teacher? Meyer Scabies will surely beat us tomorrow."

"He can go to hell," he said with a wave of his hand.

"Absolutely," I added, "that demon can go straight to hell."

We stood there a moment, listening to the birdsong and breathing in the fresh scent of the grass.

"Let's go, Samuel Abba!"

"Where to, Little Pisser?"

"We'll fly over to King David's palace."

"King David's palace? But are we allowed in?"

"I have a friend there who works as a shepherd tending the sheep on King David's estate. His name's Louie. I haven't seen him for a year of Wednesdays."

"Is it far from here, Little Pisser?"

"It's about a two-hour flight east, Samuel Abba. Our King David is extraordinarily rich! He walks about all day long with a golden crown on his head, strolling his grounds with his hands behind his back, watching over the angels who work his fields. He loves to hear his Psalms sung to him, this King David. He thinks his songs are the loveliest in the world and the angels who work for him must sing them all day as they toil."

"All right, Little Pisser. We'll fly over there and listen to the angels sing King David's songs."

We spread our wings and headed on our way. We flew eastwards. The sun was blinding. Flying into the rays of the sun made for a difficult first half-hour. But afterwards we got used to it. I was burning with curiosity about King David's palace and estate. "Do you see it, Samuel Abba?" My friend pointed.

I looked downwards and saw green fields stretching out deep into the horizon. On the right side were forests in bloom, and on the left a silvery stream like a band of silver mislaid by the Queen of Sheba.

"Oh, how beautiful!" I exclaimed, unable to restrain myself.

We descended a bit in order to see better. Working angels were on the fields, their shirts hanging loose over their trousers. They reaped and sowed as enormous drops of sweat rolled from their brows. These angels were singing:

> Dawn is breaking through the window,
> It drives us out the door,
> Out of our lowly cabins,
> The refuge of the poor.

> Cuckoo, cuckoo! Look down and see—
> How our days in toil are spent,
> Take to God our bitter tears,
> Our silent sad lament.

> We till the fields so fertile,
> And then harvest with our scythes,
> And bring home only hunger
> To our children and our wives.

> Cuckoo, cuckoo! Look down and see—
> How our days in toil are spent,
> Take to God our bitter tears,
> Our silent sad lament.

"Why are the songs they sing so miserable?" I asked my friend.

"Why, you ask?" sighed my friend. "Take a good look and see how they live and you can save yourself the trouble of asking. Anyone who begrudges them a thing should spend a day in their shoes."

He pointed and I surveyed their humble clay huts. The roofs were thatched with straw.

"They live there in those huts, these poor angels. They never eat enough to feel full or get a good night of sleep to dream a dream until its end."

"But, Little Pisser, why is their lot so grim, the poor souls?"

"Why, you ask?" Little Pisser gritted his teeth. "Why? Because life in Paradise is simply unfair. It may look like these are angels like all the others, with wings and songs of praise to the Creator, but just take a look and see!"

A tear fell from Little Pisser's eyes. I caught it in my hand and it was hot. "So, you're saying that for some folks, Paradise is no Paradise?" I asked.

"No, indeed," my friend answered. "Not by a long shot it isn't." And we flew on.

I thought about all that went on at King David's palace and wondered aloud: "Where is fairness?"

"Didn't you hear what our forefather Abraham said back on that Sabbath promenade, dumdum? 'Fair-*shmair*...'"

I remembered that conversation between the Patriarchs and blushed with shame. "But King David," I asked, "what does King David do?"

"All angels should have it so good. He lives in the lap of luxury here. He rambles idly about all day long. Sometimes, maybe, he plays his harp, sometimes he fools around with Abishag. And if he gets tired of that, he has a go at the pretty daughters of the poor angels."

"So he hasn't forgotten his old routine, then?"

"On the contrary. His whole act just got going in Paradise. After all—he is King David!"

We flew past a silver Paradise stream. Women angels were standing barefoot on its bank doing laundry. A young angel with raw, red hands sang:

How fine to be a saint,
How fine for you, how nice!
As we wash your filthy laundry,
In the streams of Paradise.

Whatever you have soiled,
We shall wash it clean,
And all that you have muddied,
We shall make it gleam.

As they bent over the water's edge, the other angel women, old and young, all answered in chorus:

Sing praise to the Creator,
The Master of the Earth,
Who with eternal justice
The entire world brought forth.

There are those who play on harp strings
And those meant for other yields:
Some must do the washing
And some must work the fields.

The cries of newborn angels rose out from the clay huts. They lay all alone in their cradles and screamed their lungs out. Bryna, the Paradise wetnurse, an angel with full, huge breasts, went from hut to hut to nurse the infant angels. King David had hired her for this so that the "little fatsos" wouldn't keep their mothers away from their work.

"Where does Bryna the wetnurse get enough milk that she can nurse so many little angels?" I asked my friend.

"Don't you get it, dumdum?" my friend grumbled. "She cuts it with water…"

Flying on, we turned to the right towards the orchards. The sun was baking. We looked for a shady spot.

In the middle of a flower-filled park stood a marble palace. The palace's windows were opened wide. Two young angel women with feathers in their hair were airing out the bed sheets.

"This is King David's palace," said my pal Little Pisser. "It has over a hundred chambers. King David lives here with his wives and concubines."

"It's a lovely palace," I said, amazed. "It would be great to peek in and see what's going on inside."

"God protect us!" cried Little Pisser. "The minute you step through the palace door you'd be grabbed by one of the eunuchs and be made a royal page right away."

"Is being one of King David's pages such a bad thing, Little Pisser?"

"May only your worst enemies know of such things, Samuel Abba. You have no clue what you're talking about. You've got nothing better to do than drag around the train of King David's robes or massage his feet?"

Both of my wings shuddered as I imagined a pair of sweaty feet with enormous corns on each of the toes. I rub the feet. The sweat is stifling and the enraged king roars at me: "Harder, Samuel Abba, rub harder! Are you a page or a blathering idiot?" *Bleurgh*… I shuddered again.

We heard the playing of a harp. Little Pisser pricked up his ears. "Do you hear that, Samuel Abba?"

"I hear it, Little Pisser!"

"That's King David playing his harp. Let's fly over and see… but quietly—on the tips of our wings so that he won't hear us."

We flew towards the sound of the harp. King David was sitting under the shade of an oak tree and strumming. Beside him sat a young girl with brown curls and a beauty spot on her left cheek.

My pal and I descended not far from the couple and I took a look at the king. He was a portly man of average height, with sharp green eyes. His reddish beard was cropped close.

"*This* guy wrote the Psalms?" I asked my friend in a whisper.

"Shhh…" He put a finger to his lips, and I understood that it would be best to be quiet and listen.

I've got to admit that King David played very well. The entire time that he played, the girl sitting next to him seemed to grow prettier and prettier. When he finished playing, I saw an eagle circle seven times over King David's head. And from amidst the trees in the orchard, a thousand voices called out: "*David, King of Israel, lives and endures!*"

The king smiled, he seemed to enjoy that. The girl beside him stood up to go.

"Where are you running off to, Shulamith? You don't have any time for me?" the king said as he took her hand.

"I have to go, Father-in-law. Solomon may be seeking me in his vineyard. I know that if I tarry even a bit, he will be searching for me. He's probably already sung the entire Song of Songs some ten times by now."

But King David wouldn't let her go. He pulled her down to him under the shady tree and held her tight in his arms. "Shula, my dove, my pet!"

Shulamith broke free from his grasp. Her hair was mussed and her face was ablaze. "Let me be, Father-in-law!" she panted passionately. "It's a sin and you profane your own Psalms."

"If you'd like, my pet," King David cooed excitedly, "if you'd like, I'd write a beautiful psalm just for you. More beautiful than the Song of Solomon, far more beautiful…"

We heard a kiss. Then a second and a third. Shulamith begged and tore herself from his grasp. "Let me go, I beg you, let me go, Father-in-law! If Solomon finds out, heads will roll!"

"I don't give a damn if he finds out, my pet. Anyway, how in blazes would he find out about me, my dove?…"

"The birds will tell him, Father-in-law. Solomon speaks the language of the birds."

"The birds of my estate," said King David breathily, "will tell him nothing. The birds of my estate are always on my side."

Again we heard a kiss. And a second and then a third. Who knows where this would have led if King David hadn't heard Bathsheba's voice: "David, now where are you, David?"

Shulamith got up. She fixed her hair and, as swift as a gazelle, she was gone—hot and flushed.

King David got up, too. He picked up his harp and started walking towards the marble palace. We watched him disappear into the trees.

From the fields, the air carried the song of the working angels and the scent of raisins and almonds, of sweat and psalms. I looked at my friend and he looked back at me. We understood each other immediately.

"If Bathsheba had found out, what would have happened?" I asked.

"Bathsheba is long used to such things. But if Abishag were to have found them… Don't even ask what she would do!"

"And what about King Solomon? Would he keep cool about it if he found out?"

"He would rip up the entire Song of Songs in a rage. It would be far better if he didn't find out. What a shame for the Song of Songs." Little Pisser waved off the very idea with a sweep of his hand: "But what the hell do I care! Let them tear each other's heads off."

We shook the dust from our wings and lifted them into the air. The sun was heading westwards.

"Now let's find Louie the shepherd angel. He's an old friend of mine. But, as I said, I haven't seen him in a year of Wednesdays."

"Where do you think we'll find him, Little Pisser?"

"Come on, I know where. There, do you see, over on that green hilltop—he's tending the sheep."

We flew towards the green hill. Louie the shepherd angel was sitting atop it, playing a pipe. The sheep grazed all around him. A dog barked below and startled me. I grabbed Little Pisser's wing with my hand.

"Don't be scared, nitwit," my friend comforted me. "That's just Louie's dog. His name's Shep and he's a nice Jewish pup—he barks but he doesn't bite."

We flew closer to the hilltop. Before we landed, we could hear Louie playing his pipe. I got a good look at Louie the shepherd angel. I liked what I saw very much. He was a blond angel with bright-blue eyes.

"This is the real King David," I whispered. "This is how King David ought to look: barefoot and beautiful, making lovely music on his little pipe."

Little Pisser looked over at me. "You're dreaming, Samuel Abba. The guy playing the pipe is Louie the shepherd angel, and the guy back there with that crown on his head was King David."

"But King David is a shepherd, too."

Little Pisser did not respond. He thought for a while, gazing at the silvery wisps of clouds that floated across the skies of Paradise. As they collided into each other they gave a thin, silver tinkle before swimming off on their way.

Louie rested his pipe in the grass and started to sing with a dulcet, sincere voice. The sheer delight of its sound made a chill run down my spine:

> The flute song sounds lovelier
> Between midday and evening prayer.
> As the pious day draws to a close,
> Now lovelier is my despair.
>
> The clouds, they grow distant
> And far, so far they fly,
> They pass along my longing
> To the stars up in the sky.
>
> Alas, alas, this longing,
> That sadness never grieves,
> Alas, alas, my sadness,
> That has no flute or reed.

Tears were welling up in my eyes. My friend Little Pisser was nearly weeping. We descended to the ground. Louie the angel ran up to my friend and they embraced. Shep the dog had a bone to pick with me: "Ruff, ruff, ruff."

Little Pisser introduced me to his friend Louie the shepherd angel: "Louie, this is my new buddy, he's called Samuel Abba. He's a good kid."

We all sat down. Shep stopped his barking and befriended me, too. He lay beside me swatting at the Paradise flies.

On King David's estate it had begun to grow dark. We all sat in silence and watched as the shadows overtook a sliver of field and then inched closer. Now they had already reached Louie's sheep.

Little Pisser asked the shepherd sitting beside him: "Louie, will you sing me the song that you sang when I saw you last year?"

Louie's blue eyes had become darker. The evening appeared to have crept into them. He sang:

> The evening harnesses its steeds
> Of shadows and of shade,
> And into the dimming darkness
> All Paradise does fade.

> You there, shepherd, play your pipe,
> Your evensong do sing,
> Make the stars begin to shine
> And the birds will rest their wings.

> The sheep are longing homewards,
> As they stand upon the lea,
> And a kindling dream is warming up
> Your hut of mud and clay.

> Your hut of mud and clay
> Is poor and it is small,
> But the dreams that you dare dream
> Are the loveliest of all.

Louie lowered his head. We all remained silent. The crickets in the grass and the frogs in the nearby marsh were saying their bedtime prayers.

Louie the angel stood up. With his pipe he called his flock of sheep together. "Time to drive the flock home," he told us. "Wait for me, I'll be right back. We can spend tonight together. A night on King David's estate will no doubt be fascinating. There's so much to see and hear."

We watched as Louie began driving the herd homewards. His blond hair was the only bit of gold that shone out of the evening twilight on King David's estate.

After Louie disappeared with the flock, the first stars appeared in the Paradise sky. As we, that is, my friend Little Pisser and I, lay in the green grass I was a bit overwhelmed by the strangeness of it all. But as soon as I remembered Louie's blue eyes and golden hair, everything seemed cheerful and familiar again.

"We won't sleep tonight," Little Pisser said. "Tonight Louie will show us around King David's estate."

"More phantoms, then," I shuddered. "What for, Little Pisser?"

"When you ask a stupid question, I can only give a stupid answer…"

The Paradise sky was strewn with stars that swayed as if they were rocking in the wind. I thought I could hear the lullaby the wind sang to the stars.

"Do you hear that, Little Pisser?"

Little Pisser lay back with his eyes closed. He said nothing.

7

Night-time at King David's Estate

THE ANGEL LOUIE the shepherd returned. The moon rose through the trees. Louie put a finger to his lips: "Hush... let's go on tiptoe so that no one will know, God forbid, that there are strangers about on King David's estate."

We got up from the grass and followed Louie on the tips of our toes. We travelled by byways and avoided the main pathway. Louie said that it was easier this way since on the main path we might, God forbid, run into one of King David's concubines or come across a eunuch and thus get pressed into service as pages.

Hearing this word "page" again, I shuddered. "Don't worry about it, Samuel Abba," Little Pisser comforted me, "let a eunuch just try to lay a finger on us. We'll claw his eyes out."

"Don't be a tough guy, Little Pisser," Louie the angel smiled. "You might get away with that if there were only one eunuch here in Paradise. But in Paradise there are lots."

We went on. At every faint noise, we froze in place, afraid that we had been discovered. There were moments when we fancied that we were being followed or that suddenly the fat figure of a eunuch might suddenly pop out of the shrubbery. He would let out a guffaw of greasy laughter: "Now I've gotcha boyo, and you'll be a page whether you like it or not and I'll get meself a nice golden star of David as a reward."

But this never happened and all our fear was in vain. Louie walked ahead and we followed as the Paradise moon watched over us. We heard the wistful call of a Paradise cuckoo and the sweet warble of a Paradise nightingale.

"The cuckoo is chewing the fat with the nightingale," Louie said. "Every night it's the same conversation. I don't understand how they don't get tired of it."

"Louie, do you understand their conversation? What could they be talking about?" Little Pisser asked.

"Of course I understand," Louie answered. "The cuckoo says: 'Look you, look you! King David's palace is so lovely!' And the nightingale responds: 'And how! Ooh, ooh, ooh, and how!'"

"But tell me, Louie," I asked my new friend, "why does King David wear the crown on his head all the time? He didn't even take it off when he was smooching with Shulamith under the Paradise oak tree."

"He doesn't only wear it during daylight hours," said Louie with a faint smile, "he even sleeps with his crown on at night. He's afraid…"

"Who could he be afraid of, Louie?"

"He's afraid of King Saul, whose blood still boils to this very day. He goes around claiming that David usurped his crown. In any case, if you both see and hear all that goes on at night in King David's palace, you'll hear King Saul's complaints and King David's response."

"Come on, Louie, tell us! How does King David respond?"

"You want to know how he responds? He's got quite the comeback, this King David of ours. To all of Saul's accusations, he shrugs and says: 'So sue me!'"

We walked on. I nearly trampled a ladybug, which, you know, would bring terrible luck. But fortunately Louie pulled me back. The ladybug said a prayer of deliverance and fled quickly, disappearing behind a hill.

Louie the angel paused at an apple tree with wide-spreading branches. We, that is, Little Pisser and I, stopped too. "You see this, fellas?" Louie whispered. "It's the Tree of Knowledge. It was from this tree that Eve plucked the apple and that jackass Adam let himself get talked into indulging. You know the story, right, it's in the Bible?"

We stood gaping at the tree. The Tree of Knowledge seemed like any other tree in Paradise, but at the same time it looked different. This tree was the cause of Adam and Eve's exile from Paradise.

A breeze rustled the branches of the Tree of Knowledge. The apples quivered, but not a single one fell.

The moon, trailing us all along, cast the apple tree in silver. It was wondrous to behold.

"Let's hide in those bushes over there," the angel Louie whispered, "and you'll see something amazing."

"What's that?" we asked. But he didn't respond. He gestured towards the bush and we ducked behind it. We lay there quietly and waited.

I don't remember just how long we were waiting. It might have been an hour or maybe less. Suddenly, Louie the angel's ears pricked up. We heard footsteps.

"Hush now"—he laid a finger on his lips—"hush… Here they come."

"Who? Who is it, Louie?"

"Adam and Eve."

We watched as two figures approached the Tree of Knowledge.

One wore a top hat and tailcoat. The other was in a crinoline ball gown. On her head she wore a hat with a long ostrich feather.

"That's it there," pointed the gentleman in the top hat with crisp Teutonic diction, "there it is. The very spot where you had me taste that damned *verfluchten* apple."

The woman in the gown sighed and put her hand to her heart. I could see tears in her eyes. "*Ja, ja*, Adam, *mein Schatz*, there you have it. That *verfluchte* snake, she talked me into it."

"And because of you, *haben wir alles verloren*, everything is gone, Eva, our inimitable Eden."

"Life was splendid in our Eden, Adam. But that *verfluchte*, she…"

"*Ja! Ganz recht*, Eva," said Adam pointing, directly at Eve, "she did, that *verfluchte!*…"

"I was referring to the snake, Adam, *mein Schatz*, and you are pointing your finger at me."

"I'm also referring to a snake, Eva, when I point at you."

Then the two began bawling each other out, using every name in the book. Eve tore at Adam's hair. She would have been in the wringer, too, had a miracle not occurred. An apple fell off a branch from the Tree of Knowledge and plunked down on Adam's top hat. The apple rolled into the grass.

"Don't you touch it, Eva!" Adam yelled, his voice faltering. "For the love of God: don't touch it!"

"Heaven forbid," Eve said with a clap of her hands. "I never got the taste of that last apple out of my mouth."

They both sat down under the tree, reminiscing about the lovely time before the Fall. "*Ach*, Adam," Eve said, misty-eyed, "*wie schön das war!* Such days will never come again."

"We were naked, unashamed and happy," sighed Adam.

"Maybe we should get rid of these clothes, Adam, and be naked once more and unashamed and happy?"

They got up and started tearing off their clothes. The stars slyly twinkled in the sky.

"It's of no use, Adam. My clothes are like a second skin now," Eve sighed.

"Mine too," Adam hung his head.

They stood there for some time with their heads low. Two lost souls illuminated by the light of the Paradise moon.

"Let us offer penance," Adam spluttered. "Maybe *He* will pardon us."

They turned themselves towards the stars: the gentleman with the top hat and the woman in the ball gown. With clenched fists they beat their breasts, piously whispering, and begged for a great act of forgiveness that would lead them back into Paradise.

The wind that had been caressing the leaves of the Tree of Knowledge suddenly leapt down from the tree. Startled, Adam and Eve took to their heels and ran off. In her haste Eve left her purse behind. We opened it and found inside a mirror, a compact and a love letter signed "your ever-loving Max".

We decided that we would give the found purse as a present to Little Pisser's lovely sister Ethel with the rosy wings, who was soon to be wed. It might come in handy.

"Did you see, fellas," Louie called to us, "how they flagellated themselves as they prayed for forgiveness? Every night they return to that spot where they sinned. They sneak into Paradise, clambering over border fences, making sure not to be seen and then they run off at the slightest noise, just like Paradise bunnies."

"But how do they manage to get in? After all, there are angels standing guard all day and night at the gates of Paradise!"

"Well, an angel is just an angel, after all," Louie explained. "And besides, the changing of the guard is quite infrequent, maybe once every three years. As soon as the exiled couple spies an angel grabbing a little shut-eye, they sneak right over the fence."

"Will they ever be forgiven?" I asked.

"Not yet. They say that when the Messiah comes, a general amnesty will be declared, but for the time being they'll keep skulking around outside the gates of Paradise."

I closed my eyes and saw the miserable couple skulking about the Paradise gates. At the gates, angels stood with sabres in their hands, waving their blades and lunging fearlessly at any unauthorized person who approached the abode of the sainted ones called "Paradise".

"God have mercy on them," I said. "If I were the Messiah, I'd come this very minute and open the gates of Paradise to them."

"If, indeed…" Little Pisser mocked. "If my grandma had wheels, she wouldn't be my grandma, she'd be a car."

It bothered me that Little Pisser made fun. But I loved him so much, I forgave him.

Louie the shepherd angel was sitting all the while, his chin resting on both hands, looking pensive.

In the moonlight, there was a strange beauty about him. We gazed in awe at the little shepherd who tended the sheep on King David's estate and waited for him to stir from his contemplation. Meanwhile, I observed the play of the shadows cast by the Tree of Knowledge on the ground below.

The shadows kept coming closer to the circle of light the moon had drawn around us, wanting to cross its border but recoiling in fear. One of the more audacious shadows dove right into the circle of light and immediately vanished, gone forever.

We heard the sound of a bugle. Louie jumped up: "C'mon fellas, the bugler is mustering the maidens of the estate, all the nymphs that reside in the woods, and the naiads that dwell in the waters. They all assemble in front of King David's palace as he, the king, sits on his balcony playing the harp as they perform the 'Goodnight King David' dance for him."

We got up. Louie walked in front with us behind him. Then he stopped suddenly. "Where did the moon go?"

The moon, which had been following us the entire time, had disappeared somewhere. We turned back and saw that it had got caught in the brambles. The angel Louie set it loose and pricked his finger in the process. The moon flitted back above our heads and we continued on our way.

We held back about a hundred paces from King David's palace. We saw King David on his balcony, the crown sparkling on his head. Bathsheba sat to his right; she was a plump woman in a wig, hiccupping all the while. On the king's left side sat Abishag, pale with deep-set, dreamy eyes. Her braids slipped down to her breasts like two serpents.

King David strummed his harp. The wood nymphs, dressed in green-leafed garb, whirled in pirouettes and sang:

> We, ladies of the wood,
> Dance for you, our King.
> We now have laid to rest
> The birds in their nests,
> The rabbits on the pasture,
> The butterflies in the aster.
> Now we lull to sleep,
> Our dear lord, King David,
> With all his kith and kin,

> Oh lord! Into our fluttering dance,
> Let blow the gentle wind.

The dance of the nymphs became swifter and wilder. King David grinned a sweet and weary smile. Abishag's eyes widened. Bathsheba suppressed a tenth yawn.

The wood nymphs disappeared. The water naiads now moved into the foreground, water lilies quivering in their hair. They sang:

> We, lasses of rivers and of streams,
> Dance for you, our King.
> We lull and bring to rest
> The ancient water maids
> The lullaby that is the sweetest
> Is the murmur of the waves.
> Now we lull to sleep,
> Our dear lord, King David,
> With all his kith and kin,
> Into our quiet fluttering dance,
> Let blow the gentle wind.

The naiad's dance quietly swished past to the tune of King David's harp. Abishag's eyes became moonlike. Bathsheba used a silk handkerchief to wipe the sleep from her left eye.

The foreground was now overtaken by the beautiful daughters of the worker angels, who curtsied before the king and began to sing:

> We, young maidens, brides-to-be
> Of peasant huts and shacks,

Dance for you, our King—
We, who calm and comfort lack,
Joy to you we bring,
The one the storm may shake,
The one stroked by the wind.
So goodnight to you, King David,
And all your kith and kin.

The poor maidens from the clay huts danced with their quivering rosy wings, curtsied and, with a bashful "Goodnight, King," disappeared.

King David stood up. He kissed Bathsheba on the hand and Abishag on the forehead. He went into his bedroom, recited a few chapters of Psalms and lay down to sleep. He left his harp on the balcony to let the wind strum it through the night.

His wives stayed a while longer sitting on the balcony, as if admiring the night sky while wishing each other a dark and bitter end. The first to get up was Bathsheba, who, without saying "Goodnight", left for her chambers. Abishag stayed gazing at the stars a bit longer before tiptoeing into David's bedroom.

"Come on now, fellas," Louie the angel said, "let's head down to the river. We'll return here around midnight for you to see something amazing."

We headed off for the river. We passed by many poor huts with open windows from which echoed the snores of the overworked angels.

Two young angel ladies were sitting on the stoop of one of the huts; one of them was holding a letter in her hand.

"Read it, Pessie, read the letter!" begged one of the angels. "I want to hear what Efrem wrote you."

Pessie opened the letter and started reading by the starlight. We listened as her voice quivered.

"My dear Pessie," she read, "I write to let you know that for the last three days our regiment has been stationed near the border of Turkish Paradise. Serving here has been quite hard. We need to be on constant guard against smugglers of Turkish tobacco. Our commander, Major-Angel Samson, told us that with the illicit import of so much Turkish tobacco into Jewish Paradise, people are using less of ours and Jewish Paradise's tobacco monopoly is suffering as a result. If any of us catches a smuggler, we have been given permission to bash his wings. We remain on duty day and night, yet so far none have been apprehended. It seems that the smugglers have got the message that the angels of the Fifth Regiment of Jewish Paradise mean business and they want to keep their wings. How long we shall be posted here on the frontier, I do not know. I only know that I can hardly wait for the day when my service is done and I am discharged. All in all, another year and two months. As soon as I come home, we will raise our wedding canopy. And until that joyful day comes, I send you so, so many kisses. Yours, Efrem."

When she finished reading the letter she folded it back up and held it to her heart: "If only I could take the weight off his bones!"

The other angel kept quiet. I could tell that she envied her friend. An angel, a soldier, a hero—why was she blessed by God with such luck?

I tugged at my friend Little Pisser's right wing. "Nice letter, huh, Little Pisser. That angel Efrem sure knows how to write a letter, don't you think, Little Pisser?"

Little Pisser did not answer.

Louie whistled faintly: "Come on, fellas, let's go!"

We set out walking towards the river. I kept looking back at the girlfriends still sitting there on the stoop. One had a letter, the other had none. The longing of the one had an address: "Infantry Private Efrem Angel, Near the Border of Turkish Paradise," while the other's longing was still looking for an address and maybe, someday, she'd find one.

"Maybe we shouldn't have been eavesdropping," I said. "I'm afraid we may have committed a grave sin."

"Huh? What's that you say, Samuel Abba?" My pal Little Pisser woke up as if from a dream. "What were you talking about?"

"Nothing, Little Pisser. You must have imagined I said something."

Suddenly, I felt that it was a sin to speak of sin at such a moment. We walked on, Louie the shepherd angel up ahead as we followed.

"*Samuel Abba!*"

"What? Are you calling me, Little Pisser?"

"Who, me? You must be dreaming, Samuel Abba."

"Maybe it was you, Louie? Maybe you called my name?"

"Are you talking in your sleep, Samuel Abba?" Louie stared at me, confused.

"But who could have called my name?" I wondered. I was sure I heard my name called. Maybe I really did imagine it, I decided. I couldn't have suspected then that there is a kind of silence in Paradise that can call you by your name, just as if it were said aloud.

We heard the burble of the river and quickened our pace. The burbling was getting closer.

The enormous clock that hung in King David's palace began to chime. I counted: one, two, three, four…

"Ten. It's ten o'clock," my pal Little Pisser said.

"We have just barely two hours to spend by the river," Louie the shepherd angel noted. "We must be back at the palace at exactly twelve. That's when it starts."

"When what starts?" my friend Little Pisser and I asked.

"Oh, you'll see," Louie smiled, but his smile disappeared in a flash.

We came close to the river. It coiled out like a silver ribbon, truly dazzling. We sat down at the riverbank. No one said a word; we let the river do the babbling.

I stretched out my feet into the water. It was cool and mild. Little Pisser tossed in a stone.

Aghast, Louie the angel grabbed my friend Little Pisser by the hand: "What have you done?"

But it was too late. The stone that my pal threw into the river had awakened Sarah-Gitta, the naiad of these waters, who swam out from the depths. Her hair was bedraggled and her eyes were still asleep.

"Who threw a stone?" she asked. "Who woke me from my sleep?"

"I did!" Little Pisser answered. "I didn't do it on purpose."

The naiad Sarah-Gitta was an old spinster who suffered from insomnia, for which she took a nightly sleeping aid before heading to sleep.

"Since you have awakened me," she said to my friend Little Pisser, "you must become my groom."

Little Pisser turned as pale as snow and his teeth began to chatter in fear. Luckily for him, Louie the shepherd jumped in.

"What do you need a groom for, Sarah-Gitta," he said to the naiad, "you've got along all these many years without a husband and you'll also do just fine from here on."

"Well then," the naiad was almost in tears, "how am I going to go back to sleep? I finished the last of my sleeping powders today and the Paradise pharmacy is already closed. How will I ever get back to sleep?"

"Nonsense, Sarah-Gitta. You certainly don't need a husband to make you fall asleep. I'll help you get back to bed." Then Louie began to meow like a cat and gave us a sign for us to start making some cat-music too, until the naiad turned a shade of yellowy green. She clutched at her head with both hands and let out a peculiar cry. We didn't let up until she had descended below the water, viciously cursing us all the while.

"Now let's scram!" Louie said. We spread our wings and started flying like a shot.

"You saved my life," Little Pisser said to Louie the angel. "It would be a better fate to become one of King David's pages than a husband to that freak."

"Louie, how did you know," I asked, "that the naiad couldn't stand meowing?"

"It's a short and sweet little story," Louie explained. "This naiad once had a husband—oh, what am I saying?—a match for a husband was being arranged for her. The prospective groom was brought for their first meeting but a cat got in the way and it all went nowhere."

"What does that mean: a cat got in the way and it went nowhere? Fill us in on the details."

"What's there to fill in? While they, the couple that is, were sitting and getting to know each other at home, a cat overturned a saucer of cream and the would-be fiancé got splattered. He stormed out, called her a shlimazel and never wanted to hear from or think about her again. From then on she remained an old maid, suffering from sleeplessness. And, at the slightest sound of a cat's meow, she's ready to leap into a pit of fire."

My friend Little Pisser said a quick prayer of deliverance and remained as pale as a sheet. There was simply no calming him down from this.

As soon as the burbling of the river was out of earshot, he was able to relax again. He spat three times, saying: "For her head, for her limbs, and for her entire body and soul!"

We all burst out laughing. Louie was clutching his sides and barely able to catch his breath: "You got away by the skin of your teeth. Be careful next time!"

We headed down below. Midnight was still a long way off and we had no need to hurry. We sat down by the edge of a field. Louie the angel softly played his pipe. Little Pisser was lost in thought and I counted the stars in the sky.

I have always loved counting the stars. I never did it in order to find out the number of stars. Rather, I counted for the sake of counting alone and I never tired of starting from the beginning.

I don't know how long we had been sitting on the edge of the field when Louie's voice interrupted my counting and Little Pisser's musing. "Come on, fellas! Time to go."

We walked a little of the way by foot and flew the rest. We arrived in front of King David's palace at seven minutes to twelve. We hid amongst the trees, stretched ourselves out on the ground, and began to wait.

The seven minutes stretched out like an eternity.

8

Midnight at King David's Estate

T HE GLOWING moon clock on the King David Tower struck twelve. We lay amongst the trees and held our breath.

What would happen this midnight at King David's estate? It is the witching hour, I thought, but didn't dare say a word.

The moon above our heads grew larger and more severe, the stars more distant and awesome. I could hear my friend Little Pisser's heart thumping.

The harp was still standing on King David's balcony. Clumsily, the wind kept trying to strum its strings. A lame, good-for-nothing wind, I thought, it would be better if it had never been born. The king himself is a far more skilled virtuoso—what a shame that he should be asleep now and allow this dilettante wind to plunk away with no talent. What a pain in the ear.

Suddenly, everything was quiet. The wind ran off to hide somewhere. Bathsheba appeared on the balcony in only a nightgown, her eyes red from weeping. It looked as if she hadn't slept the whole time.

For a while she attended to the silence and, when she was certain that all were asleep in the palace, she slowly descended the marble steps.

She stood in the open green in front of the palace, barefoot and wearing just her nightgown. I looked closely at her: she was old and ugly, her face wrinkled. Even the wind, who was not known to be particularly picky, refrained from fooling around with her nightgown.

"She's quite a hag," I said quietly.

"Once she was young and pretty," Louie the angel remarked, "but now she is old. She knows all the books of customs and etiquette for pious women by heart."

"Aha," Little Pisser declared, "I get it now. She has come to mark the hour with a proper midnight prayer of commemoration."

"You guessed wrong," Louie clarified. "She's pretty devout and all, but, you see, she's just a simple woman at heart. She knows that Abishag is with the king and now she can't sleep. She loves King David deeply and so she hates Abishag. She wishes she'd drown in a spoonful of water."

"Aha, I see!" I said, still not really understanding why Bathsheba was standing at the stroke of midnight barefoot in her nightgown out in the cold on the empty palace green. "But how is this of any use to her?" I asked Louie the shepherd angel.

"She's probably going to see her mystical healer. When poor Bathsheba sees how Abishag's beauty is more powerful than any ladies' old-fashioned book of blessings, she summons the folk healer to acquire some remedy to win back the heart of her beloved king."

"Do the healer's remedies help at all?" Little Pisser asked without taking his eyes off the fat old lady in the nightgown.

"As much as cupping can help a corpse," whispered Louie the angel. "But she doesn't give up. She still has faith that the healer will discover some elixir that will help."

Bathsheba stood fixed in her place, not batting an eyelid. She suddenly shuddered and then we heard her call out in a whisper: "Genendel, Genendel, where are you?"

There was no reply.

Bathsheba looked nervous. She took a few steps forwards and called out a bit louder: "Genendel, where the devil are you?"

"I'm here, mistress, right here."

We saw an old woman wrapped in a Turkish shawl hobble over. The limping healer approached Bathsheba.

"I'm nearly frozen to death, Genendel. Where have you been?"

The old healer did not answer. Instead, she took Bathsheba's hand and led her to the terraced lawn in front of the palace. Bathsheba sat down on a grass step and the old woman sat at her feet.

"Something troubles you, my child?" the old woman said, and a rotten tooth, the lone inhabitant of her mouth, flashed for a moment in the brilliant gleam of the moon.

"Oh, dear God!" Bathsheba sighed. "Tell me what to do, Grandma Genendel, I can't stand it any more. My heart is going to break into pieces."

"So she is back with him again, Bathsheba?"

"Yes," Bathsheba sighed. "The king barely lies down to sleep and off she goes sneaking into his chamber on tiptoe—dear Lord God in heaven, may all her days be darkened."

"Have you spoken with him," the healer muttered, "have you told him what I instructed you to say?"

"I went and cried to him, dearest Genendel. I told him that because of him, my darling Uriah, may he rest in peace, was taken from the world. Did I ever want for anything when I was with him? Such good times those were. He never called me anything but his cuddle bear. And I left it all behind for you, David, I told him, and this is how you repay me in my old age?"

"So, then," asked the healer, "how did he respond?"

"How did he respond, you ask? Don't ask, Genendel. He stroked my wig and said, 'My Basia, if only you were now as young and lovely as you were then, I would have your husband knocked off yet again. But now that you are, bless your heart, in your advanced years, I would give a fortune if only Uriah could be brought back to life. I'd lead you both to the wedding canopy with my blessing.'"

Bathsheba burst into tears. The old healer comforted her, caressed her hand and soothed her, saying: "Don't cry, Bathsheba. It'll be all right. You'll see, everything will work out, much to Abishag's regret."

The old woman took out a deck of cards, laid the cards out on the ground and stared at them for a long, long while.

"The old healer is reading cards, Little Pisser, do you see?" I exclaimed to my friend.

"In this starlight, Bathsheba is lovelier now than before," Little Pisser said, as if to himself.

"Well, it's not the first time or the last," Louie the shepherd angel explained to us. "Every Thursday, this Genendel the wonder-working healer comes here and lays out her cards to read by the light of the stars."

"And Bathsheba believes in this?" I asked.

"She does. And her faith makes her radiant again for a bit," Louie said. "It's a shame that King David never sees. It sure would please him."

The healer stood up and danced seven circles around the cards that lay on the ground. Bathsheba sat like a sculpture hewn from stone.

Then the healer suddenly turned her head towards the stars. Her grey hair in disarray, she stretched out her arms as she intoned her incantation: "Fly to me, my sparrowhawks seven from the peaks of Paradise, Auntie Genendel calls. Auntie Genendel summons you. Heed the call, my sparrowhawks, and shake the sleep off your wings. Auntie Genendel seeks your council, Auntie Genendel has a mission to carry out. You, who peck at the stars with your golden beaks, fly to me on the double! I'll count to thirteen."

She repeated her incantation several times. Then she sat on the ground, brought her knees to her chest and waited.

"Little Pisser, I'm scared." I drew close to my friend, who was lying beside me.

"Shh…" The angel Louie put his finger to his lips. "Keep quiet now."

We heard a flutter of wings. The seven sparrowhawks from the peaks of Paradise circled in the air and then descended at the feet of the Paradise folk healer Genendel.

"I have summoned you here, dear sparrowhawks"—she caressed the wings of each one of them—"I have summoned you, my faithful ones, at the very stroke of midnight, to help me. For you will bring me a cure for a sick soul, the broken spirit of Bathsheba—long may she live—who sits here on this knoll and can find no rest because of her passionate love for King David, a long and healthy life to him."

"We are at your command, Mama Genendel," said the senior sparrowhawk. "Command us and we shall bring anything within our power to you. But one condition, Grandmama: you must finish the tale you started telling us six hundred thousand years ago."

"Fine," said the healer, "I agree to it. I shall finish the tale. Now you will fly off and bring back the please-love-me flower from the Paradise peaks, the die-for-me flower, and the fall-for-me rose from the rivers of Paradise."

"All right, Auntie Genendel," the senior sparrowhawk said, "we'll fly off and strive to gather all that you need. But remember to keep your word if, God willing, we manage to fetch it all."

"Auntie Genendel means what she says," the healer snapped. "Now make haste, dear sparrowhawks, fly and search and fetch all that I have requested. When do you think you might return?"

"When do I think?" thought the senior sparrowhawk for a moment. "We can't say exactly when, but I assure you we'll return by Thursday night, hopefully sooner."

The sparrowhawks spread their wings and flew off. Genendel the healer watched after them, smiling: "Such loyal children, these Paradise sparrowhawks. You just give them a call and there they are: ready for business. Fly safe, my dear sparrowhawks, and bring back to Bathsheba the joy she has dreamt of for so long."

Bathsheba was still sitting like a stone statue. The stars shone in her eyes.

"Now go, my little Bessie, go lie down and get some sleep, my child." The old healer gently stroked Bathsheba's wig. "Go. God forbid, you might catch cold going about in only your nightgown. It will all be all right, my child. Next Thursday, you heard, my dear sparrowhawks will gather the flowers for you to brew into a tea and give to King David to drink. It will all work out, Bathsheba, it will all work out, my child."

Bathsheba stood up from the grass. Like a sleepwalker, she ascended the marble staircase. Suddenly she stopped, turned her head towards the healer, who stood below, and said: "I hope your sparrowhawks won't disappoint, Genendel. I couldn't bear it. I'd lose my mind."

"What are you saying, my child?" The healer spat three times on the ground. "May your enemies lose their minds! But you, my precious, God willing, you will find your joy again."

We watched as the old healer hobbled away and slipped out of sight in the nearby forest. At a loose end, Bathsheba remained standing on the steps. The searchlight of a moonbeam pored over her pious wig.

She stood there like that for some time. Who knows what was going on inside her? She suddenly gave a start and then was on her way once more.

King David's bedroom window was open. Bathsheba listened, too scared to peek in. She could barely contain her bitterness.

"I just hope those sparrowhawks don't disappoint," she murmured. "No, Auntie Genendel's sparrowhawks won't let me down," she assured herself, and went into her bedroom.

"Little Pisser, did you see?" I poked my friend.

"Of course. How could I not see? What am I, blind?"

"And you heard everything too, Little Pisser?"

"And how. Of course I heard, you think I'm deaf, too?"

Louie the shepherd angel put his finger to his lips again: "Shh… fellas, shh… You can bicker later."

We held our breath. "What will happen now?" we each thought, afraid to utter a word.

We heard the galloping of a horse. "Who could that be?" I wondered, too scared to ask. We saw a horseman on a white steed. He was wearing armour that glimmered in the moonlight.

He dismounted from his horse, approached King David's palace and called out loud: "Hey, David, wake up! Come on, let's spar!"

In the palace no one stirred. The wind shivered between the curtains of King David's bedroom.

The horseman in the iron-plated armour wouldn't give up. He stretched out his armoured arm and shouted even louder: "Hey! David! Wake up and come out to the open field and we'll battle!"

King David came on to his balcony, rubbing his sleepy eyes. He yawned a hearty yawn and addressed the horseman standing below: "Is that you, Saul? Have you snuck out of the World of Chaos again? What do you want from me, Saul? Why won't you let me sleep?"

King Saul burst out laughing. His laughter was sharp and bitter. "Come down, David, let's have a go right now! Let's head to the open field and battle!"

King David yawned again. "I'm not interested in fighting, Saul. I came to Paradise to relax and enjoy myself, not to fight."

"Coward!" roared King Saul. "You coward, you're too scared to battle. Now give me back my crown! You hear me?"

"Now don't get in a tizzy, Saul," King David said serenely. "Why get yourself all worked up when, no matter what, you'll never get your way? Listen to me, Saul, sit yourself back down on your horse and head on back to the World of Chaos. Why spend your time bothering the tzaddikim when they're trying to sleep?"

All of King David's tranquil talking made the horseman in shining armour flip his lid. He yelled so loud that it awakened the birds in their nests. "Oh, just look at him now: the fancy tzaddik in furs. Usurped the crown of King Saul and still he calls himself a tzaddik. Steeped in sin from head to toe—and he still calls himself a tzaddik."

King David, it seemed, was long used to these nocturnal visits. He stood serenely on his balcony and tried to calm the outraged horseman, but to no avail. King Saul grew even more incensed. His eyes were burning, actually aflame.

"Give me back my crown. You hear me? You give me that crown! I will not budge from this spot until you give me my crown back."

King Saul's screaming woke up Abishag. She ran to the window and fearfully asked King David: "What's going on, Duddy? Who is yelling like that?"

David reassured her. He gave her a kiss on the forehead and told her to go back to sleep. He'd come back soon.

Abishag looked like a startled deer. Her entire body trembling, she implored the king: "I'll go, but listen, Duddy, please hurry back."

She crawled back into bed. King Saul, on the other hand, was still standing below, shaking his fists at David, seething, threatening, demanding the return of the crown and the throne in Paradise that, in his view, had been usurped from him.

King David could control himself no longer. He lifted up his nightshirt and shouted down in elegant Hebrew: "*Yishokeini!*"

"Thief!" screamed back the horseman in the iron-plated armour. "First you stole my crown from me and now you go and plagiarize the 'Come and kiss' from your own son Solomon's song."

King David went into his bedroom, shut the window to the balcony and drew the curtains closed.

King Saul got back on his horse and galloped around King David's palace a few times. "I shall get my revenge, David. Don't think that this is over. I'll get my revenge, almighty God in heaven as my witness!" he swore, shaking his fists at the stars.

I held on tight to my pal Little Pisser and my pal Little Pisser clung closer to the shepherd angel Louie.

"You see that, fellas?" Louie whispered. "He always comes, Saul, the horseman of the World of Chaos, and wakes David up. Every time he comes, he repeats the same old story and they have the same conversation, word for word. He doesn't concede a single point in his argument until King David lifts up his nightshirt and tells him biblically to 'let him come and kiss!'"

"He's riding off like a fiend now, his brow clouded with rage. Where do you suppose he's off to?" I asked.

"Let's fly after him, fellas," Louie suggested. "But quietly! Don't let anyone hear even a rustle of your wings. Saul should be none the wiser that we're following him and spying."

We spread our wings and flapped them soundlessly, hardly taking a breath.

King Saul rode on his white horse. His tall, slender figure cast a strange and eerie silhouette against the black banner of the moonlit night.

"A troubled soul," Louie the shepherd angel whispered. "He never found any rest on Earth and no rest in the other world either. He is consumed by turmoil in death, just as it consumed him in life."

King Saul brought his horse to a halt in front of a small whitewashed house and jumped off. With his spurs rattling, he went up to the window.

"In this house here," explained Louie, "lives Samuel the prophet. He's still a bachelor, that is, he never married. He lives a modest life and doesn't get mixed up in Paradise's public affairs. Cecile, an angel with a hairy upper lip, tends to his needs: does a little cooking for him, patches up his underpants. The old man doesn't require much. Once, he even promised me that when the Messiah comes, he would hand over his own portion of Behemoth and Leviathan to me. He would keep just his share of holy wine for himself…"

King Saul rapped at the window: once, twice, then a third time, each time louder than before. All the while he called: "Samuel, Prophet Samuel, get up! It's me!"

The door opened. The old man, Samuel the prophet, came outside, his beard as white as snow, his eyes clouded by age. He was also a bit hard of hearing.

"Back again, are you?" Samuel the prophet said. "Why don't you let me sleep?"

King Saul's tall figure shrank slightly as he bent down to the old prophet. "Prophet, you've got to help me find my father's donkeys! How can I go back home without them—a pitiful herdsman like me?"

The old prophet smiled bitterly. His white beard fluttered in the wind like a distress flag. "You'll never find those donkeys, Saul. There's no use in trying, you'll never be a herdsman again. The herd has found someone else."

"Neither herdsman nor king," Saul whimpered. "So now what, then, Prophet? Tell me, give me some advice."

The old prophet waved his hand in resignation and then shook his hoary beard. The stars above his quiet, whitewashed house grew larger and sadder.

"What do you ask me for, Saul? How should I know? On Earth I was a prophet; here, in the real world, I live on the pension that I receive in consideration of my accomplishments. So, Saul, how should I know?"

The horseman in the iron-plated armour hung his head. Sadness exuded from his entire being. I thought I'd come unglued.

King Saul mounted his horse and pulled back the reins: "Giddyup, Li'l Eagle, giddyup! Back to the World of Chaos."

The steed flew like the wind; all we could see were the sparks sputtering from his horseshoes.

Old Prophet Samuel watched after the miserable horseman until he had disappeared. The old man sighed deeply and tip-toed back into his cottage, so as not to disturb his cook.

We all sat down on the wayside, each of us absorbed in his own thoughts. The stars grew paler and a cool wind was taking its first stroll around the grounds of King David's palace.

Two shadows dropped down and stretched long on the road below. We raised our eyes and saw two humble worker angels in flight. They were flying quite low and we could hear every word of their conversation.

"We just better not get caught, Zanvel," one angel told the other. "That would be a fine how-do-you-do: first the whipping we'd get and then the pain and humiliation that follows."

"Let's not think about it, Eli," the other angel responded, "and let's hope that this works out. It's got unbearable here on King David's estate. You toil the whole day and don't even get enough food to sate your hunger. And if you say so much as a word, you get beaten for it right off. We're treated like animals, not like angels."

"You're right, of course," said the first angel. "It's just that when I think about the kids, it breaks my heart. What did they ever do to deserve this, the poor things?"

"I feel the same way," sighed the other angel. "But it's a lost cause—so let's try our luck abroad; it's just too unbearable here."

The two angels vanished into the night. In sadness, we watched them go. I prayed that their escape would succeed and that they'd find work abroad.

Louie the angel seemed to understand my silent whispering. He gazed at me for a moment and said: "Such fools! Where do they think they're going to run off to? Is it better anywhere else? For their sort of angel, no Paradise is paradise."

My heart sank at Louie's words. I felt sorry both for the children left behind and for the escaping angels.

I could picture the wives of the two fleeing angels, waking up in the morning. I could hear the weeping of these two desolate, abandoned women and the wailing of their children.

The door of Samuel the prophet's house opened and the old man came out again. He could not fall back to sleep, it seemed, after King Saul's visit. He paced back and forth in front of his house, back and forth, apparently waiting for daybreak.

"What are we hanging around here for?" said Louie. "Let's fly back to King David's palace."

We flew off. One by one, the stars were beginning to flicker out. It was getting chilly in Paradise.

We landed in front of the palace. All around was nothing but dead silence, not even the slightest sound was heard. A rooster crowed and another answered it, and then there was such squawking that I thought I'd go deaf.

The chief rooster appeared upon the spire of the King David Tower, a chap with a fiery red crest. He gave quite a crowing as his flapping wings blew out the glow of the moon clock.

In all the clay huts a commotion was commencing. The angels were waking up from their sleep and getting ready for work.

Louie told us that he had to go and drive his herd of sheep into the field. In the meantime, we ought to fly ahead and wait for him to come back with the sheep. He described where we were to wait for him, right at the very spot on the hilltop where we first met him the day before.

"Get a move on, fellas. You don't want anyone, God forbid, to discover you here." He left for the paddocks and the two of us, Little Pisser and I, spread our wings and flew in the direction Louie pointed us.

We alit on the green hilltop; the grass was damp. We were tired from our sleepless night. The azure of the morning twilight flooded into all of King David's estate. The birds began to chirp their greetings, delighting in a new day in Paradise.

"What do you say about this night on King David's estate, Little Pisser?"

"What's there to say, Samuel Abba? It was a night like nothing else: a tale to tell to our children and to our children's children, too."

From far off we heard the angels singing as they walked to work. The singing was loud at first, then quieter, until it finally faded away.

"Where could Louie be, Little Pisser?" I asked my friend.

"How should I know, Samuel Abba? He'll probably be back soon. He knows we're waiting for him."

It wasn't too long before Louie returned. He was driving his herd of sheep in front of him and playing his pipe. He sat down beside us. He took some dark bread from his satchel and a hunk of sheep's cheese. We ate it up hungrily and said our goodbyes.

"Come again some time," Louie told us. "You are always my welcome guests, so see here that you don't wait too long."

We embraced each other. What a shame it was to bid farewell to this lovely, barefooted little angel, but we had to. Little Pisser's mama was probably already worrying about her rascal.

As we neared his home, I said goodbye to my dear friend. We agreed that neither of us ought to tell anyone where we had been and what we had seen. We swore on it and flew off, each in a different direction. Little Pisser went to his home and I to mine…

*

I stopped my recounting here. Day was breaking through the window. Across from me sat the rabbi. His white beard was quivering. His eyes were red from sleeplessness and astonishment.

"Will wonders never cease!" he said. "Our King David is quite the big-shot nobleman. And with such a fortune, no evil eye. May he always have such luck."

The rabbi's assistant was sitting speechless. His mouth hung so wide open that you could count all his teeth. He was unable to get a word out.

But the town magnate, Mr Michael Hurwitz, drummed his fingers on his belly, repeating the word "*sonderbar*" a good hundred times, if I'm not mistaken.

My mama smacked her hands together: "Oh it breaks a mother's heart! It's already daylight out there and my child hasn't shut his eyes all night. A bunch of bullies you are, ganging up on a child!"

"I… I… What do you want from me, Zelda? Who's ganging up on the child?"

My mama didn't answer Pop. She merely gave him a look and he started trembling from head to toe. If he hadn't stuck by the table, who knows what would have happened to him.

Mama took me by the hand. She nearly smothered me with kisses. "Come, my little kaddish, let's go to sleep. It's enough to break a mother's heart!"

She laid me in the cradle and began to rock it. I was so tired, and the swaying of the cradle made me even more sleepy. A moment before I fell asleep, I sat up and told the honourable upstanding individuals not to come that evening since I was so very tired. I would, God willing, continue my stories of Paradise the following evening.

I lay back down in my cradle. I was still listening as the door creaked open and the upstanding individuals said their goodbyes to Pop. My eyelids grew heavy and I fell sound asleep.

In my dream, I relived the night on King David's estate once more and saw my friend Little Pisser again and heard Louie the shepherd angel's lovely songs. And in that same dream I recounted all the extraordinary experiences I had in Paradise to the rabbi, his assistant and the town magnate, Mr Michael Hurwitz.

9

The Behemoth's Terrible Misadventure

I slept in all the following day. Everyone went about on tiptoe so as not to wake me, God forbid. Pop didn't even dare lift his head; speaking out loud was strictly forbidden. He cast about aimlessly like a shadow. My mama took great pains to make sure that absolutely no one should disturb my slumber.

I woke up around dusk. It was already nearly dark in the room. My pop stood in the corner silently reciting God's benedictions in the midst of his evening prayer.

I rubbed my eyes, let out a great yawn and called my mama over to my cradle. "Mama, could you nurse me, please, I haven't had a thing all day. You know, I can't eat while I sleep, after all."

I didn't need to ask my mama twice and immediately she began to nurse me. All the while she caressed and kissed me like the paragon of mothers.

"Oh, my little kaddish, they're making your life just miserable. Whoever heard of such a thing: grown people not letting a newborn baby sleep? They make him stay up all night long to tell his stories of Paradise. And *you*, you wretch"—she turned to my pop, who had just finished with the eighteen benedictions—"you are to blame for it all. What kind of papa are you? You're a no-good, stone-hearted fraud of a father."

My pop turned pale. He wasn't expecting such a condemnation at that moment. He didn't react at all, acting as if she weren't referring to him.

I interceded on my pop's behalf. "Leave Pop alone, Mama," I implored her. "He's not guilty of anything. It was me who asked for these folks to be called here so that I could tell them how things are in Paradise. Tomorrow night, God willing, they'll come again and I'll tell them more."

Then I fell back asleep, without even saying "Goodnight" to my mama, that's how tired I was. I don't remember exactly what I dreamt that night and I won't tell you anything I don't precisely recall.

When I woke up in the morning, the room was full of sunlight. My mama wasn't at home. She was off milking the goat. Our cat was warming herself on the windowsill. "Here, puss, puss," I called to the cat. She leapt from the window into my cradle. The cat licked my eyelids and I felt newly born.

The day passed without anything particularly interesting happening. We had a little something to eat, in the afternoon Pop rested a bit, and Mama chatted with some ladies outside. I played with a red button on my coverlet.

In the evening, as usual, my father headed off to shul. This time he didn't stay long and returned a short while later.

For dinner we had rice porridge. It wasn't long before the rabbi, his assistant and the town magnate came in with a "Good evening".

They sat themselves down at the table. The rabbi had grown even whiter since the last night, his juridical assistant even thinner. Only the magnate, Michael Hurwitz, was none the worse for wear. He was sparkling in his gold splendour, nodding affirmatively at everything, and kept repeating his German "*sonderbar*".

I seated myself across from the rabbi. The lamp was burning on the table. Mama drew the curtains. Everyone was ready to listen.

My mama, as usual, stood in the doorway. She put her hands to her heart and said: "Now don't strain yourself, my darling, if you get tired you should take a rest. There's no emergency, God forbid, so you don't need to be in such a hurry. And as soon as you feel even a little hungry, let me know so I can nurse you."

My mama, bless her, was so devoted to me. She looked after me as the apple of her eye.

I rested my head on both my hands and began my story. Everyone around the table sat stock-still, you could hear their hearts beating. I began:

*

As you recall, I had said goodbye to my friend Little Pisser. He flew home and I flew home. I was so tired that I could barely stand. I hardly managed to drag myself to my door.

I collapsed on to my cot and fell asleep. In my dream, King David, Bathsheba, Abishag, the naiads, King Saul and the old healer Genendel were all jumbled together. All that I had seen on King David's estate appeared there, but helter-skelter. The forms and figures were so mixed up that my dream was more of a nightmare than it had been in real life.

I woke up around four o'clock in the afternoon. I washed up, had a bit to eat, and flew right off to my pal Little Pisser.

My friend Little Pisser was still asleep. I sat down in the workshop and waited for him to wake up.

Little Pisser's pop, Solomon-Zalman the patchmaker, was standing at his big table with a tape measure hanging from his neck and a piece of chalk in his hand. He was marking up a pair of wings that had been brought in for repair.

At their benches sat the two tailor angels, Barney and Seymour, both engrossed in their work. The needles were genuinely flying in their hands. I tried to count the number of stitches each made per minute but it was impossible. I kept losing count.

Little Pisser's mama, the angel Hannah Deborah, came in from the bedroom alcove. She sat down next to me and tried to extract from me where we, that is, Little Pisser and I, had disappeared to. She had thought goodness knows what had happened to us. She very nearly went to the Paradise Police and raised a stink to file a missing angel report.

I didn't know if I could tell her the truth. I had completely forgotten to get my story straight with my friend Little Pisser about the whole affair.

I sat there awhile tentatively, shilly-shallying. Finally I came to the conclusion that I was under no obligation to tell her the truth. If Little Pisser wanted to, he could tell it. So I played dumb, telling her that I hadn't seen Little Pisser for around three days. And, as a matter of fact, I had come over to find out if he had, God forbid, taken ill.

"Taken ill!" The angel Hannah Deborah clasped her hands together. "May only my enemies take ill! The last thing I need is for Little Pisser to be sick. A mother's troubles…"

She kept trying to give me the third degree, but when she saw that I was sticking to my story, that I was no clairvoyant and had no crystal ball, she shook her head and returned to the alcove.

Little Pisser's pop was done marking up the pair of wings. The angel Seymour had just finished with another pair and was preparing them for fitting.

Little Pisser's pop flew off to his customer, the angel Henzel the miller, to try on the wings. He was barely out of the door when Seymour burst into song:

> The game of love's not worth your time,
> Now angels, I swear it's true,
> If you please, take my advice
> And let no trouble come to you.

> For love is grief, oh, it's a plague,
> That robs you all delight,
> It never lets you work by day,
> Or go to sleep at night.

Then the angel Barney, the other journeyman tailor, who was always at daggers drawn with Seymour, was, for the moment, in full agreement with his rival. He joined in, quavering:

> Its joy may glimmer for a while
> With stars and birds and daisies,
> Then it runs off a thousand miles
> And leaves you to go crazy.

> But going crazy's not worth your time,
> Now angels, I swear it's true,
> Better to say: to hell with love,
> Than let it get hold of you.

This song made me terribly sad. I thought back to the moonlit night when I saw these two infatuated tailor angels bump into one another on the sidewalk. They didn't even know that I had seen them and heard their conversation, I thought. But still, that didn't make it any easier to bear.

From the alcove, Little Pisser's sister, Ethel, the lovely angel with the rosy wings, began to sing. She apparently was none too pleased with the lessons drawn by these two unlucky-in-love tailor angels. Her song was sanguine and spirited and her voice was as sweet as honey:

> You came to me in my dreams,
> My golden one, my treasure,
> And gave to me a golden ring
> To remember you forever.
>
> The ring is of the finest gold,
> On my finger I wear it proud,
> I showed it to my dearest friend
> And said to her aloud:
>
> This is the ring my true love bought,
> An angel with sparkling eyes—
> And if my parents would consent,
> Into his arms I'd fly.
>
> And in his hold I would remain
> As ages come and go,
> Until my braids, now raven black,
> Turn white as winter snow.

Who is to say which of these was right, I thought. These guys claim one thing and then Little Pisser's sister comes along to assert just the opposite. When I grew up, I concluded, I'd know the answer for sure.

Seymour the angel sighed deeply. He was thinking about the Paradise shopkeeper's daughter and it tugged at his heart strings. I saw for myself how a tear dropped from his eye on to a broken wing on the workbench.

Barney the angel was filled with envy for his rival over the shedding of this tear. He thought long and hard about the Paradise shopkeeper's daughter and squeezed his eyes until he, too, successfully extracted a tear.

He shot a victorious glance at Seymour the angel. His glance said: "You think you're the only one sacrificing tears for the Paradise shopkeeper's daughter? Not by a long shot!"

This apparently got under Seymour's skin. He hung his head, picked up the pace of his needlework, and sang:

> Although I know you mocked me, love,
> And with my heart you toyed,
> Still I ramble through the streets at night,
> And know no peace or joy.
>
> From the moon and throngs of stars above,
> Your voice rings in my ear.
> I know I'll never feel your touch,
> Though I'd die for you, my dear.

Barney the angel stepped back from his worktable. Seymour's song had unnerved him. He felt that if Seymour were to sing even one more verse, he, Barney the angel, would not be able to contain himself. He would grab the pressing iron and flatten Seymour's skull.

Luckily, Seymour's thread ran out. The song had only two verses and Barney the angel settled down.

That is, you might say, he seemed to settle down. God only knows what was going on in his heart; from the outside it was impossible to tell.

Little Pisser finally woke up. He came into the workshop and was very glad to see me. He ran over and hugged me as if it had been ages since we had last seen each other.

"Have you been here long, Samuel Abba?"

"I've been waiting for you for over an hour, Little Pisser. You got, no evil eye, quite a snooze in…"

The two of us headed over to the open window and looked out. On the pasture fields outside, the Behemoth was grazing. The three barefoot herdsmen who watched over him were playing a round of gin rummy.

"That Behemoth," I said to my friend, "gets fatter and fatter every day. By the time the Messiah comes, he'll be so fat that they won't be able to move him out of there."

Little Pisser kept quiet. We watched as the angel Hasia strolled past the Paradise pastures. She was in her ninth month and every evening she took a walk through the Paradise pastures to get some fresh air.

"What is she doing in that red pinafore, Little Pisser?" I asked my friend. "If the Behemoth sees red, something terrible, God forbid, could happen."

"Oh, that's true, that's true," Little Pisser agreed, and we both motioned with our hands to signal the pregnant angel that she ought to turn back while there was still time.

The angel Hasia, however, seemed not to take the hint. She continued her meandering, all the while getting closer to the spot where the Behemoth was grazing.

The Behemoth spotted the red pinafore and his eyes lit up. Here it comes, we thought, he's going to pounce on the angel.

We thought wrong, however. Indeed, the Behemoth was no admirer of the red pinafore. But, to our great astonishment, he kept his wits about him. Apparently he was of the opinion that he was not just any bull: he was *the Behemoth*. And it would not do at all for him to get worked up over a little bit of red like your run-of-the mill dumb ox.

I was rather impressed by his composure. The Behemoth kept tugging at the grass and paid no mind to the foolish angel in the red pinafore.

Yet, a catastrophe was still in store. The angel Hasia wasn't the sharpest angel in Paradise. One might say that she was more of a lummox than the Behemoth. When she got even closer, barely a few steps away from the grazing Behemoth, she stopped to observe him as he chewed away on his cud with relish. She stood there wide-eyed for a while, admiring his appetite.

The three barefoot herdsmen were busy bickering over their cards. One argued one way, the second said another, and the third insisted quite the contrary. They were so absorbed in their arguing that they didn't notice that the pregnant angel had walked right up to the Behemoth and was now stroking his neck.

"Let her," the Behemoth thought, "let her pet away to her heart's content. It would be better, though, if she took off that red pinafore."

But as Little Pisser's mama, the angel Hannah Deborah, says: "Fools rush in…" The pregnant angel didn't realize just how magnanimous the Behemoth was being. She continued to pet and stroke him and then, suddenly, bent down and whispered in his ear: "The Messiah's on his way!"

The Behemoth's entire hefty body began to tremble. "The Messiah's on his way!" That would mean that they were going to come after him, to slaughter him and slice him into pieces and roast his flesh. The tzaddikim would dip their hunks of challah into gravy made of his drippings, gorging on his flesh and savouring his deliciousness: "My, it's heavenly, the taste of Paradise!"

Then the Behemoth went berserk. "The Messiah's on his way!" Danger was imminent, he had to escape, save his hide, elude the slaughtering knife.

The Behemoth, who was just an ox after all, was unaware that the pregnant angel Hasia only meant it as a joke. Until the Messiah was actually on his way, he still had plenty of time to graze on the pastures of Paradise... All at once he dropped his head, snatched up the pregnant angel with his horns, and set off running full steam ahead.

Little Pisser and I raised an alarm. We shouted at the top of our voices: "The Behemoth is on the loose! The Behemoth is on the loose!"

The three herdsmen leapt to their feet and started whistling and chasing after the raging, runaway ox. The angel Hasia, flailing, held on to the horns with such a shrieking that everybody and his cousin came out running. They asked one another: "What's going on? What happened?"

"The Behemoth took a pregnant angel on his horns and ran off."

"We've got to chase after him!"

"We have to catch him and bring him back!"

"Forget the pregnant angel, the Behemoth is what matters. What would the tzaddikim do without the Behemoth when the Messiah comes?"

An out-and-out chase was under way. Anyone with a pair of wings, no matter how old, took off flying.

The unbridled Behemoth, however, kept running like a thousand bats out of hell. No doubt, in his eyes he could see before him the flash of the butcher's knife that they would use to slit his throat. He was escaping the "Great Repast" for which the Messiah was supposed to prepare the Behemoth's own flesh to serve the tzaddikim.

The pregnant angel struggled to hold on to his horns. She flailed her arms, she hollered, she swooned, she came to and swooned again.

We chased after the Behemoth. The three barefoot herdsmen led the way and behind them were angels with beards and without. The only little kid angels who chased alongside them were me and my friend Little Pisser.

Some angels ran out of steam. They took time out in the middle of the chase, tried to catch their breath and wiped the sweat from under their wings before flying back home.

"He's got grit, that Behemoth."

"Have you ever seen anything run like him? He's faster than the fastest hare in Paradise."

"That dumb broad scared the daylights out of him. They ought to take her outside the shul and give her a spanking so that she'll learn never to monkey around like that again."

That was the way the angels talked amongst themselves as they headed home. But the Behemoth was still on the run and we kept after him.

The Behemoth left quite a bit of damage in his wake. He ran over gardens and newly sown fields, trampling everything. He knocked down a couple of little angel kids who were playing "Red Rover".

An old angel who was standing on the outskirts of a village playing a hurdy-gurdy got such a blow that he made several somersaults in the air before landing on the ground unconscious. It took great effort to bring him back to his senses.

"Look, Little Pisser, he's heading west, towards the border of Gentile Paradise."

"I see that, Samuel Abba, I see that. If only there were better news to report."

The evening began to darken. The Behemoth chase became even more frantic. He had to be caught before nightfall. Or so we thought. The Behemoth, however, thought otherwise. He concluded that once it was dark, the angels could turn the world upside down but they'd never catch him.

The night cast its shadow over the fields and the roads. And, as if just for spite, the moon didn't appear in the sky. There was no sign of a single star. It was total darkness, you couldn't see the nose of the person next to you. All you could hear was the swift beating of wings and the fearsome bellowing of the Behemoth.

"Where does he get his energy?" an angel gasped, short of breath. If I'm not mistaken, it was Hillel the nightwatchman.

"Where, you ask?" someone responded with a laugh. "He hasn't stopped grazing since the days of Creation, you think he hasn't been saving his energy?"

The Behemoth raged on like a whirlwind over the fields of Paradise. He carried the angel on his horns, her red pinafore fluttering like a flag.

"You see those green lights up ahead, Samuel Abba? That's the border of Gentile Paradise. He better not have got it into his head to cross the border. That would be a catastrophe."

"He'll probably get scared and give up." I tried to say something hopeful to my friend, even if I didn't believe it myself. Can you be sure that an enraged Behemoth will play by the rules?

I wondered. What does a beast know of borders? What's the difference for him between a Jewish and a Gentile Paradise?

The lights at the border were getting closer now. We could hear the bells of the Orthodox church ringing near the frontier. The Behemoth carried on with wild momentum, heading closer and closer to the border crossing.

The pregnant angel, still clutching the Behemoth's horns, had no strength left to scream. Her raspy voice jangled like a bell. Now you could just barely hear the creak of a groan coming from her.

The three herdsmen who had been charged with watching the Behemoth were as pale as a piece of chalk. What would they do if the Behemoth, God forbid, were to cross the border into Gentile Paradise? All indications were that this was where things were heading. The bells of the Orthodox church rang out: *bing-bong, bing-bong.*

The Behemoth sprinted and bounded so hard that he was nearly frothing. The border was right there; you could clearly see the Gentile Paradise Border Patrol angels with their blue eyes and blond hair. They wore large jaunty boots and stood leaning against their lances.

"Little Pisser, what's going to happen?"

"A catastrophe!" my friend Little Pisser moaned. "It's a catastrophe, Samuel Abba."

The Behemoth with the pregnant angel atop his horns crossed over the border. Several gentile angels tried to block the way, but he leapt over them and kept running.

Our angels, that is to say, the Jewish angels, came to a halt at the border, unable to pursue the Behemoth any further. That is, they would have wanted to, but the gentile angels would by no means allow it.

We touched down below, sad and chagrined. We didn't know what to do. We stood looking across the fields where the Behemoth had run off and disappeared.

"Maybe they'll catch him?" said an angel.

"And if they do," another answered him, "what good is that to us?"

"They might even improperly slaughter him and render him unkosher," a third said.

"He's a pretty fat beast, our Behemoth, no evil eye. They'd make quite a saint's feast out of him."

"Our holy tzaddikim will be left with their tongues hanging out of their mouths. They've been sharpening their teeth their whole lives for this and now—no more Behemoth."

"Bite your tongue!" the angel Henzel replied angrily. "What do you mean 'no more Behemoth'? He still exists after all! He's just gone into Gentile Paradise and now we've got to get him back from there." Henzel the angel stroked his sparse beard, determined to come up with a scheme to extricate the Behemoth.

"What can be done, Mr Henzel?" asked a short little angel with a thick beard. "Suggest something, Mr Henzel."

The angel Henzel didn't answer. He walked straight over to the Gentile border guard and started discussing the matter, partly in their language, partly in Yiddish, and the rest he expressed with his hands. "*Nashi* Behemoth," Henzel began, gesturing to all of *us* on our side of the border, "went off and escaped into *vashi ray.*" He pointed vigorously towards *their* Paradise.

"*Chto?*" Vasil Angelenko, staff sergeant of the Gentile Border Patrol, responded uncomprehendingly.

"*Nashi* Behemoth *do vashi ray,*" Henzel the angel attempted to clarify, gesticulating with his hands to show exactly where *our Behemoth* entered *their Paradise.*

The Gentile Border Patrol all burst out laughing. Staff Sergeant Vasil Angelenko twisted the ends of his moustache and then barked out harshly: "*Poshel von, zhid parkhatiy!*"

The "dirty Jew" just addressed, Henzel the angel, shuddered at this order to "beat it". We all stood there crestfallen, our wings dropped at our sides.

From the fields of Gentile Paradise we heard a sudden "Hurrah!" and a peal of laughter. The gentile angels, it seemed, had successfully stopped the Behemoth.

We stood on our side of the border and listened to the gentile cheers. In the chests of each of us, our hearts pounded like clocks gone haywire.

The angel Hillel the nightwatchman sighed deeply. You could have heard his sigh from seven miles off.

The three barefoot herdsmen stood as if slapped in the face. How would they respond when they were brought in for their comeuppance?

"So this is how you bastards take care of the Behemoth?" And the tzaddikim would spit right in each of their faces and with good reason, too. They were just dying for a round of gin rummy, weren't they... and while they played, the catastrophe occurred.

The laughter emanating from the fields of Gentile Paradise grew louder. Each of us could picture them, parading the Behemoth into a Gentile Paradise paddock. They would put the pure and kosher beast by a single trough alongside their pigs. Woe to those who lived to see the day!

"Goodness knows what will happen," Henzel the angel said to no one in particular. "They might go and slaughter the Behemoth with their unkosher knives. What will our holy tzaddikim say about that? A fine kettle of fish that would be to have the great feast with no Behemoth. Mercy me, tell me what to do, angels?"

"Tell you what to do! That's easier said than done."

The night was now completely dark. The angels with their downcast wings stood by the border and, frankly, didn't know where to turn.

"You know what?" said one of the barefoot herdsmen. "Let's light a fire so we can warm ourselves up a bit while we consider what to do and how we should disclose the matter to the rest of Paradise."

Everyone appreciated the plan to light a fire. It was, as I said, the middle of the night now, and we were all shivering.

The three herdsmen gathered kindling and lit the fire and we all sat around it. Everyone was scratching his head, thinking and figuring out what should be done.

"What do you say, Little Pisser?"

"What can I say, Samuel Abba? It's all pretty, pretty rotten."

"Now they've got the Behemoth and we're left with bubkes, Little Pisser."

"We'll have to do without the Behemoth, Samuel Abba. When the Messiah comes, the Leviathan will be served. And at any rate, the meat of the Leviathan is tastier than Behemoth meat."

The angel Henzel, who had overheard our conversation, was outraged. He became apoplectic and launched into a whole sermon. Punctuated by fits of coughing, he said:

"So, the youngsters are already willing to let them keep the Behemoth there in Gentile Paradise. What's that, we should let them have our Behemoth? For millennia we have tended him, and for what: to let them make a feast of their own? As if they don't have enough pigs there, they need our Behemoth to boot? The world may be brought to its knees, it may be hell and high water—you hear what I'm telling you: hell and high water—but the Behemoth will be returned to us!"

My friend Little Pisser and I were frightened. We tried to splutter out a response: "Don't be angry, Mr Henzel, sir! We didn't, God forbid, mean anything bad. We wanted... We were just saying... You see, Mr Henzel?"

But once Henzel gets fired up, it's very hard to calm him back down. He stood inflamed over the fire, gesticulating with his hands, ranting, sermonizing, droning away like a mill wheel. No one understood a word he was saying.

All of a sudden he flapped his wings, blowing out the fire that flickered in the field. He shouted shrilly: "Rise up, angels! Why are you sitting here like a bunch of old ladies around the fire? Let's wake up all of Paradise. Let's raise the alarm. Let's defy danger! Woe to all my years that I have lived to see such a day."

We all stood up, spread our wings and flew off. Henzel the angel flew ahead with all of us behind him. With a fearsome flapping of his wings he yelled: "I'll be damned if we let them have the Behemoth! The Behemoth is ours, we shall bring him back to our Paradise by any means necessary..."

The Uproar over the Behemoth's Escape

T HE NEWS that the Behemoth had run off shook all of Paradise. One bird told a second bird; one breeze told another. When we got back home in the morning, we encountered mobs of tzaddikim huddling in the street. They were distressed and angry and flapping their hands as they spoke, none of them wanting to believe that such a calamity had actually occurred.

"Did the Behemoth really run away?" the sainted Rabbi of Opatów asked the Holy Rabbi of Lublin. "Such a thing simply cannot be, it's unheard of."

The white beard of the Rabbi of Lublin quivered; one got the sense that he was absolutely beside himself. "The birds are singing it from every rooftop and all you can say is that it cannot be?"

"Maybe it's just a bad dream," the Opatów tzaddik interjected, "and all this aggravation is for nothing?"

The Tzaddik of Lublin brushed the idea aside with a flourish of his hand: "A dream, a dream, you say? If only it were just a dream."

"Well, they'll probably get him back," the Opatów tzaddik offered by way of consolation. "What do the tzaddikim in

Gentile Paradise need with our Behemoth anyway, they've got pigs aplenty and pork is certainly their preference."

The Rabbi of Lublin took a pinch of snuff from the Rabbi of Opatów, sniffed it and let out a resounding sneeze.

"You said it—you've sneezed on the truth!" the Rabbi of Opatów said, not believing it himself.

I poked my friend Little Pisser: "Now, where did those three herdsmen go, the ones who watched the Behemoth? They were just here with us. Where have they run off to?"

"You need to ask, Samuel Abba? You don't get how scared the herdsmen are? The tzaddikim are all livid with them since they took such poor care of the Behemoth. The herdsmen are probably hiding up in an attic somewhere."

We saw another cluster of tzaddikim. In their midst stood the sainted Rebbe of Sadagura. His beard looked bedraggled, his black eyes seemed to glow. He was fuming and breathing fire: "Where are those lazy bums, those herdsmen? We ought to give them what they deserve, they ought to be rooted out. They should have their wings smashed, the bastards! They should be driven out of Paradise, they should, along with their wives and children and their children's children."

The other tzaddikim nodded their heads in agreement with the indignation expressed by the Rebbe of Sadagura.

We saw the Holy Tzaddik of Horodenka briskly running over. His robe had come untied, he had lost a slipper on the way. He ran up to the huddle of tzaddikim and barely spluttered out: "What a catastrophe, what an outrage! Now what am I going to do with the golden fork and knife that I have set aside just for the Great Repast? What a catastrophe!"

The Holy Tzaddik of Horodenka was a tiny man with an enormous beard. It would be no exaggeration to say that his beard came down to his knees. My friend Little Pisser couldn't contain himself and he burst out laughing.

"Don't laugh, Little Pisser," I told him. "It's a sin."

"How can I not laugh," Little Pisser responded. "Just look at this miniature tzaddik with one slipper and one bare foot. But at least it seems like he's still got an appetite, no evil eye."

Luckily for us, the tzaddikim were all so absorbed in their conversation that they didn't hear my friend Little's Pisser's mocking.

"What to do? What to do? What will we ever do?" The Rebbe of Sadagura wrung his hands. "What kind of great feast will it be without the Behemoth?"

"We ought to raise a rumpus. We should shout it in the streets." The Holy Tzaddik of Horodenka was seeing red now. "I mean, such a thing has never been heard of."

"It is the devil's work," expounded the Holy Rabbi of Lublin. "How else would a reasonable beast like him get such a notion to make a break for it?"

"Right, absolutely right," cried the Horodenka tzaddik. "It is the devil's own work. Satan, may his name be blotted out, has infiltrated Paradise."

"We ought to inspect all the mezuzas," suggested the Rabbi of Zalishchik, who was amongst the throng. "Maybe a mezuza somewhere is out of whack and unfit for use. As a result, we have this calamity on our hands."

"Come on," whispered Little Pisser in my ear, "let's leave these Galicians here. Let them discuss mucked-up, bad-luck mezuzas to their heart's content. In the meantime, we'll fly on."

"Where to, Little Pisser?"

"I think we should head over to the holy Patriarchs to hear what they have to say about the Behemoth's escape."

We left the cluster of Galician tzaddikim and flew towards the Avenue of the Patriarchs, where the villas of the holy Patriarchs are. On the way there, we came across several other tzaddikim. They were standing in groups of five or even ten to a cluster. As we flew we heard scraps of their conversations: "Behemoth... Ran off... Herdsmen... Playing cards... Into Gentile Paradise... Must be whipped... Shatter their wings... What will the Messiah say..."

"The Behemoth sure pulled a fast one, Little Pisser. The tzaddikim are really in an uproar, right? The Maggid of Koschnitz even forgot to put on his fringes..."

"And the Sage of Shpola, Samuel Abba, did you see the Sage of Shpola? He pulled entire handfuls of his beard out and was banging his fists against his head, screaming: 'Heaven help us, folks, heaven help us! What will we do if the Messiah gets the urge to come, God forbid, on this day of all days?'"

"Explain to me, Little Pisser," I asked, "how it is that these tzaddikim have such appetites?"

"You ask the weirdest questions, Samuel Abba. By now you should already have got the picture: the tzaddikim don't lift a finger, they go around the livelong day enjoying the fresh air, and fresh air, they say, induces quite an appetite."

We landed on Prophet Elijah Boulevard. The morning sun dappled all the rooftops with gold. Prophet Elijah Boulevard was empty. The wealthier tzaddikim were still sleeping. The tzaddikim who lived on this same boulevard were out with the other tzaddikim conferring about the calamity.

Shmaya the policeman in the green uniform stood on the corner yawning, his wings down at his sides. As usual, he held his baton in his hand but, for the moment, he didn't know what to do with himself.

My friend Little Pisser and I still longed to take our revenge. He was standing there at a loss, having no one around to impress. We flew over his head, turned a couple of somersaults in the air and, holding each other by the hand, the two of us chanted a ditty that Little Pisser had composed after Shmaya filed the report on us for goatnapping:

> Shmaya, Shmaya, policeman,
> Keeps the peace as best he can,
> On the beat with his nightstick,
> He's like two short planks, but extra thick.
> His swollen head, you must have seen,
> Atop his uniform so green,
> He sure thinks that he is swell.
> Come on now, come on out!,
> Join with us and give a shout,
> And we'll tell him to go to hell!

Shmaya the policeman turned as red as a beet. He spotted us and, nearly frothing at the mouth, he shouted up at us, waving his baton: "You just wait, ya punks, I'll show you!"

He had wanted to spread his wings to take to the air and settle the score with us, but we got lucky. At that very moment, the Prophet Elijah showed up as he was taking his first stroll of the day on his boulevard.

"Shmaya, where are you off to, eh? What's got you flying like such a busy bee, Shmaya?"

Shmaya the policeman let down his wings. He was, it seemed, embarrassed to tell the Prophet Elijah that we had just unleashed our mocking ditty on him. He smiled and saluted the old prophet: "Good morning to you, Eli, sir. Have you heard the news, sir? The Behemoth has made a run for it and escaped. All the tzaddikim in Paradise are terribly upset about it, but here you are, Eli, sir, on your morning walk as if nothing happened."

The Prophet Elijah gave a smile: "I know, I know, Shmaya. I know that the Behemoth ran off and the tzaddikim are all in a stew. Well, let them stew, they have good reason. They've got, no evil eye, such healthy teeth, while I"—the ancient prophet displayed his gums—"I don't have what it takes to chew my portion of the Behemoth, all the same."

We left the old prophet to talk things over with the police-man and continued flying on our way towards the Avenue of the Patriarchs.

"You know what I think, Samuel Abba?"

"How could I know what you think, Little Pisser?"

"I think the holy Patriarchs must be at their wits' end… I'm curious how our forefather Isaac is handling this. He's quite the epicure, Isaac. He'd give who-knows-what for a good hunk of meat."

"How do you know that, Little Pisser?"

"Don't you remember what we read in Hebrew school, Samuel Abba? In the Holy Book, it clearly states that Isaac favoured Esau because Esau would always bring him a cut of meat from the hunt. And second of all, Samuel Abba…" Little Pisser reflected for a moment. "Second of all, I have seen with my own eyes how Isaac came one evening to the Paradise pasture where they tend the Behemoth with a piece of chalk in his hand."

"What did he need the chalk for, Little Pisser?"

"Our forefather Isaac made a mark on the Behemoth with the chalk—if I'm not mistaken, on his right side—to show that this cut of meat belonged to him and that he, God willing, would eat it when the Messiah came."

"Isaac is pretty blind, Little Pisser. How would he know where to make his mark with the chalk?"

"Leave it to him, Samuel Abba," Little Pisser answered. "Even blind he could feel out the fattest cut to make his mark on."

We turned on to Baal-Shem-Tov Alley. It was a squalid street but filled with sunlight. The very poorest angels lived on this alley, angels who may only have one pair of wings for the whole household. When anyone in the family needs to fly out somewhere, the others have to sit at home and wait for him to come back, take off his wings and give them to someone else.

Many wonderful tales are told in this alley. Just as they go on hungering here, they go on believing in miracles. The tales they tell are strangely beautiful, as hunger does what it does, gnawing and gnawing and keeping you often up at night.

In the alley, little angels played. They held hands and danced in a circle, singing:

> Round and round, round we go,
> Riva is the lady-o!
> Bertie is the lord so grand,
> Bert he is her loving man.
> Hand in hand, they fly and stroll
> With their wings of brightest gold,
> You must have seen these two together:
> On her cap she has a feather,
> A high top hat is what he wears,
> They have no kids, they have no cares,
> Only sweets and wine they take:
> They can go jump into a lake!

"Little Pisser," I said, pointing to the kids playing below on Baal-Shem-Tov Alley, "Little Pisser, those kids are so poor and so filthy, let's head straight down and play with them."

"Perish the thought," said Little Pisser. "Have you forgotten that we're on our way to the holy Patriarchs, Samuel Abba, so that we can hear what they're saying about the Behemoth?"

"Just for a little bit, Little Pisser," I pleaded with my friend. "Let's just play one game with them and then we'll fly on."

"No, right now we'll fly there and next time we'll come here and play with them," Little Pisser said firmly. I had no choice but to give in.

The alleyway was winding and narrow and we had to fly carefully so as not to get a wing caught somewhere.

We had just left Baal-Shem-Tov Alley and turned to the right. We recognized the street immediately: it was Brotherly Love Street. On this very street lived the rabbis Moses Leib of Sasov, Zev Wolf of Zbarazh and Levi Isaac of Berdichev, and each of these holy tzaddikim owned a piece of real estate here. Behind their houses was a cherry orchard. Needless to say, they weren't the very richest of the tzaddikim, but they didn't fare too badly either. They had no need to worry about their livelihoods and prayed their days away on behalf of the Jewish people, beseeching the Almighty to have mercy and grant all Israel a place in Paradise.

Looking down, we saw an average-sized fellow wearing a gabardine. Even though it was just an ordinary Paradise Wednesday, he was wearing a fur shtreimel on his head. He stood in the middle of the street, his head cocked towards the clouds, his arms reaching high into the air. His lips moved as he muttered.

"That's the Rabbi of Berdichev," Little Pisser whispered in my ear, "Rabbi Levi Isaac of Berdichev. He's probably making an appeal to the Master of the Universe. In times of hardship, he always stands in the middle of the street, in his finest Shabbos clothes, and weeps and appeals to God."

"Well then, let's hear how Rabbi Levi Issac makes his appeal to the Master of the Universe right now."

"All right, Samuel Abba," agreed my friend. "We can head down and listen to one of the prayers he makes in plain Yiddish. But remember, we can't hang around for too long."

"I just want to hear one of his prayers, Little Pisser. Just one and no more."

We quietly descended to the street and stood a few steps behind the Rabbi of Berdichev to listen. Levi Isaac of Berdichev was standing, as I said, with his hand stretched up towards the clouds as he made his appeal, an appeal that could move a stone to tears:

> A good day to you, O Master of the World!
> I, Levi Isaac, son of Sarah, from Berdichev,
> Appear before You with a humble plea.
> Where is justice? O Master of the World,
> And why do You torment your sainted ones?
> O Master of the World!
>
> Have they followed the path You laid before them?
> You must agree, it is so.
> Have they followed Your commandments?
> Again, it is so.
> Did You promise them eternal Paradise?
> Once more, it is so.
> With the Behemoth and Leviathan,
> With the red holy wine?
> Yet again, it is so.

Where, then, is the Behemoth now,
O Father in heaven?
Run off to the gentiles,
O Almighty Father.
So, return him to us,
O Father in heaven,
Do not turn our joy into disgrace,
O Almighty Father.

Not for my sake do I ask,
O Papa dearest,
But for all Your tzaddikim,
O Beloved Father.

I shall forgo my share
Of Behemoth and Leviathan,
But spoil not the Feast,
The repast of the tzaddikim, O Father in heaven.

The Rabbi of Berdichev bowed this way and that like a stalk of wheat in the wind. In his voice you could sense tears, earnest tears.

"He seems like a fine fellow, this Rabbi of Berdichev, eh, Little Pisser?"

"A very fine fellow indeed, Samuel Abba. But let's take off already."

So we flew on. Soon we had reached the Avenue of the Patriarchs. During the daytime, the avenue lay deserted. The benches that lined the thoroughfare sat empty. Only in the evening would the promenade start to fill with life. That's when loving couples would appear on the scene to coo and kiss and swear their love by the moon and stars above.

The Avenue of the Patriarchs is always well shaded, more than anywhere else. The dense birch trees that line the way dutifully watch over the avenue to make sure that only select sunbeams have the privilege to enter.

We saw three figures in the distance sporting shtreimels, gesticulating as they walked. From the shadows that fell as they made their way, we guessed that they were arguing about something.

The figures got closer. We could make them out now and recognized the three Patriarchs. They were moving quickly, as if in a hurry, and bickering.

Isaac was in the centre. As usual, he was wearing his dark glasses. He spoke anxiously, more yelling than speaking, saying: "And I tell ya, without the Behemoth, Paradise is just not Paradise. Whoever heard of Jewish Paradise without the Behemoth? What kind of tasteless feast would the Great Repast be without a scrap of his meat? It would be no feast at all. You hear what I'm saying: no feast at all."

Jacob our forefather, who was walking at his father's left, agreed with him. A feast without Behemoth was no feast. "Esau has all the luck," he said bitterly. "We, the tzaddikim of Jewish Paradise, tended and raised that Behemoth and now Esau gets to enjoy it. Well, that's your Esau for you, Pop. You always treated him as your little jewel and here's what you get in return. He'll gobble up your portion, too."

"Don't even mention his name to me," Isaac thundered. "Don't unkosher my ears with his unholy name."

Abraham our forefather tugged at his grandson Jacob our forefather's sleeve: "What are you getting your old man all worked up for, Jacob? Just because a parent makes a mistake, you don't need to go reminding him of it all the time! Your pop thought that Esau was bound to grow into a decent man and he loved him. If only your poppa could have known that he would turn out a goy, he would have given him the boot right off."

Jacob, however, dug in his heels. He argued that even if Esau was a "who the hell knows what" his father would still favour him, all because Esau always brought him something to eat. "My pop," Jacob went on, "loves his noshing more than the Holy Scriptures and now he…"

Isaac turned crimson. On his forehead a vein pulsated in anger. He had in mind to give Jacob both the tongue-lashing that he had coming to him and a good thrashing, too.

But Abraham didn't allow it. He stepped between Isaac and Jacob and reproved them: "I have called a meeting at the Central Synagogue to consider how to get the Behemoth back and you two keep fighting and squabbling. Phooey!"

Abraham's reproof helped. Isaac calmed himself down and he walked along in silence with his head down.

"Did you hear that, Samuel Abba? The Patriarchs have called for a meeting at the Central Synagogue. Let's fly over there and listen. But we've got to be fast about it, Samuel Abba, so that we'll be there in time to hide and not get kicked out."

"All right, Little Pisser, let's fly."

We took off into the air. The Patriarchs looked like three black specks on the ground below. "Quickly, quickly!" Little Pisser directed, and we flew towards the Central Synagogue.

A great many tzaddikim had already assembled at the Central Synagogue. Naphtali the Paradise shammes, an angel with a humpback and a goatee, had flown from one villa to the next to let the tzaddikim know that the holy Patriarchs Abraham, Isaac and Jacob were convening a meeting. The tzaddikim didn't need to be asked twice. They all took their walking sticks in hand and headed over.

My friend Little Pisser and I went into the synagogue. Nobody noticed us since they were all too preoccupied with the matter of the Behemoth. The two of us hid under a bench that was by the southern wall and watched and listened.

The synagogue was packed. There was no room to stand and the tzaddikim that came late shoved and elbowed, trampling the corns on the feet of their fellow tzaddikim, before they finally pushed their way in. It was so stuffy inside that we, that is, me and my friend Little Pisser, could barely breathe.

"What is the point of all this rigmarole?" I whispered to my friend Little Pisser.

"Shh, Samuel Abba"—Little Pisser put his hand over my mouth. "If they hear us they'll throw us out of the synagogue."

Abraham our forefather, the eldest of the Patriarchs, appeared on the pulpit. He tucked his right thumb into his waistband and brandished his left hand over the heads of the assembled crowd: "A terrible calamity has befallen us, gentlemen," Abraham said, holding forth. "The Behemoth has escaped. Now he hasn't run off like your average steer that wanders off sometimes, but rather he has escaped and absconded into Gentile Paradise. How the Behemoth got it into his head to run off remains a mystery, but now is not the time to solve that, gentlemen. Now we must think, we must reflect and figure out a solution as to how to bring him back. Back to the place he belongs. Back to Jewish Paradise…"

The crowd burst into an uproar. A fellow with a terrifying beard began elbowing his way forwards, getting closer and closer to the pulpit. "I have a parable apropos of this, gentlemen, a fine parable with a most illuminating lesson to be drawn from it," the fellow yelled out. "Once upon a time, there was a king. Now, this king had three—"

"No one wants your parables now, Maggid," the entire crowd roared. "We need a solution, not a parable."

But this was the famed parablist and itinerant preacher the Maggid of Dubno, and he wasn't going to be deterred. He shouted above the din of the crowd and, with all his might and with tremendous effort, made his way to the pulpit.

"You'll regret it, gentlemen, this is a fine parable and the lesson you can draw from it is a most illuminating one. Once upon a time, there was a king…"

The Maggid of Dubno would have prevailed and launched right into his parable if a loud "ratatattat" had not been heard from outside the synagogue door.

"King Solomon has come," cried a tzaddik standing by the window. "He is stepping down from his gilded carriage now."

The synagogue became silent for a moment. Then the buzzing started anew. "King Solomon…" "The wisest of the wise…" "He'll find a solution…" "He has the brain of a government minister…" "Idiot, a king is far greater…" "A king is the master and a minister is no more than his servant."

More bickering broke out: one called another "jackass" or "idiot" and many other names besides. Suddenly, a voice from the back of the synagogue was heard: "Make way! Make way for King Solomon!!!"

King Solomon pushed his way to the pulpit. He was sweating like a horse and wiping his dripping brow with a silk kerchief. A hush fell over the synagogue. Solomon's tall, broad-shouldered figure, his sable-red beard, his intelligent and sharp eyes demanded respect. He spoke calmly, he appeared to be in no hurry.

"As soon as I was informed about the whole incident, take it from me, I wasted no time in writing a letter to the saints of Gentile Paradise, you take it from me. I wrote them such-and-such and what did they want for the Behemoth's return, take it from me. We are ready to negotiate, I wrote, even though we can get along just fine without the Behemoth, we don't really need him so urgently and…"

At this our forefather Isaac could not restrain himself. He jumped from his seat and screamed: "What do you mean we don't need the Behemoth? We absolutely need him, for without the Behemoth… Wh-what do you mean you wrote them that we'll get along without the Behemoth?"

King Solomon gave a wise grin and calmed the outraged Isaac: "It's just a turn of phrase, Isaac, take it from me, we ought not to let on that the Behemoth is the apple of our eye… Otherwise they would demand a king's ransom, just mark my words…" At that he tapped his fingers on the temple of his own head and added shrewdly: "That's what you call *diplomacy*, Isaac, diplomacy, you ought to learn the word, you take it from me."

The tzaddikim all nodded their heads, agreeing that Solomon was right and still the wisest of men—you could turn Paradise upside down searching and you would never find his equal.

"And so, take it from me," King Solomon resumed, "I wrote the letter to them inquiring what they want and I sent this letter to them with one of my carrier pigeons. I expect that tomorrow or the day after we shall have a reply."

"What does he mean? Did he write to them without our knowledge?" An uproar started from below. "We could have at least been informed about what was in the letter… After all, we have a stake in this too."

King Solomon never could abide anyone talking back to him. He stood up to his full height, his beard blazed, his eyes on fire, and in his roaring voice he bellowed like a Russian officer: "At-ten-tion!!!"

The tzaddikim came to a halt like soldiers before their commander. No one even blinked. They remained standing like that for nearly fifteen minutes until King Solomon gave the order: "At ease! Now you can all go home, and when I receive an answer from Gentile Paradise I'll let you know." He descended from the podium and pushed his way back through the crowd. His gilded carriage was waiting for him outside.

After King Solomon departed, a debate broke out. One argued that King Solomon should have consulted with the tzaddikim. He may truly be a sage, but he was but one. The tzaddikim may not be sages so wise, but they were still many.

"That's how he's always been. He does whatever he wants and anything we have to say about it is just barking at the moon."

"Phooey, I say, phooey! You speak like this against a king… Phooey!" cried a short tzaddik with a sparse beard.

A path was cleared for the holy Patriarchs, who left the synagogue and headed homewards.

"So then, tomorrow or the day after there has got to be a reply," Isaac said.

"I assure you that the reply will be a good one, too," Abraham encouraged him.

"From your mouth to God's ear, Pop, amen!" sighed Isaac, and the Patriarchs continued on their way.

I I

Our Mission

S EVERAL DAYS PASSED and still no reply had come. The tzaddikim were terribly nervous. They recited chapters of Psalms at night and kept watch by day, looking out for the carrier pigeons bearing the reply. But no pigeon had been seen and no letter, of course, either.

"They're having a great laugh at our expense," Isaac our forefather insisted, "and what a shame that my own parents had to live to see this sad day."

"Your Esau," Jacob our forefather needled him, "your little jewel, knows his pop is just pining away for a little piece of Behemoth, but yet he does nothing."

"Are you starting up with your pop again?" Abraham our forefather's dark eyes gave a flash. "How about a little honouring thy father, Jacob?"

Mother Rachel ran in breathlessly. She was as slim and lovely as ever. A few wanton strands of her own hair peaked out from under her wig. As soon as Jacob saw her, he was like a different man. His eyes beamed. He went over to her and stroked her head: "What are you running like that for, my pussycat? You know I'd do anything for you, my beauty."

The Matriarch Rachel, all the while looking lovingly at Jacob, recounted: "I ran into Esther on the street. She was acting like a queen, as usual, wearing a silk dress in the middle of the week, a gold ring on every finger and a chain of pearls around her neck—may all Jewish daughters have it so good. I was pretending not to notice her and hoping to walk right past her, since I can't stand Little Miss Universe. And then she comes straight up to me and says to me: 'I want to tell you that we all ought to fast. If we want the Behemoth brought back, the best way is by fasting.'"

"Well, she's got a point, I've got to say," said Abraham. "We should call for a fast for all of Paradise."

In short, a fast was declared and everyone stopped eating. The tzaddikim were soon falling over from weakness but, all the same, no letter arrived.

During these days of fasting, something very strange happened. The angel Simon Bear, as was his wont, got plastered. He beat his wife savagely and dragged her by her hair through the streets of Paradise and bellowed in his drunken voice: "What do you need the Behemoth for, tzaddikim? If you want a fat cow, I got one for you right here. I'll hand her over to you for a bottle of two-hundred-proof hooch."

They tried to calm him down and talk some sense into him, telling him that the angel that he was dragging by the hair was no beast, but rather his own seven-months-pregnant wife. But he wouldn't let up and kept yelling: "For a forty-litre keg, tzaddikim, the cow is yours!"

The Paradise Police were called and several angels in green uniforms flew over and, with some trouble, they finally succeeded in subduing Simon Bear. They hauled him into the Paradise drunk tank and left him to sober up. Simon Bear's wife could hardly regain her senses. Barely conscious, she was brought back home.

"To think that precisely during such dreadful days as these he would decide to get so drunk," the tzaddikim muttered amongst themselves. "That Simon Bear behaves far more like a gentile angel than a Jewish one."

Finally, on the twelfth day, the news spread that the carrier pigeon had returned, bearing a letter from Gentile Paradise. The letter was already at King Solomon's.

Even though it was still not known what the letter contained, there was great joy at its arrival. People kissed in the streets with tears in their eyes.

The same day, King Solomon summoned a meeting. He read the response for all assembled:

To the Esteemed and Honourable Sainted Ones of Jewish Paradise!
To your letter we respond as follows:
Your Behemoth crossed the border without a passport and without a visa. According to the laws of our Paradise, this warrants six months of imprisonment, with a half-pound of hay for his daily rations. Additionally, the damage that he caused is to be recompensed by hard labour.
As for the pregnant angel, whom he smuggled over the border on his horns, we are prepared to return her. Her little angel, however, who was born on our territory, will be baptized and remain with us.
Following the completion of the Behemoth's sentence and payment for the damage he caused, we are prepared to return him to you…

After King Solomon finished reading the letter, Jewish Paradise was overcome with weeping and mourning. Tzaddikim stumbled about like poisoned mice, in a state of restless agitation. They wrung their hands and howled out lamentations.

"Who has heard of such a thing?" "Six months in prison…"

"Half a pound of hay per day…" "Hard labour for the damage done…" "There will be no Behemoth to return, just his skin and bones."

The wives of the tzaddikim bawled: "Such a thing has never been heard of since the world began… To take a Jewish angel baby and baptize him! How miserable that we have lived to see the day!"

Only one man had not given up hope. This was King Solomon. He sat down to write a second letter, making proposals and all the while flattering the gentile saints. He, the wise king, knew that flattery was an excellent means of making someone more lenient and flexible.

A reply to King Solomon's second letter came three days later. King Solomon read it before the saintly elite.

To the Esteemed King Solomon, Wisest of All the Wise!

We hereby inform you that we have accepted your proposal. We consent for you to pay the damages that the Behemoth caused with a diamond from your crown. The Behemoth, however, must serve his sentence for the illicit crossing of our border without a passport or visa. For a law is a law. So that you may recognize, however, that we are eager to accommodate, we have reduced his sentence to three months. The Jewish little angel who was born on our lands has already been baptized and given the name Petru. His mother is at your disposal. You may collect her at your convenience.

"Three months with nothing but prison rations would be the end of the Behemoth," bemoaned our forefather Isaac.

"They baptized a Jewish baby angel." Sarah our Matriarch wrung her hands, weeping, as Rebecca, Rachel and Leah joined her.

"What a catastrophe! What an outrage! And all because of those lazy bum herdsmen," groused the tzaddikim.

King Solomon wrote a third letter. He agreed that the Behemoth deserved to be punished but three months was far too much. In addition, on his prison rations he would get too thin. Therefore he suggested that they, the gentile saints, allow two Jewish herdsmen to attend to the Behemoth for the whole term of his confinement in the prison stall. "We are also prepared," King Solomon wrote in his letter, "to ship over several wagons of hay so that the Behemoth will have enough to eat. In the matter of the baby angel that you have baptized, what's done is done. I await your prompt and urgent reply regarding the Behemoth."

The carrier pigeon set off for Gentile Paradise with the letter and, three days later, returned with their reply.

King Solomon read this letter to the tzaddikim as well. This time, too, the gentile saints created no complications. They agreed to allow Jewish Paradise to dispatch two angels to take care of the Behemoth until he served out his sentence. But they warned that no Jewish herdsmen should be sent because no sooner would the Behemoth see them then he'd go wild again. It would be best if the tzaddikim of Jewish Paradise would send over two angel kids. The Behemoth would trust them and no harm would come to them. As for his sentence, the gentile saints reduced it to six weeks, which had to be served. As for the diamond, King Solomon could give it to the two kids to bring when they came to tend to the Behemoth.

The letter was received well by everyone. The gentile saints were a rather well-disposed bunch, after all, as anyone could see from this last letter.

"But whom shall we send over?" Abraham our forefather asked, stroking his estimable beard.

The tzaddikim began to deliberate. Some thought one way, others thought another, until someone mentioned the name Little Pisser: he's a clever little angel who knows a thing or two.

"But for the second one," another said, "I am wondering about the second one… It may be a good idea for the second one to be…"

"Spit it out already," grumbled the others, "you keep saying 'the second one', 'the second one' over and over, but you don't name any names."

"I think that the second should be Little Pisser's buddy, Samuel Abba. They are very fond of each other, like two brothers, and Samuel Abba, you know, he wasn't born yesterday."

In short, it was decided: my friend Little Pisser and I would fly to Gentile Paradise to take care of the Behemoth. We were told to head over to Zeidel the Paradise photographer's studio so that he could take our pictures for our passports.

We happily went over to Zeidel the photographer. The angel Zeidel was quite pleased to see us and gave each of our cheeks a pinch. "I'm glad you're here, boys, I want to read you my latest Purim play."

Zeidel the Paradise photographer, an angel with long hair and spectacles on his nose, had one indulgence. Every week he wrote a new Purim play that he'd read to anyone he could accost.

We explained to him that we had come to be photographed and that we had no time now since we were flying out on a mission all the way to Gentile Paradise, of all places. When we returned, God willing, he could read to us as much as he liked.

This made the angel Zeidel sad. He really wanted to read it, but if he had no choice he would have to wait until we came back. "By then," he promised us, "I will have six new Purim plays. Remember that, boys, and come back. You'll enjoy it."

He took our pictures and in no time developed them on the spot. Then we headed to the Paradise Police, where our passports were processed.

With passports in hand, we went to say goodbye to Little Pisser's parents. Little Pisser's mama wiped her eyes with her apron.

"Be careful, Little Pisser, God forbid, don't catch cold on the way."

And Little Pisser's pop, Solomon-Zalman the patchmaker, warned us sternly: "Don't get taken for a ride by those gentile angels, you hear me? And do not eat any pork!" He hammered a host of no-nos into our heads and ended with a gulp: "Always remember that you are Jewish angels and that it is an honour to be an angel in Jewish Paradise."

We promised him everything he wished. Little Pisser's mama sent us off with some buckwheat cookies for the journey and then we parted.

"Have a safe flight and come home safe!" they shouted after us.

"Now, Samuel Abba, we need to fly to King Solomon to pick up the diamond, and from there straight to the border."

We ascended high, high into the air and flew off. It was a bit of a long haul to reach King Solomon's palace, but we were so eager for our journey that we didn't even notice how much time it took.

"Samuel Abba, do you see the house with the gold roof? That's King Solomon's palace."

We landed below. The guard angels who stood outside the palace were informed in advance that we were coming and they let us right in. We approached a silver stream and saw Shulamith sitting at its bank. She was dipping her bare feet into the water and catching fish with a golden net.

"If she only knew that we had seen her with King David, Little Pisser, what do you think she would do?"

"Here we are on such an important journey, Samuel Abba, and look where your head is."

We crossed over a wooden bridge. Behind us we could hear Shulamith's song:

> To sit beside you,
> My heart's desire,
> I would endure
> Gehenna's fire.
>
> For hell, my dearest,
> Is sorrow and pain—
> Where prayers do not help,
> And tears are in vain.
>
> No prayers then, no tears,
> No, they're all wrong,
> 'Tis only true love,
> That ascends with a song.

We turned off to the side. Shulamith's song grew more and more distant until we could barely hear it. Another time, perhaps, we would have stayed an hour or even two to listen to her. My friend Little Pisser and I loved songs of all kinds very much, but now we were flying off on a distant journey and we simply had no time.

We found King Solomon sitting in his courtyard. He was wearing a silk caftan and on his feet he wore a pair of slippers. The crown glimmered on his head. The king was standing and discussing matters with a naked-necked turkeycock. As is well known, King Solomon understands the language of all creatures, birds and fowl included. We saw how he asked the turkeycock questions and how the turkeycock responded. Just what, exactly, we couldn't say.

We started to get impatient. He could have continued chatting away for who knows how long, and we had such a long way ahead of us.

Little Pisser nudged me: "Hey, Samuel Abba."

"Yes, Little Pisser."

"Let's go up to him."

We approached and bowed before the king. He broke away from his conversation with the turkeycock.

"Your Majesty the king, we have come for the diamond. We are flying off to Gentile Paradise to tend to the Behemoth."

King Solomon took off his crown and removed the diamond. He gazed at it with delight for a moment. It sparkled and was dazzling to behold. "Here's the diamond, fellows, don't lose it. It's a precious diamond—worth twenty-five thousand dollars."

We took the diamond. We promised to guard it like the apple of our eye. He dismissed us with a wave, letting us know that we should take our leave.

"Off we go, Samuel Abba!"

We spread our wings and headed towards the border.

In the evening, sometime between afternoon and evening prayers, we arrived at the border crossing. All the church bells were ringing.

The twilight, solemn chanting, and ringing of bells all struck us as strange and foreign. We huddled close to each other, anxious not to get lost.

An angel in a blue uniform with two crosses on his wings checked our passports. Two other angels in grey uniforms searched us to see if we were smuggling in, God forbid, a Talmud, which was considered a most terrible thing in Gentile Paradise.

They found nothing on us. Our passports were all in order. Passport control took just over an hour. The angel in the blue uniform led us to a large iron gate. He knocked three times and asked for it to be opened.

From the other side of the gate a voice was heard, and we could tell right off that an old man was there. "Who is knocking there?" asked the voice.

"I am knocking, Saint Peter. It is I, Teodor Aniol, the Border Patrol angel. I've brought two little yids here from Jewish Paradise."

We heard someone insert a key. The lock gave a groan and the enormous, heavy gate swung open. An old man stood before us with a long white beard and smiling eyes. He was bareheaded. In his right hand he held the key to Paradise.

He looked us over for a moment. The crucifix on his chest was made of the purest gold.

The angel in the blue uniform saluted. Saint Peter made the sign of the cross and told him to leave. The border was left unattended and needed to be guarded.

The old gatekeeper told us to follow him. We passed through the gate. The old man locked it behind us.

"You are probably exhausted from the long trip," he said to us. "If you'd like to rest up, tomorrow morning a guide will take you to the prison stall where the Behemoth is kept."

Not far from the gate of Paradise was the house where Saint Peter lived. A small lantern glowed in the window. The night was already terribly dark.

"You have no need to fear, boys, nothing bad will happen to you. Now, come along with me."

The old man led the way and we followed. I don't know about my friend Little Pisser, but my heart was pounding.

We entered the house. It was quite spacious. Icons hung on every wall. In the middle of the room stood a table and the old man asked us to be seated.

We sat down at the table and the old man offered us a slice of dark bread with cheese: "You don't eat any pork, eh? If only you knew how delicious pork can be... But you are going to be sticklers about it and not want any. It's a scrumptious treat, a little pork. You know what they say," he smiled, "live and loin!"

We said nothing in reply. Each of us ate our bread and cheese. We were mighty hungry from our trip.

The old man asked about our tzaddikim. The main thing he wanted to know was how the holy Patriarchs were doing. Were they feeling well or was anything aggravating them?

Little Pisser told him that everything was faring as well as possible. If not for the matter of the Behemoth, everything would have been quite excellent.

"Tomorrow you'll be taken to the Behemoth," the old man told us. "But be careful not to wander from the place where they're keeping him. Don't go flying all over our heaven. Folks around here don't care too much for Jewish angels. So be on your best behaviour and mind your manners, you don't want to get your wings broken."

We assured him that we wouldn't bother anybody. If nobody bothered us, everything would be just fine.

"It would certainly be best," advised the old man, "if you don't go creeping around where you shouldn't. When the saints are on their way to Mass, don't attract their notice. If you see them in procession, don't let them see you for dust."

A fine state of affairs, I thought. We have to hide out of sight, not let anyone see us. What's the point of all this if we're not going to see anything anyway?

I looked over at my friend Little Pisser. We understood each other perfectly. He also seemed to regret the whole undertaking.

Old Peter's eyes were starting to get heavy. He led us into a particular room that had no icons in it. "You'll spend the night here, boys, and if you need to do your angelic business, it's through the window and outside with it."

Then he went to his own quarters and left me and my friend Little Pisser alone. We looked at each other sorrowfully.

I walked over to the window and looked outside. The sky was overcast and it smelt of rain.

There was no joy in our hearts. We thought of home and prayed to God that the six weeks would pass quickly.

A bolt of lightning flashed and illuminated our room for a moment. Then a second flash. The thunder rumbled and rumbled until it landed with a crash. We made a blessing out loud. In the other room, old Peter was snoring away.

"Samuel Abba!"

"Yeah, Little Pisser?"

"Let's go to sleep. The night passes quicker when you're asleep."

We undressed and lay down in bed but we couldn't fall asleep. The thunder and lightning would not let us.

We had experienced plenty of nights like this in Jewish Paradise, but here, abroad, so far from all that was familiar, this stormy night was far more fearsome.

"Little Pisser!"

"Yeah, Samuel Abba?"

"Let's tell each other stories. Time flies by when you're telling stories."

We huddled closer to each other and Little Pisser began telling a tale about a beggar and a prince. The thunder interrupted and would not allow the story to go ahead and Little Pisser had to keep stopping in the middle.

We tried to bury our heads under the covers, but it still didn't help.

We leapt out of bed. Little Pisser opened the window and hopped outside. He stood in his nightshirt, the lightning blazing above him. If you haven't seen my friend Little Pisser lit up by flashes of lightning, you haven't beheld true splendour.

"Samuel Abba," Little Pisser yelled, "jump out the window, Samuel Abba!"

I hesitated for a while before jumping. At that very moment, rain began to pour down. We were as wet as a pair of fish. Our wings got so heavy that we could hardly lift them. We headed back into our room, water pouring off our heads and wings and soaking the floor.

We crawled back into bed and cuddled with each other for warmth. Outside the rain kept streaming down.

"Little Pisser, do you hear that?"

"What, Samuel Abba?"

"What the rain is saying..."

Drip-drip, drop—Pssh... Drop-a drop—Pssh...

With our arms wrapped around each other, we fell asleep.

In my dream I saw King Solomon before me again. He stood there chatting with the turkeycock. I understood every word of their conversation:

"What's going on, Turkey? How are your thousand wives?" the king asked.

"Thanks for asking, King. My wives are busy laying eggs, squawking away, and all are, thanks to the Almighty, healthy. How are *your* thousand wives, King?"

"Oh, no complaints here. But you know what I tell you, Turkey, amongst all these thousand wives, I haven't found the one that's just right for me."

"Really, if that's how it is with you, King, then I'm more blessed than you. All of mine are, no evil eye, just right. All of them are as fertile as can be. Take my advice, King, get yourself a couple more wives. Maybe one of them will suit you."

King Solomon thought for a moment. "You may be right, Turkey. As long as you're still breathing, you may as well go on looking and searching till you find the right one."

All of a sudden, a remarkable thing happened: I watched as King Solomon transformed into a turkeycock himself with a fire-red comb. He gave his wings a flutter and flew up on to a fence post: "Cock-a-doodle-doo!"

The crowing startled me awake. A strange dream, I thought. Outside it was daybreak already and the Gentile Paradise roosters were all crowing.

My friend Little Pisser was still sleeping. He was apparently very tired. His right hand lay on his heart. He was smiling. He was wonderfully charming in his sleep. I couldn't resist giving him a kiss on the forehead.

I crept out of bed quietly, not wanting to wake him. I went to the window and looked outside. After the night's rain, the ground was fresh, the grass was fragrant. It was exhilarating. The birds were singing songs of praise amidst the trees. "How lovely are your realms, O Lord of the Universe," I whispered. Still, I could not understand the point of three different Paradises. Wouldn't it be better if there were just one Paradise for everyone, with no passports, no visas and no squabbles?

I surprised myself with my heretical thoughts. "Well, well, fancy that," I lectured myself, "you, Samuel Abba, are going to enlighten the Creator? The wisdom he possesses in his pinky finger is more than you have in your entire body."

The sun, enormous and radiant, was rising in the east. A golden sunbeam landed on my friend Little Pisser and tickled under his nose until it woke him up.

"Good morning, Little Pisser!"

Little Pisser rubbed his eyes. For a moment, it seemed, he had forgotten where he was. Then he hopped out of bed. We washed and said the morning prayer of thanks for the return of our sleeping souls. After this, our spirits felt lighter.

We went into Saint Peter's room. The old man wasn't there. He had already gone to church for morning Mass. On the table there was a jug of milk. We drank it, accompanied with some rye bread. All the while the bells were tolling.

The old man came home. Seeing us, he smiled cheerfully. He gave each of us a pinch on the cheek. "Have you gone to Mass already, boys?" he asked.

"We said our morning prayer of gratitude. You think we'd eat before saying our morning prayer? That would be quite a start to the day."

"If so, then very well," the old man smiled. "The angel who is supposed to take you to the Behemoth is due here any minute. Remember, lads, if you are good boys all will be well for you in the world."

We considered what he said and swore that we would be good boys. He gave a satisfied nod of his head and sat down at the table. He crossed himself and began to eat.

We watched him and felt a bit more at ease with him. The clock on the wall struck seven.

12

Aniela

SAINT PETER wiped his lips, stroked his beard, and asked us to give him the diamond from King Solomon's crown. Little Pisser handed the diamond over to him. He examined it from every side and smacked his lips.

"A precious diamond, a diamond of a diamond! I can't even imagine the value of such a diamond."

The old man took a sheet of paper from a drawer and wrote up a receipt, confirming that he had received the diamond. Little Pisser took the receipt and the old man cleared the table. The clock on the wall struck nine.

We heard a knock at the door, and before the old man had even called out "Come in" the door opened and a broad-shouldered angel with piercing grey eyes came in. He bowed before the old apostle. He gave three flaps of his wing and said: "I'm here to pick up the little yids and take them to the Behemoth. Dmitry Angelenko is my name."

He cast a nasty look in our direction. His piercing eyes and the curling ends of his moustache plainly proclaimed that this man hated Jews, that he was an out-and-out anti-Semite.

The old man whispered something into his ear. We stood to the side, trembling.

Dmitry Angelenko twisted the ends of his moustache three times and with a venomous smile called to us: "C'mon, little kikes."

We had no choice and left with him. The old man walked with us to the door.

We took off into the air. Dmitry Angelenko flew in the front and flapped his big, powerful wings as he chanted:

> Kike, kike,
> Lousy Jew,
> Sabbath's over,
> To hell with you.

We really didn't care for this little ditty that he sang, but there was nothing we could do about it. We had to listen and keep quiet. Little Pisser had tears in his eyes.

Dmitry Angelenko kept looking back at us. Our wings were young and weaker than his. He railed at us, telling us we flew like a bunch of lifeless chickens and mocked us continually. "*Oy vey mama… oy vey papa…* a scrap of challah—chop, chop, chop…"

Just what we endured on that flight with that maniac, only God can tell. We cursed our fate. We would rather have had our wings broken than to have flown out there.

In the evening we descended near a forest. On the right was the prison stall, secured with bars. An angel with a sword paced in front of it. Dmitry Angelenko approached the angel on guard. He said something to him in a language we didn't understand, pointing at us all the while.

The angel on guard grunted back a Russian "All right", and Dmitry Angelenko said goodbye. He spread his wings and flew off. In the distance we could still hear him chanting: "Kike, kike, lousy Jew…"

The angel on guard opened the heavy iron doors to the prison stall with an enormous key. We entered and saw our Behemoth lying there, bound in chains. He was as thin as a rail. If we hadn't known who he was, we would never have recognized him.

Little Pisser stroked him… The Behemoth looked up at him with his huge, sad eyes.

"What good did running away get you?" Little Pisser asked him. "All because some foolish angel made a wisecrack, you go and run off?"

The Behemoth seemed to get the gist of what my friend said. In his eyes I saw regret.

Little Pisser consoled him as he kept petting him: "Just a few more weeks, Behemoth, and we'll take you home to Jewish Paradise. But next time, you should know better. We have come to take care of you. And then you'll come back with us. What a celebration we'll have when you come home. You'll see, I'm not lying."

I also went over to him and petted him, telling him how much the pastures of Paradise missed him. Ever since he ran off, the grass of the pastures of Paradise have been unusually downtrodden and the crickets have stopped singing. The butterflies started wandering aimlessly like foundlings, with nowhere to go.

"But when you return," Little Pisser said, "everything will be as it should be again. The pastures of Paradise will blossom once more, the crickets will sing again, and the butterflies will know that the pastures of Paradise are their home."

The guard angel signalled to us. We understood that he was telling us to leave. It was enough for today.

We said goodbye to the Behemoth. We promised to come again tomorrow and we left the prison stall.

The guard angel went over to lock the gate and we stood outside, not knowing what to do, where to go, or where we would spend the night.

"Samuel Abba!"

"What, Little Pisser?"

"What will come of this, Samuel Abba?"

"May I know as much of evil as I know that. I have no idea."

The evening began to get dark. Stars were trembling above the forest. They were the same stars as back home, but still they seemed foreign.

When it was fully dark, we saw a wizened old man with a long white beard. He approached us. A sack was slung over his shoulder. I regarded him for some time and could have sworn it was the Prophet Elijah.

Little Pisser, it seemed, thought likewise. He nudged me and whispered: "Look, Samuel Abba, it's the Prophet Elijah…"

"But since when does the Prophet Elijah wear a crucifix around his neck, Little Pisser?"

The old man came over to us. The guard angel drew his sword and called out "Ten-hut!"

We stood still like soldiers. The old man, however, patted our heads and smiled cheerfully and kindly: "You must be the little Jewish angels… Fine, fine… I am Saint Nicholas… I'll show you to where you'll be living… In the meantime, here's a present… Take it, take it…"

He untied his sack. To Little Pisser he gave a leaden soldier and to me he gave a chicken made of tin.

The old man spoke in Hebrew, as if from the Holy Books, and it was refreshing to hear. He refastened his sack and threw it over his shoulders.

He walked ahead and we followed. We felt more at ease with

him. We went into the forest and the old man lit his lantern. We walked slowly. By the light of the old man's lantern we could see how the squirrels leapt from tree to tree. We heard the birds of the night calling to one another. A deer ran across our way. We heard a brook burbling in the distance.

The old man looked about for a moment, then he smiled and said: "You're tired, boys? Very soon we'll be at the forest ranger's lodge. That's where you'll stay until the Behemoth has served his sentence."

The old man guessed right. We were really very tired, especially after an entire day of flying with that maniac Dmitry Angelenko. We kept on, hardly able to drag our legs along. The sound of the water was getting closer. A wooden cabin stood right at the riverbank. The old man stopped and put his lantern on the ground. He knocked: "Open up, Ivan! It's me, Saint Nicholas."

The door opened. Ivan the forest ranger came outside. He was an average-sized angel with dark, sturdy wings.

"These two little Jewish angels will be staying with you, Ivan," Saint Nicholas said. "See that you take good care of them. They won't eat our food, so give them raw milk in a clay cup to drink and some rye bread."

The old man bid us farewell and was off. We lost sight of him in the trees of the forest.

We went into the house. The walls were covered with portraits of saints. Through the window you could see the river. Ivan the forest ranger looked us up and down, from head to toe. Bewildered, he didn't know what to say to us. In the end he shrugged his shoulders and grumbled in Russian: "No matter."

The door to another room opened and a young little angel girl with blonde braids and blue eyes came in. The forest ranger angel said something to her in a language we didn't understand. We figured out that her name was Aniela.

The blonde angel went back into the other room. But before long she returned, bringing fresh milk and rye bread. We took the food eagerly; we glugged down the milk and devoured the fresh rye bread and felt well refreshed.

The forest ranger angel took his rifle down from the wall. He went over to Aniela and gave her a kiss on the forehead before heading out for the night in the forest.

We were left alone with the lovely blonde angel, the forest ranger angel's daughter. She went about the house tidying up, warbling all the while like a canary.

We took an immediate liking to her, this Aniela. Every move she made was full of charm. My friend Little Pisser, however, was absolutely bowled over. He took me aside and whispered in my ear: "I've never seen such beauty, Samuel Abba. If she just says the word, I'd stay here in Gentile Paradise. I could look at her from morning to night and never get tired of it."

Hearing my friend say such words really rattled me. That was the kind of thing you heard all the time, I thought, pronounced by the loving couples on the Avenue of the Patriarchs. I felt a pang in my heart. I thought my friend was a goner.

"But you are a Jewish angel, Little Pisser, and she's a gentile angel. It's like chalk and cheese, Little Pisser."

My friend suddenly became sad. I had said something that dampened his spirits.

Outside, we could hear the sounds of the forest and the water. In the house, Aniela moved from one place to another. Little Pisser could not take his eyes off her.

I gave him a tug at his right wing: "Come on, Little Pisser, let's get a little fresh air."

He followed me outside in a daze. We sat down by the riverside. The moon crept out from behind a cloud. Little Pisser sighed deeply.

The first symptoms, I thought. The moon has barely made an appearance and he's already sighing. Next thing you know he'll be writing poetry. She's enchanted him, this blonde angel.

Little Pisser sat for a long time in silence. I listened to the rush of the water. All of a sudden, I felt a burning sensation on my left wing. It was one of Little Pisser's tears.

"Little Pisser, God help you, why are you crying?"

He didn't answer. He put his arm around me and sang:

> The moment I saw you, my lovely,
> Sitting on your papa's front porch,
> I swore love by the heavens above me,
> And for you I'd carry the torch.

> For you I keep tossing and turning,
> Since I saw your sweet face so divine.
> In my brain a madness is burning,
> And soon I'll go out of my mind.

It was one of Seymour's songs. He didn't have his own, he was not yet so forlorn a case. We had to get far, far away from there while there was still time. As long as love is just a spark, it could soon become a fire, and then it would be too late.

"Little Pisser!"

"What is it, Samuel Abba?"

"Let's fly away from here right away, this very minute."

"What would happen to the Behemoth, Samuel Abba?"

What could I say about that? After all, we had been sent here to take care of the Behemoth and bring him home. I thought for a moment and then said to my friend: "This Aniela isn't so pretty. Your sister Ethel is far more beautiful, Little Pisser. Jewish angels are prettier on the whole, right, Little Pisser?"

"Idle words, Samuel Abba," my friend sighed. "Aniela is lovely and an angel should never denigrate any beauty, even if she's a foreigner."

He's in deep, I thought, he's already sounding pretty head over heels. May the good Lord help him, I don't know if I will be able to.

We heard Aniela's voice calling; she was standing at the open window and shouting to us in her own language: "Hey, boys! Hey, boys!"

Little Pisser gave a shudder. We stood up and went back into the house.

Using sign language, Aniela indicated that it was time for bed. She led us into a separate room and then went into her own room.

We lay down to sleep. Little Pisser talked in his sleep the whole night through and kept waking me up.

We got up the next morning. Aniela served us milk and rye bread. The forest ranger angel was back home, sleeping and snoring. Aniela drove the goats out from their pen. My friend Little Pisser and I flew off to the prison stall where the Behemoth was kept, to give him his food on time and make sure he wasn't suffering.

From the time we arrived, his daily portion of hay increased. He started to become more like himself again and to fill out a little. I celebrated every gram he gained.

My friend Little Pisser, on the other hand, went about preoccupied. In the few days that the Behemoth managed to gain a little weight, Little Pisser seemed to lose some. He was continually disappearing out of reach. He would go off wandering around the woods; he ate his food without appetite and slept fitfully.

At night when we came home to the forest, Aniela would be waiting for us. She began to become our friend; she taught us the songs of Gentile Paradise and we taught her Jewish ones.

Things were going pretty well with this lovely angel. Little Pisser could never tear his eyes off her. If he happened to sit next to her, he turned bright red.

One Sunday she invited us to gather berries in the woods with her. Her father Ivan the forest ranger angel was still sleeping. Aniela was as lovely as ever and it was impossible to refuse her.

We went deep into the forest. We couldn't fly since the trees were so dense, so we went by foot.

Aniela laughed and sang and frolicked. Every so often she knelt down and picked a few berries and put them into a little jug that she had taken from home. From time to time she would tear off a whole stemful and deliver it straight to our mouths. Little Pisser plucked the berries of the stem with his lips. His cheeks blazed redder than the berries.

He walked with his head down, silent, not saying a word. I called him over to the side and asked him if perhaps he would like to be left alone with Aniela. He cheered up at this and his eyes flashed.

"You're a great pal, Samuel Abba. I'll never forget you for this. You could clear out of here so that Aniela won't even notice that you left."

189

I obliged him. While Little Pisser and Aniela were bending down to the ground together absorbed in gathering berries, I took off.

By the time they returned home, it was already evening. Aniela was tired and my friend Little Pisser was in fine spirits.

I woke up in the night and I saw my friend Little Pisser standing by the window. He was holding something in his hand.

"Little Pisser, why aren't you sleeping?"

"I can't, Samuel Abba."

I got out of the bed and approached him. "What's that in your hand, Little Pisser?"

"Nothing… it's a secret, Samuel Abba." He clamped his hand tighter, which annoyed me. What's this, I thought, my best friend has a secret that he won't tell me about. You call that friendship?

Little Pisser could tell that I was angry. He came over to me and embraced me. "Samuel Abba, if I tell the secret, then it won't be as lovely."

"So, no one's making you, Little Pisser. I won't tell you my secrets either."

I could see that Little Pisser was wrestling with himself, not sure what to do: should he or shouldn't he tell me?

Little Pisser opened his hand. I saw a lock of blonde hair there.

"She gave that to you, Little Pisser?"

"She did," Little Pisser stammered, and I felt like the revelation of his secret had sapped his spirits. I regretted it and I gave my word that I'd never again ask him to reveal his secrets to me. A shadow had fallen over our friendship.

I crawled back into my bed. I lay there a long time with my eyes open. My heart was strangely heavy.

From that night on, as soon as I saw my friend with Aniela, I made myself scarce and pretended I didn't notice anything going on. I wandered about in the forest alone or flew out for a stroll over the river.

The days were flying by—just try and stop them. The Behemoth, in time, was becoming a more substantial beast, fattening up. True, he wasn't as he was before. There was still much for Jewish Paradise to restore.

Even if he left the Behemoth entirely to me and I had to take care of him, my friend Little Pisser was no shirk. For his part, Little Pisser carved "Aniela" into every tree in the forest, etched "Aniela" with a stick into the sand on the riverbank, and in his sleep called out the name "Aniela".

For all I know, he may even have written poetry too, but I never asked him and he never showed me any.

Every Saturday Saint Nicholas would come over with his sack on his shoulders. Since he hardly ever saw Little Pisser, he was continually showering me with various gifts.

"It would be a fine thing, Samuel Abba, if you were to stay here and be baptized, maybe, eh? Our Paradise is far lovelier than yours. You'd be as happy as you could ever be."

I did not give into this and countered it point by point. First of all, I wasn't so sure that his Paradise was lovelier. Had I even seen it? I was only allowed to fly from one point to the other and back. And secondly, what about my Jewish soul, Nicholas, sir? Is this no small matter—a Jewish soul!

The old man smiled: "You're a stubborn mule, Samuel Abba! And a stubborn mule is phooey!"

He left empty-handed. He came again, and again left empty-handed.

But, truth be told, I was very worried about my friend

Little Pisser. He had really got himself obsessed now, and Saint Nicholas could easily talk him right into the baptismal font. I prayed to God that the last couple of weeks would pass even more quickly and that we would return home with all speed.

The weeks flew by. The day the Behemoth was to be set free was approaching.

Later, my friend told me that at the same time he prayed that the days would be drawn out longer and longer. But my prayer was liked best and the weeks zipped by.

"It's proof, Little Pisser," I told him, "that the Almighty did not want you to be baptized and marry Aniela."

On the day that the Behemoth was set free, however, Little Pisser was a crestfallen angel. He was pale and Aniela went about mournfully.

Very early that morning, Saint Nicholas came to us. He woke us with the news that they were waiting to hand over the Behemoth to us.

We got dressed and headed outside. Aniela stood at the window with enormous, sad eyes.

"Farewell, Aniela!"

"Godspeed, Little Pisser!"

Two cuckoo birds called out to each other in the forest. Teardrops glistened on the morning grass, drops of dew hovered in Little Pisser's eyes.

Saint Nicholas beat a path forwards with his walking stick. The wind lifted up the fringes of his coat, his sack swung precariously on his shoulders. Little Pisser walked beside me, constantly looking back. The forest ranger's cabin could no longer be seen. The trees blocked it from view.

I stroked Little Pisser's wing and said: "Little Pisser, try to forget!"

We arrived at the prison stall. The guard angel stood in front of it, sword in hand. A few steps away was that maniac, Dmitry Angelenko. He was holding a paper in his hand. We entered the stall with the guard angel. Dmitry Angelenko unfettered the Behemoth and tossed the chains to the side. Saint Nicholas took the sheet of paper and read:

In the presence of Saint Nicholas, Guard Angel Grigori Stasiuk and Gendarme Angel Dmitry Angelenko, we, the young angels Little Pisser and Samuel Abba, hereby take possession of the Behemoth in order to lead him back to Jewish Paradise.

We are obligated to leave Gentile Paradise immediately, without pausing to dawdle or linger anywhere until we reach the border. We understand that the Gendarme Angel Dmitry Angelenko will escort us the entire way and that we shall submit to all his commands.

We signed the document and started to get ready for our journey.

The Behemoth could barely stand on his legs, he was so unaccustomed to walking. The miserable Dmitry Angelenko, of course, would not wait, tormenting us: "Come, little kikes!"

We led the Behemoth out of the stall… Little Pisser took one of his horns and I took the other, and behind us flew Dmitry Angelenko, twirling his moustache and shouting orders in Russian: "To the right, ya kikes! Kikes, turn left!"

The day was sweltering. The main Paradise highway was dusty (we had to go by foot on account of the Behemoth), and our throats were dry. But the maniac tormented us, refusing to let us rest a moment, not letting us have a sip of water. If you thought our first journey with this anti-Semite was unbearable, the return trip was agony.

"And to think you were prepared to stay with monsters like him," I said to my friend Little Pisser.

Dmitry Angelenko continued mocking us the whole way: "Challah, Challah, Challah, mommy, daddy, chopped liver," and every so often he gave the Behemoth a smack with his rubber baton.

We spent the entire day travelling. Night fell. Barefoot and hungry, we led the Behemoth by his horns as we cursed all our days and years, with no border yet in sight.

If that miserable maniac ever entered Jewish Paradise, I thought, I'd show him a thing or two. In the meantime, we had to put up with him and curse the maniac if he ever found out how much it hurt us…

But when the moon rose, Little Pisser could not restrain himself and let out a deep sigh. The moon reminded him of the forest ranger angel's daughter.

Dmitry Angelenko burst out laughing, nasty and bitter: "It's nothing, ya little kikes, nothing!"

And, truly, all that had gone on until then was nothing. Just around midnight, Dmitry Angelenko suddenly yelled "Halt!" We stood still, shuddering. He gave three twists to the ends of his moustache and ordered us to perform a "Jew dance" just for him.

At first we refused, but when he started waving his baton over our heads, we had no choice and had to dance.

Even to this day, when I remember that moonlit night in the middle of the road, I get a chill. We danced and twirled, flapping and clapping our wings. Sweat ran down us by the bucketful as he, that miserable monster, flew above us, brandishing his baton, splitting his sides with laughter.

When we could dance no more and were barely able to stand on our feet, the maniac took out a piece of pork and demanded we eat it! We tried with all our might to resist, explaining to him that Jewish angels must not eat pork. But you might as well have been talking to the wall, the maniac insisted and we were forced to taste it.

We ate it and grimaced, it was nauseating. Apparently he took great pleasure in our grimaces. He was shaking with laughter.

We started back on our way, ashamed and humiliated. I said to my friend: "Little Pisser, remember, no one in Jewish Paradise must ever know that we ate pork. We'll be expelled. Remember, tell no one."

We kept walking the whole night through and the entire next day. We came to the border crossing around evening. We could hardly stay upright.

Dmitry Angelenko handed the document to Saint Peter and bid us farewell: "See you kikes later!"

Saint Peter put on his spectacles and started to look over the paper. While he read, we rested and caught our breath. The Behemoth stood flummoxed; you could have tipped him over with a feather.

*

"A real live Haman, that Dmitry Angelenko," said the rabbi's juridical assistant. "To think that they allow such a type in Paradise—may God preserve and protect us."

"Praised be His divine name," the rabbi said, catching his breath. "At least the Behemoth was returned to our Paradise. I can just imagine the tzaddikim's jubilation when he was brought back."

"You have no idea. There was a whole parade. But I'll tell you about that, God willing, tomorrow. Now I am too tired."

My pop sat there as if dumbfounded. He did not take his eyes off me. My mama ran over to me and embraced me with kisses while bitterly cursing Dmitry Angelenko.

"May he meet with a heart attack, that maniac Dmitry, what terrible misery he put you through. He should be tossed from one end of Paradise to the other until I say enough is enough."

She took me in her arms and laid me in my crib. I heard the magnate, Mr Michael Hurwitz, several times repeat "*Sonderbar*".

I could still feel my mama's kiss on my cheek and, as if in a dream, I heard our guests say goodbye to my pop.

I fell fast asleep.

13

A Parade for the Behemoth

T HE NEXT NIGHT, when the rabbi, his juridical assistant and the town magnate Mr Michael Hurwitz were sitting once again at our house, I wasted no time and resumed my story:

*

We, that is, me, my friend Little Pisser and the Behemoth, had hardly reached the border of Jewish Paradise when we heard a bugle blast. It was Gimpel, the Jewish border guard angel, signalling that we had arrived and that the Behemoth was back on the territory of Jewish Paradise.

As if from underground, throngs of Paradise herdsmen appeared, holding ropes leading throngs of fat, dignified Paradise cows—the Behemoth's wives. The cows were adorned with colourful ribbons in honour of the distinguished guest, their husband, who had returned from abroad.

Gimpel the border guard angel motioned for us to step aside; the first encounter should belong to the family. The cows waved their tails, beckoning their husband over, and in their own language greeted him:

"Well, as I live and breathe, my darling! We wept nights

on end not knowing what to think. But, God be praised, you seem well."

We all stood off to the side, under the cover of the trees, so that we wouldn't spoil this domestic scene. We stood in the trees like that for nearly an hour during which my friend Little Pisser told the herdsmen all that we had gone through in Gentile Paradise.

When we came out from amidst the trees we saw how the Behemoth was licking one of his better halves, the charming Belle, who had a dark splotch on her forehead. "That's enough for today," Gimpel the border guard angel said. "Now we must light a fire on the hill to let the tzaddikim of Paradise know the happy news."

A few herdsmen went off to clamber up the high Paradise mountain that abutted the border. They lit a fire that could be seen from miles away. When they returned, they told us that as soon as they lit their fire another fire appeared on another mountaintop and, in the wink of an eye, fires were blazing on mountaintops and hilltops all over Paradise.

"The tzaddikim ought to know we're here by now, Little Pisser."

"Big deal," grumbled my friend Little Pisser, who could barely stand on his feet.

I looked over at the border and shuddered. Over on that side was the maniac Dmitry Angelenko. But, just by remembering all that we overcame, my spirits lifted. I saw the moon on that side of the border and came to the conclusion that their moon was an impostor and only our moon was worthy of blessing.

Gimpel the border guard angel gave a whistle. We and the other herdsmen gathered around him.

"We ought to bless the moon," Gimpel said, "and then go to bed. The parade for the Behemoth will start early in the morning."

We said the blessing over the moon and leapt before her, flapping our wings. The moon beamed with delight and grew fuller and brighter.

The moon over Gentile Paradise looked on, nearly bursting with envy. In anger, she hid behind a cloud.

Gimpel the border guard angel asked the herdsmen to corral their cows in one stable and to put the Behemoth in his own paddock, explaining: "You understand, fellas, the Behemoth is in a vulnerable state. To be penned up together with the cows would be too great a temptation. A beast is only a beast, after all."

The herdsmen did as the border guard angel requested. Then they kindled a fire in an open field, sat around the bonfire and sang:

> To fall asleep in the meadow and
> To bury your head in hay
> Seems a thousand thousand times better than
> Being eaten by fleas where you lay.
>
> In the meadow the birds are singing,
> Crickets chirp in the grass that grows—
> I'd give all the tea in China
> For the wind to come tickle my nose.
>
> Atishoo! Gesundheit! God bless you!
> Achoo! Could you ask for more,
> Than to gaze on her serene highness,
> The moon, as she charms so demure?

My friend Little Pisser and I lay on the grass not far from the fire and counted the stars.

"How many have you got, Little Pisser?"

"One million ninety-six."

"I count one million ninety-seven."

"You're lying, Samuel Abba."

"I'll swear on it, if you don't believe me…"

"Swear then."

"On my life or a shiksa's my wife… Now do you believe me?"

Little Pisser looked sad. Our old oath had reminded him of the forest ranger angel's daughter, Aniela. I gave him a poke: "You know what, Little Pisser? Let's start counting over again."

"I don't feel like it, Samuel Abba."

I scooted a bit closer to him and stroked his left wing with fondness. "Listen to me, Little Pisser, you ought to forget about it!"

Little Pisser rolled over and turned his back to me. I could tell that anything I said was futile. He would have to suffer through his pain to its bitter end. After that, he would be a different angel.

The herdsmen sat around the fire telling stories. I tried to listen to what they were saying but they were speaking so quietly, almost in a whisper, that I couldn't hear a word. I said my bedtime prayer and wished my friend a good night. But still he said nothing.

"Never mind then…" I said to myself. I turned my back to the fire and fell asleep.

In the morning we were awakened by a loud hullabaloo. We rubbed our eyes and dopily looked around, not understanding what all the clamour was. We walked over to the herdsmen, who were standing in a cluster talking. From them we learnt what was up.

As soon as the news had arrived that the Behemoth was back in Jewish Paradise, Isaac our forefather got up very early, ordered his horse and wagon harnessed, and made straight for the border. He wanted to make sure that the spot he had staked out on the Behemoth was fat enough again.

The angel Zavel the coachman gave the horses a real hiding, giddyupping and lashing them with the whip the entire way until they arrived at the border by daybreak.

"Open the stall," Isaac said to Gimpel the border guard angel, "I want to see the Behemoth."

Gimpel was reluctant. "The Behemoth is exhausted, let him sleep an hour or two more, let him rest his bones."

But Isaac was adamant: here and now! He wanted to check with his own hands—only then could he be sure that it was no dream.

We, that is, me and Little Pisser, ran over to the Paradise paddock, where we found Isaac with the border guard angel. They were still arguing. Isaac was already hoarse from so much shouting.

"Now, you open the stall as you've been told. This very minute!"

Isaac could really hold his own. Gimpel opened the stall and let Isaac in along with his coachman. We watched through the fence posts to see what he did.

"Do you see a chalk mark on the Behemoth, Zavel?"

"I do, saintly master," answered Zavel with his bass voice.

"Where is the mark, Zavel?"

The angel Zavel the coachman took Isaac's hand and guided him to the spot that was marked with chalk. Isaac ran his hand over and over and then shook his head: "This is not the spot, Zavel. The spot I marked was fat."

Zavel assured him that this was the only spot marked with chalk. There was no other. On the whole, the Behemoth was not as he once was. Now he was mostly skin and bones.

Isaac our forefather collapsed on the ground and wept. Tears streamed down from behind his thick dark glasses.

Zavel the coachman tried to console him: "Don't worry about it, Holy Tzaddik, we'll fatten him up, this... what do you call him... this big-he-ass."

I poked my friend: "Did you hear, Little Pisser: big-he-ass! That Zavel's got a pretty asinine head on his shoulders himself."

We watched as Isaac stood up and the angel Zavel dusted off his coat.

"You'll see, Holy Tzaddik, in a week you won't even recognize him."

"From your lips to God's ears, Zavel," sighed Isaac.

They left the paddock. Zavel the coachman angel guided the blind Isaac by the arm. "Easy now, Holy Tzaddik, there's a rock on the ground there!"

The sun was heating up. Over our heads birds were chirping. Blue Paradise swallows circled in front of the sun. It smelt of home, familiar, and all felt right with the world.

We said the morning prayer in the middle of the field. The angel Zavel the coachman made so many mistakes that we could barely keep a straight face.

Just as we finished praying, the klezmorim, the musicians of Paradise, arrived. They had been sent to the border to accompany the Behemoth with music along the whole route. Leading the klezmorim was Miriam the prophetess. She was a small and slender woman, with freckles on her face. How she was able to carry her enormous drum was really a wonder.

We, my friend Little Pisser and I, led the Behemoth out of his paddock. His horns were adorned with blue and white streamers. We waited for the signal to head out.

Gimpel the border guard angel organized it all: first went the klezmorim, after the klezmorim the Behemoth. I stood on the right side of the Behemoth and Little Pisser on his left. Behind us followed the herdsmen with the cows, and last—but by no means least—Father Isaac in his silver carriage.

Gimpel the border guard angel gave three blasts with his horn. Miriam the prophetess cued the klezmorim; all at once the music blared and we started out.

I am not capable of expressing the pitch of jubilation that overcame us. If you can imagine all the most joyous celebrations—from the festivities of Simchas Torah to the revelry of Purim—rolled into one day, you might get a sense of a tenth of the holiday we rang in.

The klezmorim led the way, playing, as Miriam the prophetess danced alongside us, pounding on her drum and singing:

> How good you have it, Israel's saints
> You, who were in dire straits,
> Now good times are back again
> The Behemoth to his home we bring.
> With joyful tears we dance and sing,
> We have what we lacked again.

If you never saw Miriam the prophetess dance, I'm sorry to say that you have never lived to see true beauty… She pranced along the entire way, not resting for a single moment. Sweat poured down, her modest wig was askew, but she looked none the worse for it. She beat her drum and kept dancing and singing:

Come blow your horns,
Let trumpets blast,
The Behemoth is coming,
The Behemoth, at last.
Oh tzaddikim, how fine it is now,
How happy and divine it is now.

The Behemoth walked along solemnly and ceremoniously, trotting with one hoof before the other. He presumably sensed the prestige bestowed upon him with the dancing and music. Every so often he kept turning his head back towards his wives, the cows who walked behind him, as if to say: "You see the honour I'm being paid here?"

The cows nodded their heads in reply—"We always knew that you weren't just any Joe Bull"—as they proudly littered the way behind them with fragrant cowpats.

We approached the Paradise City gates. "What's that shimmering up there, Little Pisser, do you see it?"

"I see it, Samuel Abba, it's a rainbow. It looks like it's been hung over the city gates in honour of the Behemoth."

"This is going to be some parade, Little Pisser."

We stopped before the gates. The city watchman angel known as Simcha the Red blew his horn: "*Toot-too-too-tooo, Toot-too-too-too-toooo*, the Behemoth is here…"

The gates opened. The klezmorim moved off to one side. Abraham our forefather, the oldest of the Patriarchs, came out first, followed by a pack of tzaddikim pushing their way forwards. In one hand Abraham clutched a bundle of hay and in the other he held a bowl of salt. He walked up to the Behemoth and offered the hay and salt. The Behemoth tasted the hay and gave the salt a lick and Abraham delivered an address:

"In the name of all Jewish Paradise and in the name of the municipality of Paradise City, I greet you, Behemoth…"

A blind man could see that Abraham had jitters, but he marshalled all his fortitude and continued:

"Even though you caused us a great deal of aggravation in running away, nonetheless we won't punish you for it. You have already received your comeuppance from *them* and we receive you here with joy. In your honour we have illuminated rainbows all over Paradise City. Each rainbow may have cost a fortune, but we did not bother ourselves about the expense in order to show just how dear you are to us. See here, Behemoth, no more rotten pranks from now on, please. Live the life you were destined for, a life of ease. And behave with dignity, of course. You are the Behemoth, not some average horse."

Out of sheer nervousness, Abraham's speech began to devolve into doggerel. He was as white as chalk. His beard quivered as if it was making to fly off and he clutched it with his right hand. Breathlessly he concluded: "You are warmly welcomed, Behemoth, amongst the holy tzaddikim!"

The Behemoth wagged his tail a few times, and in this way offered his gratitude for the great honour. The cows standing behind him gushed with pride.

A shoving and commotion broke out behind Abraham's back. "Apropos of that, Abraham," someone was shouting, "apropos of that, sir, I have a parable. Once upon a time, there was a king. Now, this king had three—"

"Knock it off with the parables, Maggid," Abraham said. "Keep them for some other time. This is not the moment for them."

"Oh, but you'll regret it, Abraham, sir. It is a fine parable with a most illuminating lesson to be drawn…"

"No one wants to hear it!" people yelled from every side. The Maggid of Dubno's voice was drowned in a sea of shouting voices.

The angel Simcha the Red gave another blast on his horn: *Toot-too-too-too, Toot-too-too-too-tooo*—the Behemoth is here. Welcome!"

Miriam the prophetess raised her hand and all the klezmorim struck their instruments at once. With the Behemoth in their midst, they all marched through the gates into Paradise City.

Rainbows in a variety of colours fluttered everywhere. In the wealthy neighbourhoods, every building was lit up with rainbows. In the poorer quarters, each alley had one. Lights flashed and sparkled, dazzling the eyes. The music played on and on. Everything was like a dream.

On the Avenue of the Patriarchs we came to a stop. Now the great procession was to begin. An honour guard of select tzaddikim took their places by the Behemoth.

"At-ten-tion!"

First to march was a contingent of Paradise fowl, led by the chief turkeycock from King Solomon's estate. The turkeycock crowed out his orders, vigorous and sharp: "Cock-a-doodle-doo! Cock-a-doodle-doo!"

After them came the Paradise goats. Their leader was an old billy goat with big horns and a short beard that looked very much like the goatee on Little Pisser's pop, Solomon Zalman the patchmaker.

A company of oxen was followed by a company of geese; the most first-rate were selected. Each species was represented in the procession by the best and brightest. The parading lasted for a good three hours. The entire time, proud Paradise eagles circled the sky above.

I myself heard Abraham tell Isaac that he had never seen such a parade in all the time he'd been in Paradise. "Never before has such an honour been bestowed as the honour bestowed on this Behemoth."

"When the Messiah comes," remarked someone standing behind Abraham, who had been listening to the conversation, "there will be an even bigger parade."

"May he come yet in our lifetime," sighed Isaac.

And the great procession carried on. We, Little Pisser and I, led the Behemoth by his horns. A guard of honour marched at our side and behind us was the rest of the crowd.

The tzaddikim behind us pushed and shoved. Each wanted to be as close as possible to the Behemoth. They elbowed their way forwards and stepped on each other's toes.

"Why don't you watch where you're going, mac?"

"You watch where you're going!"

"Youch, fellas, he stepped on my very best corn."

"You should keep your best safe at home, my dear tzaddik."

"Well, who asked you anyway?"

I felt intoxicated by the music and the lights that flooded us from all around. "Isn't it great, Little Pisser?"

"'Great', you say, dumdum? It's greater than great!"

We approached the town square. The Behemoth was placed in the very centre of the huge plaza. The tzaddikim made a circle, wrapping their arms around one another, and danced. The Behemoth watched on wide-eyed. He had never seen so many flying feet and beards as long as he had lived.

"Step it up, now, fellas! Make it even more merry, tzaddikim!"

Those who were standing outside the circle of the dancers clapped along with their hands. Miriam the prophetess beat on her drum.

Isaac our forefather broke into the middle of the circle. With a shoe on one foot and the other foot bare he leapt, throwing his head back. He snapped his fingers, yelling: "More joy, folks! Even merrier, tzaddikim!"

Isaac considered himself to be the real beneficiary of this joyous occasion. No one was more of a connoisseur of delectable cuts of meat than himself. And no one longed for a prime cut of Behemoth as much as he did, our forefather Isaac.

The dancing became wilder and more reckless. The tzaddikim panted, barely able to catch their breath, yet no one left the circle.

Around twelve o'clock at night a great banquet got under way. Tables were set up in the streets, barrels of beer and liquor were carted out. White-aproned angel women dished out roasted goose, chicken and duck. A small cask of holy wine was set before the Patriarchs.

The tzaddikim toasted each other a "l'chaim" and wished for only the best for all Paradise. May the recent aggravation be an affliction the likes of which they would never see ever again.

Lovely young angels flew above the tzaddikim's heads. The fluttering of their wings cooled the sweat-soaked tzaddikim, who ate and drank and went to town.

"Let's have a song," said Abraham our forefather as he dusted the crumbs out of his beard.

"What good is a song, Abraham, sir?" started in the Maggid of Dubno, who was sitting on the other end of the table. "Better I shall tell you a parable: once upon a time, there was a king. Now, this king had three—"

"No one wants it, Maggid," Abraham cut him off, "so quit badgering with your parables."

The Maggid of Dubno got sore. He stood up from the table and disappeared.

Our forefather Isaac, who was already on his third goose, laid down his knife for a moment and burst out singing:

> When Messiah comes at last,
> What shall we eat at the Great Repast?

And the tzaddikim all answered in chorus:

> Leviathan and wild Behemoth,
> The wild ox and the great sea beast,
> Shall we all eat at the Final Feast.

From a distance, an inebriated voice belonging to the Holy Jew of Przysucha could be heard singing in a Polish hodge-podge:

> To you, oh Abie, our papa dear!
> To you, oh Izzy, you're our papa dear!
> To you, oh Jakey, you're our papa dear!

Little Pisser and I also took a swig or two. Pretty inebriated ourselves, we clung tightly to one another. "Take a look at the moon, Little Pisser. She's swaying a bit, do you see?"

"Sh… sh… she's drunk," Little Pisser barely spluttered out.

"You know what, Little Pisser? Why don't we fly around a little to sober up?"

We ascended into the air. Little Pisser flew a bit staggeringly and reeled in flight, but put on a brave front.

In every street, on every boulevard, tzaddikim were sitting around tables and singing. They clapped their hands and all were on top of the world.

Little Pisser sobered up a little. He tugged at my wing: "Let's fly over to the Avenue of the Patriarchs, it's quieter over there."

We flew towards the Avenue of the Patriarchs. All of a sudden, Little Pisser hung back: "Samuel Abba, do you see over there… there… by the street lamp?"

I looked down and saw an angel with a red beard standing by a lamp post. He was wavering on his feet and having a chat with the lamp post. "It's the angel Simon Bear. He's plastered, Little Pisser."

"What did you think, Samuel Abba, that Simon Bear would miss a chance to tank up?"

We dropped below to listen to Simon Bear as he stood by the lamp post pounding on his chest: "We would be so right together," Simon Bear was vowing to the lamp post. "Today I'll divorce that old bag of bones of mine and right after I divorce her we'll raise a canopy, you and me."

"He must have downed a ton and now he's going to marry the lamp post," I said.

"*Mazel tov*, Simon Bear," shouted Little Pisser, and we flew off.

The Avenue of the Patriarchs was teeming with drunken tzaddikim. They kicked up a racket with their singing and clapping. Even the Rabbi of Czortków was out dancing in his threadbare long johns.

"They're everywhere! And everywhere they're drunk!" deplored my friend Little Pisser. "There's no place to find a little peace and quiet."

We turned on to another street and found the same; a third, a tenth, but again it was all the same.

On Johanan the Sandalmaker Street it was quiet. We heaved a sigh of relief and headed downwards. We walked by foot, even though the air there was not the freshest, but, still, we caught our breath.

"Little Pisser, look over there!"

Standing on the corner of Johanan the Sandalmaker Street was our Talmud teacher, Meyer Scabies, with his whip in hand. He was holding forth before a cluster of goats.

"Recite, you little bastards, or else I'll whip the daylights out of you."

The goats' beards were trembling with fright. The Talmud teacher brandished his whip, barely able to stand on his feet.

"He's drunk, too, Little Pisser. This is just too much to take!"

We watched our teacher standing and holding forth before the goats for a while. "Let's wake up his wife," I said to my friend. "When she sees her treasure with these goats, he'll get what he deserves."

"I don't want to, Samuel Abba," Little Pisser shrugged. "I want to fly home, I'm tired. Come along with me."

We left our Talmud teacher with the goats and flew towards the pastures of Paradise, where Little Pisser lived.

As we got close to the pastures of Paradise, we noticed the Maggid of Dubno. He walked along, deep in thought. The Behemoth stood grazing on the pasture. The Maggid of Dubno approached him. He stroked the Behemoth and said: "I shall tell you the parable. It's a fine parable with a most illuminating lesson. Once upon a time, there was a king. Now, this king had three…"

14

With Zeidel the Paradise Photographer

AFTER THE EXTRAORDINARY parade and the extraordinary banquet came the extraordinary hangover for all Paradise. The tzaddikim had really overdone it. They went about for several days with heads wrapped with damp cloths.

Only one angel, namely Simon Bear, was out and about the following day as if nothing had happened. He had even forgotten the vow he made to the street lamp that they were to be wed.

But who in the world is like Simon Bear?

A run of terribly tedious days passed in Paradise. One day was followed by the next, the second day the same as the tenth. The tzaddikim prayed their usual three times a day, their wives decked out in their finest jewellery. The poor angels toiled away, the rich ones still ran the show. The Behemoth was back grazing in the pastures of Paradise.

Dull, dull days in Paradise.

Every Thursday was market day and village angels would come from the surrounding countryside bringing their best: eggs, butter, fruits, vegetables and their choicest chickens, geese, ducks and young calves. Market day was the most colourful day of the Paradise week.

But after all the remarkable experiences we'd had, even market day now paled in comparison. All of Paradise seemed to us to be one enormous yawn.

I felt very restless, and Little Pisser all the more so. We rambled through the streets and boulevards of Paradise like outsiders. Little Pisser at least had something to long for: the forest ranger angel's daughter in Gentile Paradise. But what was there for me?

We went back to school with Meyer Scabies, the Talmud instructor. His whip whistled over our heads. It was the same routine day in and day out. We silently prayed to God that the Behemoth would escape again so that we would have something to do.

But the Behemoth did not escape. He stood serenely in the pastures of Paradise, grazing and getting fat. The misery that he was subjected to in Gentile Paradise had taught him his lesson once and for all.

And so the days went on, as monotonous as the chewing of the Behemoth's cud.

Little Pisser went about daydreaming. In these tedious days, his longing grew even stronger and more painful. He didn't respond when spoken to, and when he was yelled at he started as if waking from another world: "Huh, what?" He was one seriously distracted angel.

Once, Meyer Scabies stopped short in the middle of his lesson: "Little Pisser, what have you got there?"

Little Pisser, roused as if from sleeping, said: "I've got, erm, teacher, it's a…"

The Talmud instructor got furious, his eyes were sharp and piercing. He waved his whip. "You've got, you've got… Let's just see what you've got in your hand, little bastard."

Little Pisser did not want to open his hand. The Talmud angel pried his fist open and smiled. "Oh, so that's it, then, you brat? The hair of some unknown lady. Hmm… hmm… whose could it be… Let me just think for a moment: your mother has dark hair… so does your sister… hmm… hmm… and this is very blonde… So that's how it is, eh? You don't pay attention because you're too busy playing with some shiksa's hair."

Little Pisser blushed and the teacher looked at the lock of hair, sniffed it, tasted it and then barked: "Little Pisser, lie down!"

Little Pisser screamed, wept and shrieked, but to no avail. The Talmud angel began thrashing him with the whip, all the while singing out: "Playing with the hair of some little shiksa, the little bastard… *twelve, thirteen, fourteen*… Playing with such a vile abomination… *fifteen, sixteen, seventeen*…"

The teacher returned to his seat. He took the lock of hair and wrapped it into a scrap of newspaper. He then rolled it into a cigarette. He lit it and began to smoke.

"My, my… a fine smoke! It's been a long time since I've had such a tasty cigarette."

Little Pisser watched as the keepsake that Aniela had given him went up in smoke. The smoke slithered out the window and vanished into nothing. He gritted his teeth and in his heart he vowed vengeance. That villain, that Talmud angel Meyer Scabies, would pay for this—Little Pisser would remember it his entire life.

Little Pisser did not come to school for a few days after that. I was terribly sad without him. Maybe he was sick, I thought, and went to his house.

"Where's Little Pisser?" I asked.

"What do you mean 'where'? He's at school," Little Pisser's mama Hannah Deborah told me.

I understood straight away that Little Pisser had said nothing about this at home. He told his mama that he went to school but was really wandering around the streets and boulevards.

After six days out, he came back to school. His face was glowing. He pulled me to the side to whisper in my ear: "Look, Samuel Abba, Abinadab the post angel brought me a letter today."

"From whom, Little Pisser?"

"Dummy, don't you see? From her, from Aniela."

"From Gentile Paradise?"

"I had some luck, Samuel Abba. No one happened to be around when the post angel brought me the letter otherwise I would have got the third degree: 'Why are you getting mail from Gentile Paradise out of the blue?'"

"Show me the letter, Little Pisser!"

"Well, I won't let you read it, Samuel Abba. But you can have the stamp."

Little Pisser peeled off the stamp and handed it to me. It was a green stamp and on it was depicted a dove wearing a little crucifix around its neck.

"Be careful, Samuel Abba, don't let the Talmud angel find the stamp or you'll get a beating."

"To hell with him, Little Pisser. You take care to hide that letter well. The Talmud angel could roll himself another smoke with it yet."

"Goddamn him to hell, Samuel Abba!"

The rest of the day Little Pisser was a star pupil, a totally different angel than before. You wouldn't even recognize him.

Our Talmud instructor Meyer Scabies thought that the blows he delivered had done the trick. The fool had no idea that a couple of words scrawled by a blonde "abomination" could do more than a million blows.

In the evening, as we were leaving school, Little Pisser could keep it to himself no longer and he showed me the letter. All in all, it was just a few words: *"Little Pisser, When are you coming back?—Aniela."*

"You know what, Samuel Abba? We should see to it that the Behemoth escapes again."

"He'll never run away again, Little Pisser. You know that in Gentile Paradise his legs were chained and he was given half a pound of hay a day, while here there was an enormous parade for him. Do you think that the Behemoth doesn't know the difference between good and bad?"

"So what should we do, Samuel Abba?"

"You have to wait it out, Little Pisser. It will either happen or it won't."

That evening we flew over Paradise as happy as larks. We caught some butterflies to play with and they wriggled in our hands. We set them free and laughed heartily.

We flew by the house where Zeidel the Paradise photographer lived. Sitting on a bench in front of his house were Zeidel's three daughters: Shifra, Slova and Treina, three unmarried, grown daughters with sour faces and high bosoms. They were talking amongst themselves and, as usual, badmouthing all of Paradise.

On the roof of Zeidel's house, a dozen or so black tomcats paced around with upraised tails and green eyes. In Paradise these tomcats were known as "Zeidel's grandsons" since his daughters took care of them.

The angels and tzaddikim who lived nearby went about cranky and sleep-deprived. The cats mewled all night long and let no one rest. But whenever mice showed up, everyone came running to the angel Zeidel, begging: "Mr Zeidel, please loan me a tomcat!"

To which Zeidel could only shrug his shoulders: "They're not my cats… you'll have to ask my daughters."

"Mr Zeidel, rats have gnawed my best holiday wings, please lend me a tomcat for the night, at least. You'd really be doing a good turn."

The angel Zeidel shrugged his shoulders as if to say: "What are you hounding me for? Are they my cats? If they were mine, I'd have drowned them long ago in the Paradise River."

"What a nasty angel that Zeidel is," said his neighbours, but wrongly. The nasty angels were actually his daughters, the three old maids who had raised the tomcats and who, on pain of death, would never help a neighbour in need.

The angel Zeidel the Paradise photographer was a hopeless case, entombed with his daughters. They paid him as much mind as a yapping dog. If any of them insisted on anything, he gave in immediately, content—lucky even—that they hadn't snatched one of his Purim plays and torn it to shreds.

Ever since his wife, the angel Sima, had left him and their three children to run off with a gentile angel to Gentile Paradise, the angel Zeidel consoled himself by writing Purim plays. He treasured them like jewels, and all who came over—whether they wanted to or not—had to listen to one of Zeidel's Purim plays.

"Little Pisser, let's go see the angel Zeidel!"

"I don't want to, Samuel Abba. He'll bore us with his Purim plays."

"But we promised him we would, Little Pisser."

"Let him call us welshers for all I care."

Zeidel's daughters noticed us circling above the house. They shouted up at us: "What are you flying around our house for? You're scaring the cats."

"Go protect them from the evil eye then," Little Pisser shouted back down at them.

"Quit it, Little Pisser, getting on their bad side is worse than getting sent to hell," I told my friend. "Is the angel Zeidel home?" I shouted down to Zeidel's daughters.

"He is," they shouted up. "Now come down, you scamps, you can see the cats are frightened."

I tugged on my friend's wing: "Come on, Little Pisser."

We descended. Zeidel's daughters looked us over and we them. Up close we could see first-hand how hideous they were.

"Where's your pop?" we asked.

The three hideous angels burst out laughing, nudging each other with their elbows. It was a nauseating sight to behold.

We went into the photo studio. The angel Zeidel was sitting at a table retouching a negative. The lamp over the table was dim and Zeidel's shadow, with its long hair and spectacles at the tip of the nose, danced on the wall like a character out of one of his Purim plays.

"Good evening, Zeidel!"

The angel Zeidel was thrilled to see us. He set down two chairs and told us to have a seat.

"It's swell that you've come, boys. Just last night I finished writing a new Purim play: 'With Noah in the Ark'—you'll just love this Noahide romp, boys. Would you like anything? I mean, what can I offer you? A glass of tea, maybe, with jam? Shifra, Slova, Treina, what are you up to? Put on the samovar, we have guests."

The three beauties outside paid as much attention to their father as did the mewling cats. They didn't even respond, but rather remained sitting outside, slandering all Paradise. The angel Zeidel had to see to it himself to fire up the samovar. He came back with his hands and face sooty and gave a groan: "But they don't lift a finger around here, those daughters of mine, and won't do anything they're told. How well they observe the commandment 'honour thy father'—but what can you do? If only they had cleared out together with their mother, I wouldn't have had to endure such disgrace."

"What are you grumbling about in there, Pop?" shouted one of his daughters through the window. "Is something wrong again?"

"Who's grumbling, Slova? You're imagining things, my girl! May a grumbling come only from my enemies' mouths…" answered the angel Zeidel.

His daughters continued their cackling outside; the tomcats meowed on the roof. And the angel Zeidel poured our glasses of tea.

"Drink up, boys, and afterwards I'll read you my new Noah play."

We sipped the hot tea. The angel Zeidel sat down with us. "Why haven't you married your daughters off, Mr Zeidel?" Little Pisser asked him.

"*Why*, you ask?" sighed the angel Zeidel. "It's an easy thing to ask, but a harder feat to marry them off. Who do you suppose would take them? They don't have looks and even your most humble angel demands a hefty dowry these days. And where would I get that, eh? These days are not like they were. Once, you could marry off a daughter and no one asked a thing. But today it's 'Hand over the cash!'"

A genuine shlimazel, this angel Zeidel, I thought. His wife, who he wanted to stay, runs off and his daughters, who he wishes he could be rid of, never leave. When I grew up, I decided, I would write my own Purim play about this here angel Zeidel.

Zeidel began to get impatient; our tea-drinking was taking too long. He could hardly wait for us to finish our glasses.

"You don't want any more tea, do you?" he said, worried that, God forbid, we would say yes, then added, "Too much tea isn't healthy, especially in the summertime."

We obliged him and told him we wanted no more tea. The angel Zeidel invited us into his house. It would be better to read in there, here the table lamp really ruins your eyes.

We went into his home. Zeidel rummaged in a drawer for a while and returned with his manuscript. We sat down on one of the three beds that were in the room. The angel Zeidel sat on another bed across from us. He cleared his throat and said: "Now don't interrupt while I'm reading, boys. You'll see, you'll enjoy this."

"We're ready and waiting to hear, Mr Zeidel."

The angel Zeidel buried his nose in his manuscript and began to read. The tomcats on the roof continued to meow.

> *On* NOAH's *ark.* RIGHTEOUS NOAH *is lying dead drunk on the floor.* HAM *and* JAPHETH *enter.*

HAM: Look, now, Jaffy!

JAPHETH: What's that here?

HAM: Right there sleeps our father dear.

JAPHETH: Seems he's gone and drunk his fill,

How much rotgut can he swill?

Now he's snoring like a sow.

HAM: Know what I say? Listen now:

Let us play a little gag…

JAPHETH: … And with this straw give him a stab,

So he'll think the fleas all bite him?

HAM: Heavens no, don't you remember,
Papa's got a nasty temper.
He would whip us, don't incite him…
JAPHETH: What else then?
HAM: I have a plan.
JAPHETH: Well, then, let us hear it, man!
HAM: Why don't we strip all his clothes off?
JAPHETH: Sounds good to me. Don't make a peep:
Let's make sure Pop stays asleep.

> HAM *and* JAPHETH *walk on their tiptoes. They undress*
> NOAH, *who lies sleeping like a corpse. Afterwards, the*
> *two take each other by the hand and dance as they chant:*

HAM AND JAPHETH: Tee-hee, Papa, tee-hee,
We see your thingummy!
Noah in all his glory unbound,
Come, every girl and every boy,
Come and see his pride and joy,
Let's all sing and dance around!

> *As they dance,* SHEM *enters, carrying a holy book under*
> *his arm. Seeing his younger siblings, he rages:*

SHEM: Scram, now, punks, do you hear me?
HAM: Aw, go to hell, you hook-nosed sheeny!
JAPHETH: The nerve of this Jew, mercy me!
SHEM: I'll tell Papa what you've done.
HAM: Try it and we'll have some fun.

> *At this,* NOAH *wakes up and rubs his eyes. He looks all*
> *around and spits disdainfully three times.*

SHEM: My, what a dream! I was perched atop
The roof of the Temple, like a bird,

Two, then three, four days non-stop
Immersed in Torah, the Holy Word,
When a crash and bang I then heard…

> NOAH *clutches at his heart and turns to his* SONS, *who have gathered around him.*

NOAH: Fetch me some water… I'm quite perturbed!

> SHEM *runs to bring his father a glass of water.*

SHEM: Here, Papa, take and drink.

> NOAH *drinks the entire glass. Feeling a bit better, he pinches* SHEM *on the cheek.*

NOAH: Shem, you're a first-rate son, I think.

> NOAH *takes a small teacher's whip off a hook on the wall. The* SONS *sit on the bench at the table.* NOAH *asks in the melodic style of a Talmud teacher:*

NOAH: Where in the Torah do we read this week?
JAPHETH: Genesis 12: "Get thee out…"
HAM: That's not it, you dumb lout!
SHEM: Papa, Papa, does it go, uh?
    "This is the genealogy of Noah…"
NOAH: Yes, my children. Now, line by line:
    Genesis 6, start at verse nine.

> NOAH *brandishes the whip. The three boys bob their heads over their holy books and recite, singing:*

SHEM, HAM, JAPHETH: The line of Noah this way passes:
    From chimney flues rise smoke and ashes,
    Strength is drawn from whisky glasses.

A DELEGATION OF DOGS *enters. They wag their
tails as they bark:*

DOGS: Bark bark, Noah, bark!
We, too, live on this ark.
With food you must endow us
Yet your wife, your Mrs Noah,
The cruel old Mrs Noah,
Has forgotten all about us.

THE DOGS *move off to the side to make way for* A
DELEGATION OF PIGS *to enter. Each pig holds his
right trotter outstretched:*

PIGS: Greetings, Noah, sir, good day,
Please pay heed to what we say:
We may not be strictly kosher,
But your wife, your Mrs Noah,
The old, cruel Mrs Noah,
Is a nasty witch, you know sir.

THE PIGS *move off to the side.* TWO WHITE CATS,
looking emaciated, enter. They meow:

CATS: Meow, Noah, sir, meow,
Please tell your good hausfrau,
If you should run across her,
Please bring my Kitty darling
Some milk, for she is starving,
or some sweet cream in a saucer.

The angel Zeidel could read no more. The tomcats on the
roof started in with such a caterwauling that we couldn't hear
a word he said. We stopped our ears with our hands; the angel

Zeidel was in a state of despair. The Noah play trembled in his hand. He groaned: "It's one thing to live exiled with your daughters—at least they are your daughters—but to live in exile with these cats, that's beyond the pale."

The three daughters came into the house. The cats leapt in front of and behind them. One jumped on my lap and I threw him off me. Shifra, the eldest daughter, glowered at me and grumbled: "You ought to be thrown on your head, little angel."

The other two took to driving us out of the house. "Out you go, boys, it's getting late. We've got to get to bed."

The angel Zeidel was unhappy. No sooner had he stumbled upon some willing listeners to his Purim play than his daughters—may they meet with a disaster—appear and prevent him from finishing.

"What are you scamps still hanging around for?"

The eldest daughter blew out the light with a wave of her wing. We stood in the darkness. We had no choice but to leave. We felt our way along the walls and with some difficulty found the door.

"Goodnight, Mr Zeidel."

The angel Zeidel let out an anguished groan. He was still sitting with the Purim play in his hand. His daughters went about cursing and unfurling the bedclothes. The tomcats' green eyes twinkled in the darkness.

When we got outside, we smoothed out our wings and caught our breath. The sky was full of stars. A wisp of a cloud sailed across it.

"You know what, Samuel Abba? Let's sail a bit on a cloud!" Little Pisser said.

We flapped our wings and ascended high above. The wisp of a cloud was sailing slowly, it was in no hurry. Why would it need to hurry and where would it even be hurrying to?

We grabbed the edge of the little cloud and—just like that—we were astride and sailing.

Little Pisser was happy, his eyes gleamed. From below, they probably looked like two stars. Little Pisser sang:

> Nothing beats a cloud to ride,
> Above the blue horizon,
> It's better than the fastest horse
> You ever set your eyes on.
>
> The fastest racehorse and the best
> Runs till he grows tired,
> But on a cloud you can sail away
> For as long as you desire.

I looked down below. The houses of Paradise City seemed like toys. I tried to pick out the houses and villas of the tzaddikim. Little Pisser kept singing:

> Hyah! My pony, my nimbus-steed,
> Fly, fly, and don't you stop now,
> Hyah! Don't you buck or bolt
> Or to the ground we'll drop down.

"What a shame, Little Pisser, that the angel Zeidel the photographer isn't with us. Here on the cloud he could read us the end of his Purim play and pay as much mind to his cat-loving daughters as howling cats themselves."

"You haven't had enough of that old bungler already?" Little Pisser brushed the idea aside with his hand. "May he sleep well there tonight."

"Still, it's a pity for him," I said, "and his Purim play is a pretty fine Purim play, after all."

Little Pisser sang on:

> Hyah! My pony, my nimbus-steed,
> We'll ride off to distant lands,
> Where the milky spider of the moon
> Spins her silken silver strands.

We glided on the little cloud for quite a distance. Around midnight we hopped off, and just in time too. The little cloud was heading towards Turkish Paradise. We waved at the cloud as it sailed off and we sang:

> Send our best wishes to Hagar,
> And her son Ishmael, don't forget:
> Tell them, Cloud, to send us please,
> Some Turkish cigarettes.

We flew back home. When we approached the pastures of Paradise, we descended. I said goodbye to my friend. "Remember, Little Pisser, back to school tomorrow!"

Little Pisser burst out laughing:

> Back to Meyer Scabies the Talmud beast,
> More pious than the parish priest...

He went into his house and I flew home. I hesitated for a moment by the angel Zeidel's house. I could hear no sound. The angel Zeidel, his three hideous daughters and the dozen tomcats were all asleep. The Purim play lay shamefully in its drawer.

I felt deeply sorry for this ne'er-do-well angel with all my heart. But there was nothing I could do for him except to offer a sigh.

A star fell over Zeidel's rooftop. A good omen for him, I thought, or maybe just more bad luck. I went back home to sleep.

15

Conjurors in Paradise

O UT OF THE BLUE, a band of conjurors appeared in
Paradise. Nobody knew where they came from. One fine
evening they drove into Paradise City in a crude wagon: two
men and a lady. The men wore red Turkish caps and the lady
had on a blue dress with red polka dots.

In the centre of the marketplace their wagon came to a halt.
The Turks pulled some boards out of their cart and began to
tinker about. In under an hour they had cobbled together a
stage in the middle of the market square.

The lady went about in the streets with a drum and called
on the crowd to come and see the conjurors, unparalleled in
any of the three Paradises. These conjurors had already performed for the greatest saints in Gentile Paradise and Turkish
Paradise. The Prophet Muhammad had even conferred on them
an honour—a gilded crescent on a green ribbon—and anyone
so enticed may come the following morning at ten o'clock and
see them with their own eyes.

The lady spoke with a deep voice. The tzaddikim could
have sworn that this was a man who was disguised as a lady.

"It's the voice of a man," the Holy Rabbi of Lublin said, "but in the garb of a woman. What could she be?"

"You yourself said 'what could *she* be,'" contended the casuistic Rabbi of Opatów, "and *she* is in the feminine, which means we are dealing here with a female."

"Who is this 'we' you speak of?" snapped the Rabbi of Lublin. "Maybe *you* are dealing here with a female, but don't go speaking about any 'we', my dear Opatów Tzaddik."

"Right, absolutely," chimed in the other tzaddikim in agreement, who had been listening to the discussion. "The Rabbi of Lublin is right, what are you going around saying 'we' for?"

"It's only a manner of speaking, gentlemen," the Rabbi of Opatów responded. "I didn't mean anything by it, God forbid. Why make such a fuss? Have you ever heard such a thing?"

The Holy Jew of Przysucha tried to settle things: "By all indications, gentlemen, I believe we have here what our ancient Talmudic sages would call an androgyne. From the voice you would think him a man, but from the dress you'd think a woman and, as both are in one, you see, gentlemen, and do not match, the case remains, you see, that of an androgyne."

The lady with the man's voice acted as if she heard nothing and continued ambling through the streets and beating the drum: "All who wish to see sights never seen before in all your lives: come one, come all to see the great conjurors Mehmet Ali and Ali Mehmet. Tomorrow at ten o'clock in the morning. All who miss it will regret it, for such a wonder has never been seen before—even here in Paradise…"

We, that is, my friend Little Pisser and I, were sitting just then, studying with the Talmud angel Meyer Scabies. Suddenly, the Talmud angel set down his whip and exclaimed: "Conjurors!"

The students needed no more encouragement. Some flew right out the window and some out the door, leaving the Talmud teacher standing alone in the classroom with his mouth agape.

We flew towards the lady with the drum, marvelling at her mannish voice and her blue dress with the red spots. I elbowed my friend: "There's going to be some fun in Paradise."

Littler Pisser was overjoyed. He had heard a great deal about conjurors but as yet had never seen any. Tomorrow he would see them with his own eyes. He was over the moon.

The Turks, including the lady, spent the entire night getting drunk at the Righteous Noah. Even Simon Bear had to admit that these conjurors had throats lined with diamonds and could really knock them back. You should know that Simon Bear isn't an angel who doesn't mean what he says. If he says someone could, you can take his word on it. Simon Bear is an expert in such matters.

The angel Simon Bear got quite chummy with the Turkish conjurors. The night that he spent at the Righteous Noah tavern was, according to Simon Bear, one of his finest nights in Paradise.

"I was just flying by the Righteous Noah," Simon Bear recounted, "and I heard singing. Who could that be singing, I thought, and decided to check things out. As soon as I opened the door I saw the Turks, the conjurors. They had two bottles of whisky on the table and several more were lying empty on the floor. The Turks had their arms around each other and were singing:

> Wine is all right
> But whisky surpasses
> Bless us, O Allah,
> With bottomless glasses.

Allah, you are great
There is none who is bigger,
Of all that man drinks
What compares, then, to liquor?

So, friends, now let's drink up,
And give praise to Allah,
Till the night tells the dawn:
Good-day and ta-ta!

"As soon as the Turks saw me," Simon Bear continued, "they shut up, thinking I might be a police angel or something. I gave them a friendly wave of my wings and winked at the bottles: 'Drink up and drink hearty, conjurors. You are welcome here!'

"The Turks were delighted with my words. They invited me over to their table to have a glass. Well, you know"—Simon Bear scratched the back of his head—"when you're asked nicely, you really can't refuse. So we kept toasting until dawn. Those Turks can really drink, but that lady—blast her!—she could drink better than either of the men. She poured it down like it was nothing."

Everyone could tell that what Simon Bear had told us was not the whole truth. He had certainly drunk with the Turks, in that there was no disputing the angel Simon Bear. That Simon Bear later flew all over Paradise, stopping everyone he met and telling them, for the love of God, to go and see the conjurors, now that seemed most peculiar.

"The lady clearly put a spell on him," whispered some older women angels. "Turkish beauties are known to be great enchantresses."

"The wisdom of the weaker sex," scoffed the angel men. "Right away they claim sorcery. Simon Bear would sell you all of Paradise for a couple of shots of whisky."

"Who could forget," recalled an older angel with hoary grey wings, "when Simon Bear pawned his wings at the tavern? He went a whole year on foot before he was able to scrape enough handouts together to redeem them."

However it came about, Simon Bear had gone flying all over Paradise, praising the conjurors to high heaven and urging angels big and small to go and see them.

"Where are we supposed to get money to buy tickets?" asked the little angel kids.

"Jimmy it out of alms boxes," Simon Bear enlightened them, "or sneak it out of your pop's trouser pockets at night."

All of Paradise was in a whirl. Everywhere and anywhere, the conjurors were the only subject of conversation.

I couldn't sleep all that night. As soon as day broke I got dressed, washed, said my morning prayers and hied it over to my friend Little Pisser.

Little Pisser dressed in a flash and we tiptoed outside. Little Pisser showed me a handful of coins that he had liberated from the charity box. "It's enough for two tickets—for me and you, Samuel Abba!"

Everyone in Paradise was still asleep. We flew over the empty streets and boulevards. We didn't even see a single dog out, not to mention an angel or a tzaddik.

Even Shmaya the cop, whose beat was guarding Prophet Elijah Boulevard, was off somewhere with a cook in her kitchen, leaving the entire boulevard unattended.

As we flew by our forefather Abraham's villa on the Avenue of the Patriarchs we saw the oldest of the Patriarchs wrapped

in his tallis and tefillin. He had just finished reciting the benedictions of God in his morning prayer.

Through the open window of Jacob's villa, Bilhah was
dumping out the chamber pots. Mother Rachel pushed open
the shutters and yawned right into the morning's face.

"Little Pisser!"

"What, Samuel Abba?"

"Let's take a walk down by the Paradise River."

We flew over to the Paradise River. We spent a while there
skipping stones until the Leviathan woke up. As soon as we
caught a glimpse of the Leviathan's head emerging from the
water's surface we ran off, and as we did we chanted this little
ditty:

> Leviathan, Leviathan,
> You want a life of quiet, then?
> Find yourself a wife to marry,
> A top hat, and cane to carry,
> Every Tom and Dick and Harry,
> Will come with all their shouts and jeers:
> This bridegroom's wet behind the ears!

Luckily, the Leviathan couldn't chase us. If he could have, he
would have swallowed us whole without even first making a
blessing and we wouldn't have seen the light of day until the
coming of the Messiah. Being stuck in the belly of the Leviathan
for that long is no laughing matter.

We flew back into town. Tzaddikim were running all over
the streets with their wives and children. Everyone was rushing.
Each wanted to get to the market square as early as possible
to grab the best seats and get the best view of the conjurors.

Our forefather Jacob had marched his whole family out: all four of the women of the household along with his twelve sons. His daughter Dina, as usual, was painted and powdered like a doll.

Angels big and small were hovering in the air with coins in their hands. Only a few residents stayed back home on squalid Baal-Shem-Tov Alley or on blue-collar Johanan the Sandalmaker Street.

We, that is, my friend Little Pisser and I, also began to hurry. We flew at high speed and collided more than once with an older angel or a younger one. We had hardly enough time to excuse ourselves and say sorry before our wings carried us onwards.

We had a bit of a run-in with one angel, Charna the shrew. Little Pisser had accidentally crashed into her and the harridan started cursing at him, as was her custom. She swore at the top of her voice, as if she had never been so offended. "May your eyes be plucked out, you little bastards. They fly right into your head and they think a simple 'Sorry' is enough. You ought to fly straight to hell with your 'Sorry' and not come back until I say so."

Charna the shrew heaped abuse on abuse. Once she got started, she knew no limits or bounds. Fortunately, the angels who flew behind her urged her on: "Don't block the way, Charna. Either keep flying or let us fly. The conjurors start at ten o'clock sharp."

The marketplace was filled with tzaddikim. The lady conjuror in the blue dress with red spots collected the money on a platter. Hovering in the air above, Simon Bear manned the box office. "Quickly, hurry now, the conjurors are getting started," Simon Bear prodded.

We arrived at the last moment… On the stage stood the Turk, Mehmet Ali, pulling ribbons from his nose and from his ears. He placed the ribbons in a large box and straight away—"*Allons, passez!*"—the box with the ribbons disappeared.

The tzaddikim stared open-mouthed, rapt. They shook their heads and smacked their lips: "Oh wow! Oh my! How truly marvellous!"

But that was absolutely nothing compared to what the second conjuror, Ali Mehmet, had in store. To say nothing of how he could swallow fire like so many tzaddikim swallowing stuffed cabbage rolls, if you'll forgive the comparison. This Ali Mehmet performed absolute miracles, such that the tzaddikim had never seen in their lives—and these tzaddikim are something of experts in feats of magic.

Ali Mehmet took the red cap off his head and, with a smile, bowed and asked his esteemed audience if they would throw objects into it. The crowd hesitated for a moment, clearly afraid to take the risk. But as soon as King Solomon took the gold signet ring off his finger and tossed it in the cap, Queen Esther pitched in the gold hand mirror that Ahasuerus had presented to her on their wedding day, Abraham our forefather his fancy tobacco case, Mother Sarah a golden earring, and our forefather Isaac his cufflinks.

Ali Mehmet gave the objects in his red cap a good shake. Everyone waited, mouths open wide, for what would happen next. All those who threw their items into the cap trembled anxiously for their belongings.

Ali Mehmet gave his usual smile, said "*Allons, passez*, straight away, come what may!" and shook out his cap; not a single thing was in it. Queen Esther nearly burst into tears: "My mirror, my gold mirror! King Ahasuerus gave that to me on our wedding day…"

Ali Mehmet smiled and bowed to Abraham and said: "I beg your pardon, Mr Abraham, please give your beard a shake!"

Abraham our forefather shook his beard and—lo and behold—Queen Esther's golden mirror fell out.

"And you, Mr Solomon," Ali Mehmet said to King Solomon, "would you be so kind as to look at Mother Rachel's finger in the third row behind you?" And, sure enough, on the finger of Mother Rachel's hand was King Solomon's ring. Rachel seemed deeply embarrassed. In front of a whole crowd looking on, another man's ring was wrenched off her finger.

Abraham's tobacco case was found tucked in the bosom of Jacob's handmaid Zilpah, and Isaac's cufflinks were in Rahab the harlot's left stocking.

All were amazed and laughed, and they marvelled at the great conjuror Ali Mehmet, who with such skill could have been the greatest tzaddik of the entire province of Galicia.

Suddenly Mother Sarah let out a cry and began wringing her hands: "My gold earring, goodness gracious me, my gold earring is gone!"

Ali Mehmet pointed his finger at the Maggid of Dubno, who was standing in the tenth row: "Tsk, Maggid of Dubno, since when have you been wearing ladies' earrings? Please give it back to Mother Sarah."

Hanging on the Maggid of Dubno's left ear was the golden earring and it was extracted with great difficulty. The Maggid of Dubno was beside himself: "Pertaining to this, I have a parable, gentlemen. Once upon a time, there was a king. Now, this king had three—"

"No one wants to hear it, Dubno Maggid! We came for tricks, not for parables," the crowd roared.

"You'll regret it, gentlemen, it's a very fine parable with a most illuminating moral," the Maggid of Dubno admonished. But the crowd cared as much about his parable as about the snow that fell last year. The audience's eyes now turned to the stage where the lady with the man's voice stood. Now it was her turn to show her tricks.

The lady with the man's voice said: "*Ranna, kapanna, allaranna*," and at once she was wrapped with seven colourful veils. The veils were dazzling. The tzaddikim sat staring with their mouths agape.

The lady then spoke to the seven veils, which fluttered on her: "You, white veil, fly to Mother Sarah. You, red one, to Mother Rebecca. You, green one, to Mother Rachel. And you, blue one, to Mother Leah."

The four veils separated from the others and flitted over the audience's heads until each veil wound up at each of the four holy Matriarchs.

"And now, return to me!" the lady with the man's voice commanded, and immediately the veils left the Matriarchs and flew back to the conjuror.

Again, the lady with the man's voice shouted out: "*Ranna, kapanna, allaranna*," and the veils disappeared. Nobody knew where they had gone.

The two other Turks came back onstage and took their places opposite the lady with the man's voice. With a German-flavoured declamatory flourish, one said to the other: "This is my Frau! I know it and now, behold: she has hair of gold." All at once, the audience saw that the lady now had golden hair.

Apparently dissatisfied with this, the other Turk continued with a similarly Teutonic-tinged elocution: "*Allons, passez!* But this is my Frau! I know it and here's how: her hair is red! Witness the truth of what I've said."

Then we looked again at the lady with the man's voice and, indeed, now she had fiery red hair.

The two conjurors began to bicker. One said one thing and the other contradicted him and each time the lady would become something different. They argued and argued until one of them shouted: "*Allons, passez*: spirit away!" and the lady disappeared. The two guys gestured obscenely at each other before turning to the audience to announce:

> Now our show has reached its end,
> So put your hands together, friends.

The tzaddikim enthusiastically applauded. No one wanted to leave. They wanted even more tricks. The conjurors, however, had decided that was enough. They dismantled their little pavilion and packed up their things. The lady with the man's voice materialized once more as if resurrected. All their gear was loaded on to the wagon. The lady pounded on her drum. The wagon began rolling and the conjurors headed out on their way to who knows where.

The Turks on the wagon waved their red caps as they said goodbye to the crowd. "So long, tzaddikim," the older-looking of them shouted, "we'll come again with brand-new tricks for you!"

The whole audience accompanied them to the city gates. Abraham our forefather bade farewell on behalf of all Paradise City and invited them to come back to break up the monotony of Paradise a bit. "You will be deserving of merit for such a good turn," Abraham concluded his little speech. The lady with the man's voice was so moved by his words that she threw her arms around him and wanted to give him a kiss…

"Come now, ugh, bah!"

The lady had no other choice. As soon as she saw that Abraham would not allow himself to be kissed, she hopped back on the wagon. One of the Turks spurred on the horse, "Hyah!", and the wagon was off.

The tzaddikim watched after them, waving their kerchiefs as long as they could still see the caravan. Once it had vanished amidst the clouds and the highway they turned to each other and said: "They're gone! Just like that, really gone."

"What a shame! What a shame!" they all sighed as they started to make their way homewards, each to his own household and habitation.

My friend Little Pisser and I also started flying home. I already missed the cheery conjurors. In my mind, I relived the magic act of the three Turks. Then I felt downhearted. "When do you think the Turks will come again, Little Pisser?"

"How should I know? Am I some sort of prophet, Samuel Abba?"

"Don't you miss the Turks, Little Pisser?"

"Like a hole in the head," grumbled Little Pisser. But I could tell that he was lying. He was just putting on a brave face and really he missed them just like me, maybe even more.

As we flew over the hallowed Avenue of the Patriarchs we heard a clamour. We descended to find out what was going on.

We could not believe our eyes. The holy Patriarchs were running around like a bunch of proverbial headless chickens, their beards in disarray. The holy Matriarchs were wringing their hands, weeping and wailing: "We've been robbed! Our houses have been cleaned out. There's not a single thing left!"

Mother Sarah tore into our forefather Abraham: "Oh, he just had to have Turks here and, in the meantime, they go and rob us blind. Your Turks, Abie! As if anything decent could come from the line of your Ishmael."

With tears in his eyes, Abraham pleaded with her: "Simmer down, Sarah, you'll see: everything that's been stolen will turn up again. Now, just simmer down!"

On the other streets in Paradise, things were pretty bleak too. The tzaddikim and their wives were running around like mad. The hue and cry rose to the uppermost reaches of the heavens.

"To think that thieves could enter Paradise," lamented the sainted Rabbi of Opatów.

"To the devil with those Turks. If only someone had beaten the hell out of them before they dared to come here," cursed the renowned composer of prayers Sarah Bas Tovim, her headdress fluttering on her head like a crazed dove.

"Maybe this is just another trick of the Turks?" suggested a diminutive little tzaddik with a short yellow beard.

"A trick of the Turks, you say? Yeah, sure, a trick. Those Turks conned us all right, performed their tricks and cleaned us out in the meantime."

"Please, Sarah darling, simmer down already," Abraham begged. "What good will come of busting my chops about it? It certainly won't help find what's been stolen."

The Paradise Police flew over in their green uniforms. The tzaddikim began to take stock of all that had been pilfered.

"All the bedding, our silver candlesticks, a gold brooch, even my wedding ring."

"The mirror from right off the wall, my embroidered Shabbos frock, even my husband the tzaddik's slippers."

"All our holiday clothes, my silk parasol and my album of good deeds."

"A silver chandelier, the antique head-covering that I inherited, a tallis with a gold-threaded lining from Leipzig."

"My silver spice box, my oldest daughter's silk stockings and my niece's wedding lingerie."

"The garden swing, my handkerchief, my tobacco case and the chamber pot (pardon my mentioning those together)."

The tzaddikim inventoried the loss with the assistance of their wives and the Paradise Police wrote it all down. It was an enormous heist. Not a single home was spared. The reporting of everything stolen took the entire day. The tzaddikim were so distressed that they forgot to pray the afternoon prayer.

"Those Turks have got to be caught," Abraham said to the chief of the Paradise Police.

The police chief angel twisted the sides of his moustache as if to say, "You may be a great tzaddik, Mr Abraham, but it's better to leave it to someone who knows the ropes when it comes to larceny."

Someone mentioned the name of the angel Simon Bear and the police chief pricked up his ears: "What's this about the angel Simon Bear?"

"Simon Bear spent an entire night getting drunk with the Turks. The next morning he helped collect entrance money from the little angel kids who came to see the conjurors."

"Aha!" exclaimed the police chief, and tugged one side of his moustache. "Aha!"

He repeated this "Aha" maybe ten more times. Then he ordered that the angel Simon Bear be brought to him.

Two police angels went off. They found Simon Bear dead drunk at the Righteous Noah pub. They dragged him in. He could hardly stand on his own two feet.

The police chief angel gave him a mouthful, sharply telling him he was in this deep and that he, the police chief that is, advised Simon Bear to reveal where the Turks were to be found and quick.

The angel Simon Bear swore that he knew nothing; how should he know where they were? The Turks had ordered him a couple of rounds and he drank them. Maybe the police chief would be so kind as to explain where in the laws of Paradise it was written that one mustn't drink the whisky a Turk orders for you.

The police chief angel began screaming at him and told him plain and simple that he wouldn't stand for any monkey business. He was, after all, an expert in such matters and Simon Bear was an accomplice to the larceny. Collecting the entrance money from the little angels was solid proof that he was in cahoots with the Turks and doing their bidding.

Simon Bear went crazy at this. He screamed back with such fury that more than one tzaddik jumped out of their skin. Call him a drunk, be my guest and call him a drunk. But a thief, a thief! Whoever dares call him a thief, he'd teach them a thing or two. He grabbed the police chief and shook him until he was gasping for breath.

"A thief, you say?" Simon Bear shrieked, "a criminal? I'll break your damned wings, you son of a bitch, you... you..."

With difficulty, they managed to pull Simon Bear off the police chief. They cuffed his wings and hauled him into the Paradise clink.

The next day he was released. Simon Bear kept insisting that he thought the Turks were just Turks. How was he supposed to know that they were thieves, crooks? He thought they were just having a drink; could he imagine that they were planning a heist?

A sense of doom had set in amongst the tzaddikim. They slept on bare mattresses, ate with their hands, and swallowed their tears.

The police searched and scoured. Every day new reports were filed until Hyman the stationery shopkeeper angel had nearly run out of paper and yet the thieves had not been caught.

"What will come of this?" the tzaddikim asked the chief of the Paradise Police. "Is everything stolen gone for good—a hopeless case, Master Commissioner?"

The chief of the Paradise Police twisted the ends of his moustache and said with a shrewd smile: "What do you mean 'hopeless', eh? The Paradise Police don't know the meaning of the word hopeless."

"The thief's end is the gallows," declared one of the tzaddikim.

And they kept searching and scouring, investigating, arresting suspects, releasing them and arresting more…

How the heist was resolved, if they ever caught the thieves or not, I cannot say. A few days later, my friend Little Pisser delivered the news that Simon Bear was taking me away from Paradise to be born on Earth.

*

I fell silent. The rabbi across from me sat as if hewn from stone, his juridical assistant's eyes enormous. The town magnate, Mr Michael Hurwitz, searched for words for these remarkable stories from Paradise and finally he sputtered out: "*Sonder… sonderbar!*"

Pop sat with his elbows on the table in wide-eyed wonderment.

"A most peculiar world, this Paradise," said the rabbi. "A topsy-turvy world full of malice and theft, mercy me! How can it be, my boy? I simply don't want to believe what you told us is true."

"Everything I told you is the truth. I saw it all with my own eyes."

"Maybe it's just a flight of fancy," broke in the rabbi's assistant. "You merely imagined it and you think that it's true. How could it be possible that the tzaddikim are left sleeping on bare mattresses and their wives are unable to light candles because thieves nicked their candlesticks?"

"Maybe it is indeed a flight of fancy," said the rabbi like a drowning man grasping at a straw.

"It is no flight of fancy at all, gentlemen, but the honest truth. Perhaps the Paradise that you have dreamt up is a fantasy, a work of fiction. But the Paradise I come from is the real Paradise and, even though it may have its faults, it's lovely all the same. The proof is that I miss it and, if they'd only let me, I'd go right back."

My mama rushed over to me, grabbed my hand and pressed it firmly to her heart. "What are you saying, my little kaddish? What do you mean you're ready to return to Paradise? You, my darling one, will stay here with your mama and I'll claw out the eyes of anyone who tries to take you away from me."

Man, oh, man, I thought, just try and mess with an earthly mother and right away she's clawing out eyes. They think that life on Earth is a bed of roses and that nothing could be worth leaving it. It isn't for nothing that there's an expression in Paradise: she is kind and dumb, like an earthly mum.

The rabbi stroked his snow-white beard and asked me: "How is it, then, that of all angels you were sent to be born and not your friend Little Pisser? After all, you were an angel just like him."

I told him that it seems that I was not a true angel, but rather a provisional one. The difference between a true and provisional angel is that true angels can never be born on Earth. When a true angel goes astray, they send him to the World of Chaos or even to hell for some time. As punishment he has to rake blazing coals there by hand for however long it takes to atone.

The rabbi stood up. His entire body was trembling. "Make the preparations for his bris, Feivel," he said to my pop. "I suggest that you name him Samuel Abba, just as he was called in Paradise."

"Absolutely," Pop agreed. "What else could it be besides Samuel Abba?"

My mama kept me held fast in her arms. The magnate and the rabbi's assistant took their leave of my pop: "You've got a real gem there, Feivel. Treasure him as the apple of your eye. A whippersnapper like Samuel Abba ought to be treasured."

Mama embraced and kissed me. Tears twinkled in her lovely eyes. "My darling treasure, my golden boy, my little Sammy Abba!"

The guests kissed the mezuza on their way out the door. The rabbi called out, "Goodnight! God willing, we'll see each other again at the bris, Feivel."

My mama laid me in the cradle. Pop paced the house for a good long while. His shadow, a disbeliever, wavered on the wall.

Translator's Note

The last decade has seen a glut of guidelines, manifestos and treatises on the translation of Yiddish texts, ranging from the programmatic to the pedantic. In this new translation I am confident I will disappoint all authors of such statements to a certain degree. Instead of following a variety of newly established conventions for Yiddish translation and transliteration, I have tried to follow Itzik Manger's own statements on translation and tone to find an idiom suitable to the author's inimitable style. Translations of Manger into English often have an overly quaint, almost ethnographic feel to them. This is undoubtedly because of Manger's commitment to a neo-folkist, anti-elitist poetics. Although the complexity of his simple-seeming style may have resonated with Yiddish readers, when rendered in English his modernist folkism can sound flat and folksy.

In a letter to his friend, the New Zealand-born English writer Dan Davin, Manger recommended that Davin read Sholem Aleichem to get a better sense of a great Yiddish writer. "Surely, there are translations of his works in English," Manger wrote, "but very bad ones, because *Yiddish is such an idiomatic language that in taking away the idiom it loses all.*" Manger writes quite a bit about "idiom", meaning both the peculiarities of a given language and also unique expressions, collocations and linguistic usages. Throughout this translation I have relied heavily on English's incredible arsenal of idioms with the hope of giving at least a taste of Manger's richly expressive idiomatic Yiddish.

Following Manger's radical domestication of ancient texts and characters into the Eastern Galician language and landscape, this translation also aims to recreate the homey, familiar quality of Manger's Yiddish so that it reads smoothly in English without the need for a glossary or countless footnotes. This applies not only to the distinctive features of Jewish culture and religious references, but also to the names of characters. Although some may contest that I have run the risk of de-Judaizing the text, I tried to walk a fine line between maintaining accuracy while eschewing obscurantism and pedantry in rendering names that could make the text unreadable or superfluously foreign.

In general, I have used biblically allusive names as they are commonly received in English and standardized by the King James Bible. So rather than using highly academic transliterations like *Yankev* or *Shloyme*, for example, I have opted for the more commonplace Jacob and Solomon, which carry with them all of their associations in English. I'll admit that I have gone a step further in anglicizing some of the more difficult Yiddish and Slavic names in the text. In the way that an Eastern European nickname like *Syomka* has its roots in the biblical Simon—moving from the Hebrew *Shim'on* and Yiddish *Shimmen* to the Slavic *Semyon*, and then shortened and colloquially diminutivized—I chose to use familiar English versions of some names that may otherwise trip readers up. So just as members of my own family may have embraced Seymour for Syomka, Simon for Shimmen, or translated Perl as Pearl after settling in New York in the early twentieth century, so did I for a handful of characters in Manger's novel, whose names might cause trouble in pronouncing them and hinder reading.

I confess that I did this for our protagonist as well. In Yiddish, Shmul (locally pronounced "Shmil") Abba's double-barrelled first name, merges Samuel, like the biblical prophet, with Abba, an ancient Aramaic rabbinical name, and also references Samuel-Abba Soifer, the editor of the *Czernowitzer Bletter* newspaper, a popular figure in Manger's home town. Samuel Abba's surname, *Aberwo*, is really more an exclamation than an appellation. *Aberwo* is a uniquely Bukovinian German expression of surprise or disbelief. Its particular usage was so widespread in Bukovina that it grated on the ears of metropolitan speakers of Viennese German, and its usage was disparaged in volumes dedicated to the uplift of German dialects in the Habsburg Empire. I have rendered *Aberwo* here as Strewth, which captures a similar regional oath of surprise.

Acknowledgements

Most of the credit for the appearance of this new translation of Manger's work goes to others. My friends Boris Dralyuk and Moriel Rothman-Zecher helped this along at every stage. My gratitude to them has no bounds. I also want to acknowledge my family—Nomi and Tomek—who let Samuel Abba and Little Pisser join our pandemic bubble; my parents Nancy and Marty Peckerar, who have always been my first readers; Chana Kronfeld, with whom I first swam in Manger's great intertextual sea; Michael Casper for all his advice and friendship; Madeleine (Mindl) Cohen, for her initial encouragement; and Clare Fester (*strewth!*).

I would also like to thank Avrom Nowersztern and the Itzik and Ghenia Manger Fund for generously granting permission for this edition of Manger to reach new audiences.

Finally, I dedicate this to the memory of my dear friend David Shneer, with whom I travelled over the landscapes described in this book and beyond. *Zolstu hobn a likhtikn ganeydn*, may his Paradise be radiant.

THE BOOK OF PARADISE
ITZIK MANGER

THE ALLURE OF CHANEL
PAUL MORAND

SWANN IN LOVE
MARCEL PROUST

THE EVENINGS
GERARD REVE